A DUPLICATE
DAUGHTER

by

Randy F. Nelson

Harvard Square Editions
New York
2017

A Duplicate Daughter, by Randy F. Nelson
Copyright © 2017

Cover design by J. Caleb Clark ©

ISBN 978-1-941861-49-3
Printed in the United States of America

Published in the United States by
Harvard Square Editions
www.harvardsquareeditions.org

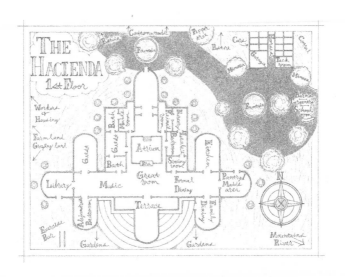

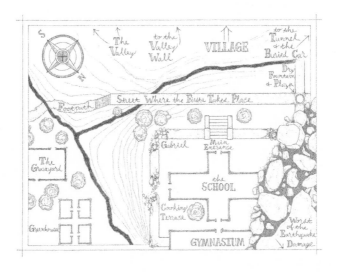

PRELUDE
September, 1948

AT ONE END of one hallway a staircase had come undone. It had folded like an accordion, its handrails dangling into space. There was a crumbling pile of debris in the stairwell itself, where a metal corrugation jutted upward at an absurd angle. From a distance it looked as though the north end of the school had been jammed against its neighboring mountain with such force that boulders and shale had become part of the architecture.

On the afternoon that the stranger came, twelve year old Mía was perched at her window, a dusky hiding place among broken rafters in the attic of the school. From there she could see the dry fountain in the plaza, the pathway to the gray-green valley floor, and the road that cut through the next range of mountains. She imagined that it was thousands of miles to the buildings in the distance, but her friend Quentin had told her no. That it wasn't even a village, just another mining camp. But who could know? Quentin was five years older than Mía, seventeen and boastful, quick to dismiss daydreams and make-believe worlds.

The school itself was like a ruined castle from one of Grandmother Reina's tales, now with a stranger coming from some place beyond the mountains. Dogs were baying and romping in circles, announcing the man before he had reached the footbridge at the turn of the trail. He wore cowboy boots, jeans, and a corduroy jacket. In one hand he carried a briefcase, and he sported a black Stetson hat. The man came picking his way over the unfamiliar route as if he expected the school at any moment to break loose from the earth and slide past him.

By the time the stranger reached the rock terrace in front of the building, there remained only Gabriel, the old drunk, sitting next to his broken wall and holding a bottle by the neck. The rest of the village seemed deserted. The cowboy took in his surroundings. Walked toward the figure slouched in the courtyard. Then squatted on the balls of his feet, speaking softly in a heavily accented Spanish. They talked for a few minutes, then finally Gabriel made a small **O** with his mouth and pointed toward the main entrance to the school.

"*Gra-see-us*," the man said.

Mía hurried down to the shadowy third floor of the school and then down again to the second floor and its abandoned classrooms. There, where the main halls intersected, two curving stairways, like gestures from a bygone era, rose up to a balcony. From this open space Mía could hear the stranger approaching. Once in sight, she watched as he drew a notebook from his briefcase and consulted some papers.

The man cocked his head and listened, hearing only the pigeons that gathered in a shaft of light at the far end of one hall. He turned in the opposite direction and peered into a few of the vacant rooms, his boots echoing as he inspected the ruin of the still-beautiful building. There were blackboards with primitive chalk drawings and undecipherable writing, stacks of books in some of the hallways, rolls of butcher's paper unfurled in certain rooms, and furniture: a teacher's desk with no legs, a row of metal stools, a dented globe without its stand that someone had kicked into a corner.

Walking back into the rotunda, he surprised an old woman peeping from behind a door.

"*Bonus dee-us*," he said. "*Yo booze-kway-da* ... " he looked at one of his papers ... "*Amedeo Muñoz. ¿Esta aquí?*" The woman slammed her door. The man pushed back his hat and looked at his watch. "Shit." He continued farther into the school. At the next intersection he flicked the light switches outside an office door. Nothing happened. Finally he simply called out, "*¡Hola!* Looking for Amedeo Muñoz! Señor Muñoz! Anybody here speak English?!"

Which was when he found Quentin.

The boy had a light complexion but also the strong facial features of northern Mexico, a mixture of European and Nahuatl ancestors. In his shoulders and arms were the first promises of manhood, but at seventeen he had not yet mastered the balance of his frame.

The two of them talked in a mixture of English and Spanish, Quentin keeping one hand on the knife in his pocket, the man referring frequently to a folder of papers. There was something important, he said, that needed to be signed. Legal papers from the north. Very important. Was Señor Muñoz in the building? Quentin nodded and pondered what to do. The man might be here to hurt Amedeo or to take one of the children. Maybe someone from the north was trying to move them all away from the school. Quentin thought and coughed and rubbed his eyebrows, reflecting on the bundle of sins he would be carrying into the next world if he drew the knife. And then he reached a decision.

On the back of one of the papers, he drew directions with the man's pen. Then Quentin slipped into one of the vacant classrooms as the man walked away. Moments later Quentin found Amedeo in the auditorium working at the base of a wet wall.

"There was a gringo," Quentin said, "bringing papers. Maybe forty or fifty papers, with writing on every page. They were in a folder, these papers, so that you could open it and turn the pages like a book. And the folder had been taken from a leather satchel with two straps and a handle. It could be something bad," Quentin went on. "Or something good. Who would bring papers to the school and ask for you by name?"

Amedeo sat back on his heels and looked ahead as if inspecting a riddle. His face was weathered and dark. The hair and eyes were a lustrous shade of black, but the first touches of gray were appearing in the eyebrows and in the stubble of his face. The mouth and chin were wide and unreadable. In appearance he seemed to be in his mid-forties. In manner, he seemed older than the mountains. "Did he say what he wanted, this man?"

"Signing the papers," Quentin replied. "He wants for you to sign. That is what he is saying."

Before they could continue, a shadow stretched into one of the aisles of the auditorium and a deep voice filled most of the empty space. "You know, I guess I could have followed your map, son. Which I found to be a pretty good representation." The man eased himself beneath the balcony and put his hand on one of the broken support columns as if testing its strength. "But, hell, I figured why waste my client's valuable time when you were probably rabbiting right here yourself. Does that make sense to you? 'Cause it makes sense to me."

The stranger patted the column and walked away from the sagging overhang, stopping to look back at the balcony. "And, you know what else? I'm working against a deadline here. So I'd just like to get right to it, Mr. Muñoz and me I mean." He turned back around and strolled down the aisle, glancing into each row as if he expected to be surprised. He did not hurry, but he kept one arm unnaturally still at his side while holding the briefcase loosely in his left hand.

The cowboy continued to the front of the auditorium where he paused for an admiring look at his surroundings, resting his free hand on the lip of the stage. "This looks like one of them New York City Broadway theatres, don't it? Balcony like the front end of a lacquered sleigh. I can't believe they put this kind of detail into schools anymore, the times being so bad and all. It's a bygone age. Down here, I mean."

The man patted the stage twice, just as he had patted the column, and then walked the rest of the way to Quentin and Amedeo, stopping some ten cautious feet away. "You know what else I find amazing? How easy it is to bring a handgun across the border. I find that amazing. It's like all the attention is focused in the other direction, you know what I'm saying?"

Quentin withdrew his hand from the pocket with the knife.

"Good," the stranger said. "I was hoping there wouldn't be no language barrier. Now. Are you Señor Amedeo Muñoz-Navarro, and do you speak enough English for me to make you a very rich man?"

"What do you want?" Amedeo asked.

"Now see? We making progress already. So I reckon I ought to innerduce myself." He held up something that looked like an American driver's license. "And then here's my business card, which you might want to keep in case you find yourself in need of my services any time after today. Feel free to call." The smaller card read "Gerald Manley, Private Investigations, 204 Parkway, Suite 3-A, San Antonio, Texas, Telephone BE-6642."

"Señor Manley ... what do you want?" Amedeo asked again.

The detective took a moment to study the banks of wooden seats around him, row after row, like a cemetery. He contemplated the slow trickle of water undulating from a dark patch on the wall. The repair work reminded him of untenanted apartments and abandoned houses and the general misery of human existence. And the war of course. In '44 and '45 he had witnessed the bombing of whole cities throughout Japan, but never once had he walked through a building that had been shaken out of its gentility such as this one. The little stream flowed along a curving baseboard, across a stretch of floor, and into a shallow orchestra pit below the stage. Already it had formed a pool that shimmered in the half-light.

"Do you mind if I sit down?" Manley continued. "I come a long dang way and you folks got a hell of a stony staircase down the side of that mountain." The man placed himself in one of the seats on the front row, settling the briefcase across his knees and closing his eyes for a second.

When Amedeo did not speak, Manley finally lifted the Stetson from his head and wiped the inside with his handkerchief. "I mean, if you don't mind my asking, what the hell's going on here? You people look like you're coming in from the Ice Age or something. You look like you collided with a glacier. Did we just not get the news up north?"

"There was an earthquake," said Amedeo Muñoz. "Years ago."

"And you just now digging out?" the detective asked.

Amedeo shrugged. "The government does not know us. We have been digging out for some time."

"Sorry to hear about that. I don't mean to make light of another man's misfortune."

"Señor Manley...."

"Yeah. You're right, I talk too much. I been told that, so I'm not going to take up a lot of your valuable time here. I just got a little something... something I wanted you to take a look at if you don't mind." Manley fished in the briefcase, keeping his calm eyes fixed on Amedeo. "I been working on a case for a client of mine up in California. Disappearance of an eight month old girl." He drew forth a manila envelope, eight by fourteen inches, the flap already open at one end. "There you go! I knew it was down there somewhere. The problem being that all this took place a long time ago. Ten or twelve years ago to be exact. Kidnapping is what everybody thought at the time. You know, like the Lindbergh baby." Without dropping his eyes or changing his expression, Manley handed the envelope to Amedeo Muñoz, who seemed surprised by its weight.

"Yeah," the detective continued, "that's the way that most people react. Go ahead, take her out."

Amedeo lifted one end of the envelope and let a thin metal plate slide into his hand. It looked as if it had been crushed and then hammered flat a second time. When he turned it over, Amedeo could see that it was a California license plate with the abbreviation CAL and the year 1936 stamped in half-inch letters across the top center. Below were black numbers on a yellow background, 8W 31 29. The paint had been chipped away from much of the background, but the raised letters and numbers were easy to read. "1936," Amedeo said.

"Twelve years ago. Can you believe that?"

"What does it mean?" asked Amedeo.

"Well now there you got me. I don't have no idea at all. I'm just kind of making the rounds, village to village, asking folks if they might know anything about it. Cause you see, there's this one little detail to the story. It's interesting really, the kind of thing that gets in your mind and just won't fall out. This very plate that you're holding in your hand right now? It was mailed in a manila envelope like this one, about a month ago, from a town twenty-five miles west of here, name of Zalcupan. You know the town I'm talking about?"

Amedeo nodded. "I know Zalcupan, yes."

"Not a lovely place, let me tell you. Anyhow, it was mailed

from there, Zalcupan, to the home of my client. Whose eight month old baby daughter was the one that just happened to disappear. Back in 1936, as coincidence would have it. And this unlikely looking piece of tin that you are holding, Mr. Muñoz, was at one time affixed to the bumper of a 1935 Nash Ambassador 4-door sedan, also owned by my client. Crème colored. Beautiful car if you ask me, eight cylinders. I got a picture of it down in here somewheres. I mean, they didn't make many of them, brother. You see what I'm getting at?"

"I'm afraid not." Amedeo stooped once more and began to search through the tool bag as if looking for something particular.

"Well, I guess I'm not explaining this too good," Manley went on. "Cause it aroused a real consuming interest in my client. The man who owned the car? His name is Cruz. Alejandro Cruz. And his wife of course. I mean you can probably imagine what the sudden appearance of a clue like this would do to a woman who had lost her only child."

"Cruz?" Amedeo stopped rummaging in the bag, turned his head to one side long enough to think, and then shook his head once.

"Yeah, he's a wealthy landowner, maybe you heard of him. Up along the Arosotape River, in California, between San Pedrillo and the mountains. Owns almond trees. Oranges. Cotton. Winter wheat. Horses. You name it. I mean, whoever thought there was money in almond trees? Anyhow, him and his wife, they seemed real interested in why somebody would mail them the license plate of a car that was stolen at exactly the same time that their baby daughter was stolen. I guess you can understand why."

"Yes. I can. What do the police say?"

"Nothing." After a pause, Manley leaned forward and lowered his voice as if sharing private information. "In fact, as far as I know, the police, the FBI, are unaware of anything I have just told you. I mean, the car *was* used in the kidnapping, but the car itself was never recovered. And there wasn't any note or ransom demand in the mailer. She's the one who actually got it in the mail, Señora Cruz was. No return address other than the postmark. No communication of any kind. Makes you wonder, don't it? I guess that's why I was called in. On account of I sort of specialize in missing persons."

Amedeo held the other man's eyes and showed a puzzled face. "It makes me sad for the family. But why do you come here?"

"Because I'm a detail kind of person, Amedeo. Do you mind if I call you that? I get paid to focus my attention on details, like the eight villages that're within twenty, twenty-five miles of Zalcupan. I'm making a little stop in every one of them. Talking to the head man, a few of the folks in the plaza, seeing if they can tell me anything that might put my client's mind at rest. Except, you all, you don't have much of a plaza nowadays, do you?"

Amedeo shrugged again. "We are no more than two hundred and fifty people, maybe forty families in all, and we have very little. But we are not child stealers."

"So I don't reckon you got anything for me then? No information?"

"I am sorry," said Muñoz.

"It's a real mystery all right. I mean, why would anybody mail a junkyard license plate from one country to another country and then not even include a note? That's what I keep asking myself."

Amedeo made his face neutral and slightly lifted one shoulder.

The detective put the license plate back into its envelope and the envelope back into his briefcase. Amedeo turned his attention to the canvas tool bag once more. And Manley turned to leave. Quentin followed the stranger like a watchdog, pausing when Manley paused, taking in the panorama himself as Manley gave a parting scrutiny to the stage, the columns, the scrolled elegance of the woodwork. "They don't make buildings like this anymore," he said to Quentin. "No pride of craftsmanship in the modern world. I admire what he's doing up here, I really do. Takes a whole different attitude."

Quentin looked back toward Amedeo and then considered the possibility that the kneeling figure would have an attitude about anything. It was not a word that Quentin associated with men. And just as unexpected was Manley's reaching out to shake the boy's hand, a gesture, Quentin realized, that no one had ever offered him before. It made him feel tall and straight, as if the world had looked at him from a distance and nodded at last. "Just a word of advice," Manley said. "If you don't mind."

"Sure," said the boy.

"If you ever go to pull a knife on a man...."

Quentin stiffened.

"Just do it. Don't telegraph it. Just make it one smooth easy move. That way you don't lose advantage. Remember that. Smooth and easy."

A wave of humiliation swept over Quentin, and his face burned. He tried to drop Manley's hand and back away, but the detective did not let go. Instead, the cowboy winked and patted Quentin's shoulder with his free hand. "Don't worry about it. You did the right thing. You just got to learn from Amedeo down there. Smooth and easy. Like when I told him I was going to make him a very rich man? Did you notice that he never once asked me how?"

Amedeo stood and turned in one motion, even began to speak again, but the detective had already disappeared.

1

THERE WAS NO PANIC in her movements, but her hands were restless and quick. It was the early morning, and she was packing the baby's things—the bottles, the nipples, the pacifiers, the diapers, rubber pants, baby oil, the tins of powder, some light blankets, the stuffed monkey and duck—into a diaper bag. Into the large green suitcase went the baby's gowns, the tiny socks, more diapers, the bonnets, shoes, singlets, a few more blankets, and three or four washcloths. What else? A water bottle so they wouldn't have to stop on the way. A banana that she could mash for solid food. What else? A baby spoon from the kitchen. Leala's mind rushed through possibilities, but she kept seeing the same list of items over and over. She left the baby's bags open and went to the closet for her own suitcase. Flung it on the bed and began to fill it from her dresser. Hose, underpants. One slip. No jewelry. Brush and comb. One lipstick. Brassiere. Sandals and shoes from the closet. The brown riding skirt. The gray full skirt and the white blouse from the armoire. Money. She would need money. And went to the bottom drawer of the dresser where she had hidden the cash. From the corner of her eye, she detected a shadow in the doorway.

And suddenly he was there, as silent as some beast from the field, unmoving but unyielding too, as if blocking her escape were his sole intent. He was just there, with no warning or explanation. It was the fright that she felt first, a flush that ran through her cheeks and up to the roots of her hair. Then the humiliation of being caught. And then the panic of being trapped. Her fear for what he would do to her now was almost rational. It settled into her ankles and calves. She could barely stand, barely turn to face him. But it was not Alejandro. And in a way, it was worse. It was the man who owned her soul.

Amedeo, she knew, could be cruel without calculation. She had seen him fight other men for sport and had watched the way he stood over the fallen, daring them to move. She knew the strength of his arms, the rush of his breath upon her as if she were about to be consumed. She told herself that she had never loved him, but that was not true. At one time he had seemed to be all that she desired. Now he was standing in shadow, and his eyes were all that moved. They were set well apart on his face and flicked to the merest movement, the tiniest variation in the light.

"What are you doing here?" she whispered, the urgency in her voice readily apparent.

"I've come to look at you." Amedeo spoke in a low baritone that somehow lingered after his words had been spoken.

"We agreed that you would never enter the house," Leala hissed.

"And yet here I am."

Now she put herself urgently close to him. "I told you yesterday. I need to be away from you both. It's impossible for me to live like this ... the two of you. I don't even know what Alejandro knows. But I am certain that it has to be over between you and me. And that I need to go somewhere quiet and think for a moment."

"What you said yesterday is not true. You love me. And I love you. And I have come to find out why you spoke to me as you did."

She looked past him into the hall, listened for the slightest hint of a sound. "Amedeo, you have to leave. What I told you is the truth." She made herself wait for another instant. "I don't love you."

"Then I've come for my daughter," said Amedeo Muñoz.

It was a pronouncement so simple and outrageous it could only have come from a peasant, from someone who saw in terms of black and white. His daughter. His honor. His woman, taken from a weaker man.

"Maria Anita Cruz y Sanchez is not your daughter." The intensity of her words came through even though she kept her voice at a whisper.

"Not in name," he said.

"She is not your daughter in any way. Now leave before I call my husband, and ask him to bring a gun."

He did not move. In fact, he hardly seemed to be breathing at all. His face was placid, curious, alert but not alarmed. His hair had been combed straight back, and his clean shirt had been rolled twice at the sleeves. He smelled faintly of aftershave. Now she wondered if anyone else inside the house had seen him, smelled him, heard him speaking his low, flat accusations. How maddening, she thought, that he should be so composed.

"Leala," he whispered.

"No."

"A word you have never said to me before."

"Amedeo, please go. You are making everything worse. I am confused. You are a danger to me ... and to the baby. Just go. You should not be here at all."

"No." It was not unkind, this finality from Amedeo Muñoz. In fact, it was the same manner in which he had spoken to her nearly a year before.

•

It was April of 1935, and love was no longer a word she used in her marriage. Even as she packed the saddlebags, she did not mislead herself. Leala didn't love the carpenter either, didn't allow for the possibility of it. None of her conversations with him had been of love. Still, she had found reason to talk with him more frequently of late. He was hardly handsome in any conventional sense. Plus he was arrogant and unrefined, in many ways the negative of her husband. Yet inevitably there she was, walking to the corral where she told the groom that she'd be taking Cesare out for the day.

Leala assured herself that what she needed was neither selfish nor absurd. That if she could not have love and intimacy within her home, then at least she deserved a momentary escape. It was what Amedeo Muñoz would be for her. A distraction from a lingering disease. Nothing more than that.

Do you want somebody to ride out with you, the groom had wanted to know. There are coyotes and cougars in the uplands he insisted. At least take one of the rifles. And Cesare, he has been hard to handle lately with some of the mares in heat. He threw Reynaldo to the ground yesterday and kicked loose a plank of his stall.

No, Leala told him. I'm taking the long ride out to the river. To look over some property my husband is buying. And Cesare will be fine. I will let him run. Then I'll walk him through the river at noon.

Perhaps the groom had pondered a reasonable reply. Perhaps he had conceived a litany of unasked questions, but he'd reached the limit of what a groom could do. She was the Señora after all, and she wanted what was hers to have. Cesare came out of his stall wild-eyed and anxious, but as soon as she was in the saddle, Leala had him in a smooth paso fino; and as they left the hacienda a touch of the spurs put him into a hard gallop.

Leala turned the animal north and west, in the direction of the mountains, where the river was shallow and where the hunting lodge had been undergoing repairs for the fall. The carpenter had been there already for a week, alone. And those who stayed behind at the hacienda had not thought of him for days.

Leala gave the horse his head and let him pound through the chaparral until they reached the road that marked the first rise into the hills. Cesare took the ditch without breaking stride. Even after an hour he had not lowered his head an inch. It was Leala who had to slow the pace. She brought him down to a cantor as they neared the river, then to a trot where the soil turned rocky. And then to a walk when he reached the willows and their weeping limbs. It was like parting a curtain to get down to the water. His hooves made sucking sounds in the bank, and she let him wade out a few feet to get a drink of clear, unmuddied perfection. Higher up, the water would be running shallow, and the riverbed would be nothing but rock and sand.

In another hour they were within sight of the lodge itself, no more than a cabin really, with a stone foundation and a log construction. It had not been built at a high elevation but rather set on a low ridge at a bend in the river so that there was water on three sides and a spectacular view of sharp, purple cliffs in the near distance. The shallows were a cascade of crystalline light, scattering the sun like a chandelier that had fallen to earth. Cesare lifted his ears when he saw the truck. Nickered when he saw the man staring back at them. Amedeo Muñoz was shirtless, wearing dungarees, boots, and gloves as he carried stones from the back of the truck to a hole in the foundation where he had been working. His chest and stomach were scratched and caked with mud from carrying rocks as wide as his shoulders. There was a swath of red-brown grit where he had wiped his cheek. He did not seem surprised by his visitors and greeted the horse by taking the headstall in one hand and caressing Cesare's cheek with the other. The woman dismounted without a word and dropped the reins. Together they led Cesare down to the water, where Amedeo uncinched the saddle and laid the blanket on the ground. Leala stretched. You can let him go she said. He won't wander far.

People will know that you're here is the first thing that Muñoz said.

No they won't. She sat on the saddle blanket and breathed the water-rich air. A dragonfly hovered and then drew hieroglyphs in front of them. It's peaceful here, she went on. Look, up there in the sun, not even the aspen are trembling. It was as direct as she could be. An admission that perhaps she had feelings for him after all.

Amedeo took Cesare to the little corral and rubbed him down with a burlap sack. Filled the water trough and found a sorry blend of oats and corn in the wooden bin. There was no gate. He had to take down three rails and slide them back in place. Soon he saw smoke rising from the little metal flue of the woodstove and also from the great stone chimney on the far side of the lodge. But before going in to her, he finished laying the new cornerstone and leveling it with mortar and fill.

Then he took out the beam and the carjack that he had been using to support the old joist. Cleaned his mortarboard and trowel. When he finally went inside, she was pumping water into a wooden bucket, the iron handle working up and down, squealing in protest. There were pots of water steaming on the stove, a cauldron in the fireplace sitting among low flames.

We're having water for lunch? he asked.

She laughed again. Told him to take off his boots. I like to hear you talk she said. It's as if you are amazed by every little thing you see but not at all surprised by the big ones. What will you tell us when the cyclone comes? She took the bucket from the pump and carried it to an alcove where there was a copper bathtub, a bed, and a wooden chest.

He noticed that she was already barefooted, her boots and socks beside the door. So he dumped his armload of firewood into the bin and sat in one of the chairs next to the small table. Watched her empty her bucket into the copper tub, already half-filled from the sound of it, and come back to the stove for two pots of boiling water. He pried off his boots, watched the steam rise from the tub as she poured. Watched her return for the kettle and a third boiling pot. Then refill them all and set them back onto the stove.

As he stood, Leala Cruz made slow work of washing his face and chest with a damp cloth. It was the first time they had ever touched deliberately. She stepped one naked foot between his legs and lifted the hem of her skirt so that she could stand closer to him. Folded the cloth as she washed away sweat and dirt, kissing his neck and shoulders and nipples as she worked. He pulled her to him and put his lips to hers. Then she drew away, let him look at her and let herself look at him, noticing how she seemed to have washed away the hard edges of his face.

Leala put both her hands inside his belt, pulling him into the alcove as if he were no more substantial than a lover she had dreamed. Unbuttoned his jeans and tugged them to the floor. Kissing him again. Until he was naked. Then pressing herself against him and whispering an answer to his earlier question. No, she said, we're cooking you for lunch. And pushed him gently until he'd backed into the tub. He went in without resisting and with only a minor splash. When he reached up for her, she slipped his grasp and backed away, laughing, putting both hands between her knees and bending over until he can see the fullness of her breasts. And then she let the laughter subside into a calm and delicate smile.

How is it? she wanted to know.

It's wet he said. And warmer than I expected.

She poured drops of amber into the water, swishing it until the suds rose up. I think I'll let you soak a while. Well, maybe not too long he said. But she went back to the kitchen table and covered it with the tablecloth from her saddlebag. Found plates in the cabinets. Two cups which she filled with cold water. Tin forks from one of the drawers. He watched her working, the rhythmic motions of her hands, the sway of her hips as she walked. He motionless, she holding his eyes with hers as she unwrapped the food, arranging it on their plates with the slow ceremony of a child exacting tea from her play-setting. It was, he realized, perhaps the first time she had ever done this without servants and the familiarity of wealth.

Beneath the low arch of the alcove she undressed for him, dropping her clothes beside his jeans, letting his eyes linger over her, the rich abundance of her breasts and the thick dark hair between her legs. When she leaned to touch the water, he kissed her nipples, sliding his hand from her waist to her hips and back again. When he reached to embrace her fully, she pulled back again and began to walk away. What now, he said. What now, would you drive a man to madness before he has the slightest taste of you?

Not nearly warm enough. I need you steamed and starched.

She took the empty kettle to the fireplace and filled it from the cauldron. He surveyed her hips, her legs, the falling waves of her hair. Her nakedness did not make her shrink from the flames. She seemed to bask in them, and they leaned in her direction. Her face and arms took the glow, transforming her skin from human brown to golden luminescence. When she dipped the kettle, it went into the water with one smooth motion; and when she lifted it, it came out steaming, droplets slipping down the cauldron's sides and hissing. She carried the kettle as casually as a basket from her garden, holding it over the center of the tub and smiling like a mischievous child. You'll want to be careful with that, he said. And she poured.

Warmer now?

A good bit, he allowed. You'll probably want to give it a try yourself.

She did something to her hair, but he could only see the lifting of her arms and breasts.

When she stepped into the water, it caused barely a ripple; and when she sank upon him, the heat rose to his shoulders and spread anew throughout his body. Her first touch was surprisingly cool. She kissed his face and leaned back to look at him again, scooping water and dripping it over his forehead and eyes and nose.

He closed his eyes and put his arms around her waist. Pulled himself into her. Dropped his hands to her hips and pushed with his foot against the end of the tub.

Slowly she said. Do it without spilling a drop of water.

No man can do such a thing.

Slowly, she insisted. Like little waves.

No. He stood up, still holding her against him, throwing a storm of water across the floor. Making her gasp and wrap her arms fully around his neck. He put his hands beneath her hips and carried her to the bed. There she kissed him, both of her hands grasping at his hair, pulling her shoulders and face up from the pillow. He kept one arm beneath her back, pressing the two of them together while his other hand squeezed her hip, slid down the flesh of her thigh, and lifted the knee until it was almost touching her shoulder. She said a word to him that he did not hear. In fact, did not hear her say the word again and again as if it gathered meaning with repetition.

Leala was suddenly overtaken by the knowledge that Amedeo Muñoz might not be the man she supposed. There was a gentleness beneath his ferocity, a hidden need beneath his own desire. She could see this in his face. She could sense it in his slow descent. In his reluctance to draw away from her when he was done.

Days later, after they had returned to the hacienda, he remembered but still did not understand what the afternoon had meant. One morning, while the men were hanging new doors for the stable, she took Cesare for another long ride, bringing the stallion back through the chaparral. Slowing him to a walk for the last quarter mile and then turning him into the stable yard when she saw that Amedeo Muñoz was alone. He had hammer and shim in one hand, sleeves rolled tight and past his elbows. In the sharp slant of light he appeared to be sweating as much as the horse. But rather than look up at her, he finished framing the door of the tack room and went back to his truck for hinges. Neither of them spoke. She guided Cesare around him, the way she had seen her husband's men inspecting cattle from horseback, until he stopped and frowned. I'm only teasing you she said. Softly, so that the words would not carry. Her back straight, her eyes on the horizon so that any onlookers would think she was merely giving orders.

But on her second passage, he dropped the hinges and took the bridle in one motion, his hand like the flick of a paw. Cesare stamped nervously, trying to travers. The three of them throwing one shadowed tangle on the ground until Amedeo soothed the horse, stroking his neck, standing close enough to him that man and animal were chest to chest. Amedeo kept the bridle tight against his shoulder and the beast's great head next to his own. He whispered to Cesare, and at the same time reached his hand beneath her skirt. He did it as naturally as he had calmed the horse; but a shock went through her body. Her knees jerked inward. She spurred Cesare on one side so that there was another flurry of stamping, of nearly losing her balance. She realized now that she could not snatch the reins or raise her voice. That she could not push away his hand. For an instant she wanted to use the crop, to slash him across the face, but that too could be seen from the house, from the terrace, from one hayloft or another or from the shambling perspective of a truant maid. But before Leala could calm her mind, he had calmed the horse, and his hand was caressing the fullness of her thigh.

It was shocking to hear him say it. It was dangerous and

arrogant and stupid. To repeat her words in this open place, but that was what he did. He said them back to her as if the two of them were still inside the cabin, still aching for each other's release. And, yes, he said. I want all of you as well.

•

So that now, in the slippery present, Leala was realizing that the brown skirt, lying half in and half out of the suitcase, was the one she wore that day in the stable yard; and she wondered what Amedeo Muñoz was remembering. For a second he was staring at the bed, and then he shifted his eyes to hers as if he deserved an explanation. She turned her back and took more items from the dresser drawer, random ones, and threw them at the suitcase before slamming down the lid.

"I'm going with you," he said.

"No. No, Amedeo, you are not."

"Why?" he wanted to know.

Leala tried to sound as if her own mind were certain of what she was saying. "Because you do not love me. And you do not own me. And I do not love you."

"How do you know?"

A sudden sympathy came into her voice. She stepped close to him and laid her face against his chest. "Because, Amedeo, you are no one. You are from nowhere. You have no future or past. You are always only now; and, even if we did love each other, then where could we possibly go? What could you offer a daughter, or the wife, of a wealthy man?"

He sounded genuinely surprised when he said "Together we are not enough?"

"No," she answered. "Not enough in any way that matters. Maybe you were my revenge for some insane, petty cruelty on Alejandro's part. I don't know what I'm feeling now, but you have to go."

He didn't seem to hear. He said, "I have been seeing you the way a husband sees for longer than a year."

"You have to leave," Leala told him now. "Someone will be coming. Someone will see."

"You put her in my arms. Yesterday, that is what you did. You put her into my arms, and she looked into my eyes."

This time she was more insistent. "So that you could tell her good-bye."

Never before had someone struck him so hard with words. He blinked, rubbed his brow with one hand, and then looked down at his fingers as if he expected to find blood. He thought about leaving her to whatever madness it was that was scattered on the bed. He thought about shaking her senseless, about trying to find his own words, the right ones that will make her care. It was in this wordless instant that he was surprised from behind.

Reina came rushing from the hall. She was buttoning the last buttons of her dress and almost collided with Amedeo, putting out her hands to stop herself and moving him a step farther into the room. Leala was nearly startled into a noise that would bring half the household, but the older woman had already pushed past Amedeo, and took Leala by the hand. "He's awake," she said. "Your husband is getting dressed, and he's been asking for you. He may be on his way here already."

Leala could feel the rush of fear that was rising from her shoulders to her neck. She could see the red flush spreading across her face in the mirror, brightening the humiliation that she already felt. Here was the carpenter Muñoz, dressed in his church-bound best, standing in her bedroom and arguing in hushed syllables over the paternity of her child. It took no more than a breath for her to regain control. "Call Gabriel," she said to the other woman. "Send Rosa, and tell him to bring the car now. To bring it now! And, Reina, get your own bag. Hurry!" She turned her back and finished with one of the suitcases, latching it and setting it next to the wall.

"What is happening?" Amedeo asked.

She folded the diaper bag and snapped it shut. "Nothing that concerns you any longer."

"I can help you," he said.

"Good. Take these bags to the kitchen. Give them to Gabriel. And then leave. Go somewhere farther north. Find a woman and make a life. You no longer have a place here. Maybe neither of us does." Leala dragged the second suitcase from the bed and raised a shaking hand to her mouth, wiping hard at her dry lips. It was strangely calming to see Amedeo stoop to pick up the bags, and she felt some hope that they might all escape.

But Reina returned with her own bag and a look of alarm. "He is coming," she managed to say. "Bajardo is finishing with him. And he is coming. I heard him call your name."

Now Leala listened to herself again saying certain words. They came to her in an oddly muffled echo, in what seemed to be, at first, the voice of her own mother, but from such a distance that the words were barely audible. It was as though her mother were speaking from the grave. And Leala listened to herself saying, "Take the baby."

The look on Reina's face. Her lips already forming an incomprehension. And Leala trying to bring her own voice into the room, trying to make someone hear. "Reina! Take the baby now. And go. Gabriel knows the way." Trying to make herself sound calm and reasoned.

Still the older woman did not move. Reina looked toward the nursery and then toward the hall. Leala had to take her arm and propel her toward the baby's room. "Reina, hurry! I'll take one of the other cars later. And I'll meet you at the cathedral. In Sangre de Cristo. Tomorrow. Or the day after."

The baby didn't wake. Reina lifted her from the crib, and the baby stirred, but she did not wake. Amedeo followed with the bags, three of them. He followed after having taken something from the bookshelf on the wall, an item that he placed inside his shirt. As soon as he had gone, Leala sensed that the room was somehow bigger, more disheveled than it had ever been. There were clothes hanging out of dresser drawers, clothes still draped across the bed. One of the small suitcases, part of a matched set purchased in Madrid, was tipping out of the closet door. The mirror for some reason was hanging off-center. Leala reached to straighten it, and what she saw made her examine her tattered self. She was barefooted and wearing a slip. She was red-eyed and suddenly shivering. Her hair had need of a brush; a long strand of it was spiraling past her chin. From very far away she heard her husband calling out her name.

2

ALEJANDRO CRUZ WORKED himself higher in the bed. He did it by rolling his hips and walking backwards on his hands, pushing with one, then with the other. He made it into a graceful, grotesque motion, like a ballet dancer with a broken spine. He pressed the button that summoned Bajardo, his valet, while looking down at the twisted sheets. Then he began to massage his thighs, thinking how could the sheets be twisted if he had not moved his legs during the night? Where was the sheet-twisting wench who visited him? The lingering scent of her, where was that?

Alejandro worked a reassuring ache into his right leg. There was no feeling at all in his left. He wiggled some toes, pulled the right leg up to his chest and let it go. Watched it replace itself among the satin wrinkles and waves. He pulled up the left leg. Visualized the problem in this leg as a broken wire that needed some jiggling to reconnect, but he didn't particularly care to give the problem a name. Didn't need to dignify it with acceptance. There. Ah, there. Alejandro took a jolt of pain so white and electric that it momentarily blinded him, made the salty remains of dinner rise into his throat. It was a lovely feeling. But then soon enough.... Soon enough it receded. And here now was Bajardo bringing his own numb presence into the room.

Bajardo looked like a movie actor whom no one would recognize, someone chosen to play the part of friend. A vague pleasantness had settled upon his face. Would you like something, he wanted to know, perhaps an aspirin and a glass of water?

"No," Alejandro said.

A man who dressed well, he reasoned, was a man who had not surrendered to the indignities of age. Or disease. A man who took pains with his appearance had not yet acknowledged that pain itself could defeat him. Nor the mortification of falling in the night. Nor the shame of being betrayed within a marriage. A man who dressed well, one could assume, raised the expectations of all around him. And so he had Bajardo help him with the gray gabardine slacks. And then with the cordovan cap toes, the ones with the black laces, and also with one of the new Arrow shirts. What else, he mused. What else? The navy blue belt of course, the wristwatch with the leather strap, the glasses. Would he be needing the cane this morning? No, he said to Bajardo. He didn't need it now. In the mornings he had energy enough, even a certain amount of feeling in the leg. It still took an entire day to wear him down, to drive him into the dark recesses. And, who knew, it might yet take years to kill him. Maybe not even then. Look at Roosevelt, the stricken president, who seemed to be running an entire country without running a race.

He had sweet sensation in the leg today, plus an implausible optimism, as he did nearly every morning. His arms, well, they were thick and toned from compensatory use. His back was strong, was it not? His mind was as clear as a cloudless sky. His appetites, with one or two exceptions, were as sharp as any man's. And his other senses, a peculiarity of the disease perhaps, had grown more acute than ever. He could almost hear her breathing in her sanctum. He could almost taste her when she undressed for the night. It was his other feelings that had grown complicated. His desire for Leala Anita Sanchez de Cruz had never entirely dissipated; but it had changed. Ah, God, a man's wife sees the best and the worst of him, is it not so? This was the thought that struck him, and it seemed profoundly poignant and poignantly profound. So he repeated it aloud. "A man's wife, Bajardo. She sees the best and the worst of him."

"That is true, Señor."

"A man should acknowledge that much," Alejandro continued.

"A generous man would do exactly so." Bajardo took a brush to the trousers and then gave a quick whisp to his master's shoulders.

"Yes. I like that. A generous man. Because marriage

demands commitment, yes?"

"I believe they say it does, Señor. And also that a man can be happy with any woman, as long as he does not love her."

"You're a wit, Bajardo, a refreshing wit. Who, I promise you, will be horsewhipped in the stable yard on the very day that I believe you are talking about me." Alejandro smiled and patted his man upon the shoulder.

But Bajardo never smiled, never betrayed an inner feeling. "You will be having breakfast now, Señor?"

"No. I want to see if my wife is up already. We'll take breakfast together."

A man should be generous, Alejandro thought. And he should acknowledge, should he not, that Leala had been the first to suspect that something medical was wrong. She saw the changes in him. In the midst of all the headaches, the loss of appetite, the inexplicable bursts of anger, she saw a sickening man. They had to stop sleeping together when she was pregnant with their baby, the first one. Then they had grown more formal after the miscarriage. His mind after that tragedy had drifted toward the abstractions of money and politics. She became childishly enamored of art and horses. But she never blamed him for his own despair. In an odd way, she had blamed herself, perhaps because she had lost his first child. So a man should be generous, even forgiving, if the woman became childishly enamored of other things. So that even now he longed for her.

In her cloistered bedroom, in the center of the house, he could almost picture her shoving clothes into dresser drawers and straightening things—mirrors and metal hangers—while finding a ring of diaper pins that she did not pack. He could imagine her haste as panic came creeping forth, its tentacles uncurling. Because Bajardo had told him everything, even about the carpenter who had come to call so quaintly. And so Alejandro gave forth her name, sweetly, and made his way to the door unencumbered by cane or careless, injudicious thinking.

Leala. A voice as distant as an echo was sounding out her name.

Li-la he usually called her. But today it was all three syllables, and they startled her more than anger or the cold calculation of his way of speaking to other men. Her eyes flitted to the window where she could see the open trunk of an idling car, which was partially obscured by overhanging leaves. Several shadowy figures were next to the car moving about like thieves, for that was what they were. She had to force herself back into the room, where she saw a single hose and a garter belt across the arm of a chair. Rolling them together with nervous hands, she stuffed them into the wrong drawer of her dresser. She came close to stumbling over two shoeboxes on the floor and kicked one of them beneath the bed. She scanned the room for further signs of flight. Her arms were cold. Her stomach was beginning to feel like sloughed cement. When he called again, she was looking into the vacancy on the bookshelf and saw what Amedeo Muñoz had taken. It was the picture that was missing. Her and the baby, the one in the silver frame.

"Leala."

The voice was nearer now. She could hear his disease. The irregular footsteps, the pausing from time to time so that his hands and arms might help him along. In the mornings, without the cane, he went about like a man tilting into a storm, the expression on his face somehow more frightening than pain. Even his smile seemed to have been chiseled out of wood.

"There you are," he said.

She could feel him suddenly in every corner of the room.

"Here I am. Yes."

Alejandro was looming in the hall, leaning a bit against the buttresses of his arms, both hands on the doorframe at shoulder height. Breathing through his nose like a runner who's just battled his way uphill. "There you are. Let me look at you."

And she was thinking that the world had gone insane. Another man who wanted to stand and look at me as if I were something that he owned. As if by living in his house I had become his decoration and his property. But his voice was gentle and undemanding. "I've not always appreciated that I have the woman that every man desires," he said. "I've been thinking about that lately. And being grateful."

His words colored her face. She looked about for her robe and then remembered that she'd already put it back into the closet. "You're up very early" was all she could think to reply.

"I couldn't sleep. Besides, I wanted to talk with you," Alejandro said.

"Alejandro, I'm tired. The baby kept me up last night. And now isn't the time for--."

"It's all right," he went on. "I wanted to apologize. For my behavior lately."

She waited, looking around the room with swift glances and a secret fear that she had left something obvious in full view. There was bric-a-brac and jewelry still scattered on the dresser, expensive trinkets that at the last minute she had decided not to pack. The lacquered door of the armoire was winging open, some of the clothes mashed together on their hangers. A few baby items still on the bed. She pressed her lips together and waited. Trying to seem as if she were merely petulant.

"I realize I have not been kind to you lately."

She looked at him still but did not speak.

Alejandro put a great deal of sincerity into his next words. "And. I want you to know. That I intend to be the man you want me to be."

"We've had this conversation before," she said.

"I know. I know. But I came to you. I came to *you* this morning, Leala. To say that I am sincere. I swear to you that I am sincere. The disease, it pulls me down into blackness. It takes me away from myself at times. You have no idea how deep it can drag your soul."

Leala was too quick with her reply. "Your disease has made you cruel?"

"Ah, my grandfather used to say that a woman can draw blood using only her tongue. It's true, eh? But I would say to you, my dear wife, do not mock what you do not know. I tell you that you have no idea. And yet, I have never, *never* raised my hand to you. Is it not true?"

"What do you want, Alejandro?"

He took a step into the room as if gathering his legs beneath him. The two of them became like adder and mouse. She moved a step backward and to one side, as if protecting the nursery door. And so he stopped, calculating the geometry of her fear—the distance between them, the distance to the nursery door, to the windows, to the lighted door into the hall. Leala combed the hair out of her eyes with her fingers, although her hand was trembling. Her own eyes could not stay fixed on one place. They were seeing every detail that was presently out of order. She was drawn to the bookcase beside the nursery door, where the familiar order of the room had been precipitously altered, a detail that could not be explained away.

"I want you to believe me," Alejandro said. "I want you to hear my sincere apology to you, my wife. And I want us to face our lives together the way we vowed to do when we were married."

She heard his low and calming voice. She felt the rhythm of it, how his intention registered before the words make their way to her brain. And it was a voice that she still wished she could trust. "You've made it impossible to live with you," she murmured. "I cannot take a breath without the servants whispering to you. And you treat me like one of your possessions." Then she placed her hand on the bookshelf, pushed two fingers along the polished surface as if checking for dust, and moved one of the smaller pictures into the vacancy that Amedeo Muñoz left behind. The place where the picture of her and the new baby, the one in the silver frame, had once stood.

He made an elaborate shrug. "I have offered you my apology. I didn't realize it would be this difficult for you to accept."

Leala knew that the words were hardly words at all. They weren't intended to mean; they were merely placeholders in some menacing equation, tossed off, discarded, scattered about the room like the leavings of an earlier dispute. He was not even looking at her anymore. He was looking at the room itself. And then at the window. And then at something on the other side of the window pane. Alejandro pulled himself closer to the bed, his right leg going up and down mechanically and being helped along by his hand. He stood himself next to the bedpost, grasping it with casual determination, not bothering to explain his interest in what was happening beyond the room. She did not dare to turn her head. Neither of them spoke. Finally Alejandro looked down at her bed, taking up one of the pillows and holding it to his face as he inhaled deeply. Then he dropped it to the floor.

"I have always loved the scent of you," he told her. "The mingling of perfume and *coño*. It's the most erotic, most irresistible force on earth. I can understand why men are made into fools. I just don't understand why women are."

She tried to stage-manage her fear, to transform it into the semblance of anger. "Why don't you leave now?"

"Do you always sleep like that? In your slip?"

"Of course not. I was getting dressed when you came in."

"This early?" he wanted to know.

"I told you. The baby kept me up."

"Yes, you did. Colic, they say, will keep a baby awake."

"I don't know what it was, Alejandro. It was a difficult night, that's all."

"I should check on her," he said.

"No. Let her sleep."

"I'll just peep in. I can be very quiet," he insisted.

"Alejandro, for God's sake, what do you want? Why are you bothering us like this?"

"Nothing. I want nothing from you. I just came to say that there's breakfast on the terrace. Bajardo is putting it out now. You can join me if you like." He offered a smile and began to limp away.

She glanced toward the window, but she was standing at the wrong angle to see what he had seen. Still frozen at the nursery door, she told him to wait in a voice that was too tremulous and too loud. "Just let me put on something, and

I'll.... I'll go with you."

"Slip into your robe. That'll be enough." He stepped past the closet where the suitcase was still visible and opened both doors of the armoire. "Oh. Were you going somewhere? Were you planning on a trip?"

His tone of voice brought clarity. She realized that he'd been toying with her and enjoying his interrogation. But his last question had an odd effect. Leala felt a surge of anger and with it an almost unrecognizable burst of courage. "Alejandro, look at me," she said. "And answer me one question. Why don't you just divorce me? It would be the simplest thing for us both."

"Because. I do love you. And because no man takes what is mine."

"And what if I divorced *you*?" she asked.

Alejandro seemed to consider the proposition. "Well, then. I would have to promise you, wouldn't I, that you would never see the child again. And, as you know, I never break my word."

"This isn't about your child! You don't love Maria any more than you love one of your horses or cars or bank acquisitions."

"Only half true, my dear. I loved my child, I truly did. You still remember her, I expect, and the little funeral we had."

"Don't you dare!"

"I loved the child that *I* put into your womb. Who was buried before she was born."

"Don't you dare mention that baby! Don't you dare push me back into that pain!" She was at his face before he could move, hitting him with both hands. Reaching into the bookcase for any kind of weapon, finding a wooden frame that fitted into her hand, and striking him until the glass had shattered and gone raining to the floor.

But Alejandro did not move, did not resist, until at last he took her forearms into his hands and forced them to her side. As if explaining to a child, he told her, "I loved the baby who almost made us into a family. Even in my grief I loved her. Until you became a carpenter's whore."

She let go of the picture frame. Her shoulders drooped.

He released his hold on her, and she turned very deliberately to look across the great room and out to the terrace where Bajardo, in the pale pink light, was preparing a small table for breakfast and pretending not to notice the open bedroom door. Then she gave a fleeting glance to the window that had so attracted Alejandro's attention. She could make out Gabriel now, who was loading the trunk of a crème colored car and arguing with someone just out of sight. She could make out Reina, who was seated already inside the car and holding a blanketed bundle in her arms. The trunk went down with a *chunk*. Then Gabriel walked toward the front of the car, and there was another *chunk* as the driver's door slammed shut and then another on the side that she couldn't see. It was Amedeo, she was certain. The car eased away from the hacienda, and she could only see silhouettes.

•

When Gabriel arrived, the sky was dark and the air was cold. There was a light in the Señora's bedroom, and hushed voices were coming from her open window. Even though it would be warmer for him inside the car, Gabriel stood outside, next to the open trunk, shivering, because he believed that they must hurry. The chauffeur wiped his lips with one hand. He willed his feet to be still in the noisy gravel. But when the kitchen door swung open, it startled Gabriel enough to make him stagger. A man emerged from the house, followed by a woman holding a bundle to her breast. It was Reina and the carpenter named Muñoz. Reina's sputtered whispers and hisses were bouncing off his back. When Muñoz answered her, it was only with a word or two. By the time they reached the car, the baby had begun to stir. Muñoz dumped the luggage into the trunk next to Gabriel's overnight kit and said, "I'll be coming with you."

"No! He won't." This exclamation from Reina was not quite a shout, but the intensity was clear. She had now grasped the man's sleeve. He turned back, looked down at her hand, and after a second she released her hold.

"But the Señora?" was all that Gabriel could think to say. "The Señora is coming too, yes?"

He said it because he had polished the car, chrome and glass and leather, until every surface gleamed. And he had dressed himself with careful attention to creases and cuffs. He was ready for the favor he had been asked to perform. For the Señora. Who had not yet appeared and who had sent no message. And so, what was he to do? Who would decide for them when to leave and when to return? Gabriel looked to the house as if it owed him an explanation, but he could only see the one light inside the kitchen going dark. A feeling began to grow and slosh inside of him like a balloon overfilled with water.

Muñoz closed the trunk with a soft click and nodded for Gabriel to get behind the wheel. "She won't be coming with us," the carpenter said. Then he opened both doors on the passenger's side, putting one foot on the running board and waiting for Reina to choose the front seat or the back. She glared at him, finally taking the baby into the back, adjusting the blanket and making hushing sounds until the little legs stop kicking.

Now the thing inside of Gabriel, the formless fear, began to press upward against his lungs, to bear downward on his unsettled stomach. He tried not to let his imagination sink further; but Reina had said nothing more to him, and still the Señora had not appeared. Perhaps something bad was happening. Perhaps something bad was happening inside the house and leaving now would be the worst thing that he could do. Even as he brought the engine to life, he kept his eyes fixed on the kitchen door, waiting, as if he expected some sudden alarm to keep him from making a mistake.

"Let's go," Muñoz said. "Now."

"I can't. Without the Señora we cannot."

"Now," the carpenter said.

On its own the car rolled out of the shadows and into the first hint of day. To the east were pink-tinged mountains and, high above them, the silhouettes of migrating geese. To the west there was only ghostly chaparral. Gabriel steered the car toward the main highway as if he were leading a funeral procession. And to no one in particular he announced that he did not want to raise a cloud of dust or make a clatter of gravel.

"He already knows," said Amedeo.

"He? Knows? The Señor?"

"Just drive."

Gabriel rubbed his forehead and eyes, let the car slow to a creeping uncertainty. How could a man think before the sun itself was awake? The tires gave off a delicate crunch, as if grinding corn, until, *bump, bump*, they reached the pavement running north and south. There, for the last time, Gabriel considered turning back. Reina still had said nothing, only some hushing sounds to the baby. Muñoz had folded his arms and leaned against the door as if asleep. And now the road brought the choice into his hands. If he turned back, he might be making the moment worse. If he turned south, he might be leaving the tack room and the comfort of his cot forever. Because the Señor was not a forgiving man.

"Go," said Muñoz, with his eyes closed and his head resting upon his shoulder. "Go wherever it is she told you to go."

It was an oddly comforting phrase. Gabriel turned south, because the lady herself had spoken, and he eased down on the accelerator. The Ambassador parted the air and settled into a smooth thrum that soon lulled the baby to sleep. The sun finally rose into its full circumference burning away low clouds at the foot of the mountains. It was then the landscape began to form itself into the pillars and foundations of the continent, revealing a thousand shades of brown and blue and gray. They drove until another highway took them more sharply south and west. Finally they joined a line of cars being waved along by a single soldier carrying an ancient Springfield rifle across his shoulders like a wooden yoke. He gave Gabriel an approving nod as the car inched across the border, and Gabriel raised four fingers from the steering wheel in a half-salute. They were funneled through a mongrel town, some of the cars stopping at bodegas that were selling gasoline and souvenirs. Finally the baby woke, and for the first time Amedeo Muñoz heard her cry.

"She needs water, a dry diaper," Reina said. "And you put her bag in the trunk."

They parked in the shade near a public fountain, and Reina handed him the baby as if passing off a bag of groceries. "Here. You want her? She is yours. Or so you say." Amedeo lifted the baby high and then brought her down close to his face. A little hand reached and patted him at the bridge of his nose. Then both her hands were entangled in his hair. The crying stopped. She pulled herself closer to the voice that was whispering to her.

"Maria Anita," the deep voice was saying. "Whose child are you? Mía. Who is the man made happy by a daughter's smile?"

Then Reina was back with a diaper, changing the baby on a bench beneath cottonwoods. "You are a fool," she said to Amedeo. "You are a reckless, arrogant man who barely thinks beyond the end of the day. You have no purpose in life other than your own appetites."

"I am a father," he said.

Reina barely let him finish. "You are a fool who will ruin lives."

"I am a father."

"Even if you are ... even if you are Joseph the father of Our Lord, do you expect her to acknowledge you? Do you think she will even for a moment look at you in a public street? Do you think that a rich woman from a landed family will leave her husband for an *inútil* like you? A carpenter who does not own his own tools? Is that what you think?"

Before Amedeo could answer, before he could calm her or make a joke, Reina rushed on. "Or maybe you expect her husband to throw her out into the world so that she can raise her child in poverty with you? So tell me. I want to know. What do you think is going to happen in Sangre de Cristo when you meet the mother of this child at the doors of the great cathedral? Because I would like to find out now if you are insane or merely so prideful you are willing to ruin all our lives."

Amedeo Muñoz spoke in the same soothing tone that he

had used with the baby. "I want to talk to her."

"If she follows us at all. Is that what you think will happen? That she will follow us in a day or two?"

Still calmly he said, "I want her to say the truth. And if she does not love me, all she has to do is say those words."

"Then," Reina answered, "let me spare you the pain. She does not love you. She loves her horses more."

"Reina. Of all the people I have known at the hacienda, you are my favorite. And do you know why? Because you are honest and true. That is what you are. And I am thankful for you always. But do you know why you are angry at this moment? Because you are afraid. You see me look into my daughter's eyes, and you see a man who is full of joy, a man who is not afraid of what the future holds." Amedeo smiled and kissed Reina on her forehead. "Now. We have a long way to go. Gabriel! Water and gasoline, my friend! Your señora is already waiting for you at the cathedral in Sangre de Cristo."

"You are a reckless, prideful man," Reina said.

"Every father is full of pride," he allowed. "Why don't you have a nap in the back? And I'll take Mía in the front. We can see the birds and the white clouds and the ocean when it comes."

3

THEY PASSED A HAND-LETTERED SIGN marred by bullet holes, the post leaning away from the road as if staggering into the desert. The words said something about a bridge ahead, so Gabriel slowed and finally stopped when he saw a man and a burro farther along. Yes, the old man told them, the bridge was gone, washed off its foundation on one side and the beams stolen for lumber.

"Sangre de Cristo?" Gabriel asked.

"You take the old road into the mountains," the man told them. "Pretty far up I think, and then come down by Zalcupan and then over to the ocean road. Another hour or two I believe it must be."

They drove east for a time, ascending to the level of pines and plateaus. In the near distance they could see snow on the highest peaks, a white reflection so bright that it seemed colorless, as if they were driving into the sun. The scrub oak and piñon of the lower elevations gave way to fir with ancient, arterial branches. Clouds hugged the mountains' shoulders. Soon there was a solid wall of stone on the left and a vista for an artist on the right. They passed a stream leaking from the ponderous northern wall and gathering itself into a blood-dark pool before continuing through a culvert and emptying into the air fifty feet below the car. Gabriel took them through a short tunnel and then along a ridge that dropped away on both sides. "Down there," he pointed. "The road to Zalcupan."

They passed a boy in a sleeveless shirt, his goats scattering to the slope as the car made its way through the herd. They came upon the stone foundation of a house. When they reached the outskirts of another village, they saw girls carrying water jars from below, round clay vessels held against their hips by bright broad sashes and a single guiding hand. As the car glided around them, the girls stopped and stared because the car was an omen, like all things from the outside world.

The water girls strained to see inside the vehicle where there was a man in the front and a woman in the back staring out at them. They were as solemn and still as corpses these passengers; and the driver, dressed for a funeral cortege, looked neither left nor right. But it was the wondrous car itself that caused a sensation. Not one of the girls had ever seen such a thing, a motor car which was not completely black. And yet this car wore two colors, the shades of butter and gold. It glided almost soundlessly past them, disappearing around a curve and headed toward the upper tunnel and the village store. One of the girls, named Hermosa, said that the painted car was really hers, that her driver was taking the long route down to the stream. She laughed. The other girls laughed too. And then, unaccountably, Hermosa felt water upon her leg. She looked down to see her water pot swinging in its sash, falling away from her hip, and then crashing to the ground. A second girl, Marianela, was unexpectedly upon her knees. Another one screamed. Then they knew. And they all began to run.

Gabriel slowed to a cautious stop in the middle of the road.

Below them were rows of peasant houses stacked against the mountainside as close as the shingles on a roof. There were narrow streets forming terraces like the layers of a cake. An adobe church where someone was ringing a bell as if he had seen a fire. Some of the people in the plaza stilled themselves; others had already started to run. Inside the car Gabriel turned his head left and right, rolling down his window and stretching to see the tires.

"What is it?" Amedeo asked.

"I don't know. I felt something beneath the tires."

"We hit something?"

"No," Gabriel was almost musing. "It was like ... wrinkles in the road."

Amedeo handed the baby to Reina and opened his door to check beneath the car. "I see nothing. We can stop down below. I'll drive for a while if you like."

"It was something. I felt it in my hands," Gabriel said as

he drove them toward a waterfall, a narrow shimmer against the rocks ahead; the car rolled smoothly past a general store with a wooden porch, past a storage shed, past two houses perched only inches from the road. It was then that they all felt it, a gentle vibration, no more than a shiver on a chilly morning. Then in the following instant there came a violent shaking of the earth. A belching cloud of dust and a hail of pebbles fell onto the hood of the car. A crevice opened in the road, and no one had to say the word. Gabriel had the car moving in reverse even before the first women down in the village had begun to shout their children's names.

They drove no more than fifty feet before Reina screamed, "Stop! Stop!"

Gabriel could see it in his mirror, the general store sliding toward them into the road.

Amedeo watched a fist-sized stone ricochet off a boulder just below them. It flew out over the village in a thousand foot arc before exploding like an artillery shell onto a red-tiled roof; it hit one of the lowest houses. A man rushed from a doorway higher up, hoisting suspenders to his shoulders and falling into the street, scrambling to his knees, and then falling again into an animal pen where he flopped like a fish. More and more people thickened the streets, many of them headed for the only large building in the vicinity, a gray stone-clad hospital or school on the north side of the town. Some melon-sized stones had begun to tumble and bound from much higher up the mountain. They skipped and ricocheted. One of them barely missed a child standing in the plaza, while another leapt over a flock of chickens that seemed frozen where they stood.

"We can't stay here," shouted Gabriel. "The road could fall away at any time."

"Keep her in the car," Amedeo said into the back seat. He and Gabriel climbed out, shouting now in order to be heard. "You look up ahead," Amedeo said, as he pointed and pushed the older man. "Try to find a pathway down. I'll check back here." But his words were muffled by a deep thunder from inside the earth and a fresh shower of hail from above. Amedeo jogged back to the store that had been shaken

completely off its foundation—still bulldozing its way into the
road. Glass shattered in one of the front windows and the
wooden telephone box on the front porch jangled like a
lunatic's laugh. There was no way down.

A brown sludge began to pour from inside the store. The
smell was of fresh-tilled earth, but the sight was obscene, like a
river of sewage flowing through the building. The front door
bulged. Several boards creaked, splintered, and flew away from
the side of the store. Amedeo turned back toward the car
where Gabriel was waving and shouting into the storm. Reina
was outside the automobile with him, tugging at one of the
door handles. "No! Wait!" Amedeo called back. "Wait! She's
safer in the car until we can find a..."

Stones interceded. Far above them an island of broken
trees began to slide downhill, loose, liquid dirt spreading like
the first waves of an incoming tide. Houses down in the village
began to buckle under the assault. The first few were simply
submerged. More people ran into the streets, some of the
fortunate ones joining clusters of eight or ten and fleeing
together while others cowered individually in corners and
doorways like small, frightened animals. The noise from
beneath the ground changed from the low rumble of a
mountain storm into something industrial. It came out of the
earth like the grinding of factories, like the roar of steel mills
and engine rooms. Amedeo tried to make out what Gabriel
was shouting toward him, but the din had grown too loud. The
shrieks from humans and animals, once indistinguishable, were
now merely swallowed up.

In one convulsive gulp the waterfall in front of them
disappeared. Amedeo watched it as he staggered back to the
car, and the reality was more than his mind could imagine.
Where there was once a magnanimous flow of water, there
now was nothing. Amedeo felt his dry lips moving. He felt
them forming two incredulous syllables that his ears could not
hear. "It's gone," he said to himself. He turned his eyes toward
Gabriel and Reina, pointing with a half crooked finger and a
numb incomprehension. They could not hear him over the
pandemonium, but he spoke to them in calm and

conversational tones. "It's gone," he said. "The river. It went away." Even as he made the words, the cliff face was changing again, reforming itself into an indentation, a natural amphitheater now of dirt and stone. The water had been erased somehow, and the convulsive force of that collapse finally reached them, shaking the car like a toy and throwing Amedeo and Reina to their knees.

The ground ahead of them began to crumble. What was once a single crevice across the road had fractured and grown to a gap of several feet. Crackling veins had spread beneath the Ambassador's tires. Gabriel was working at both door handles now. He could pull both at the same time because it was a rich man's car, the doors opening outward like a book. But a heavy stone had partially crushed the roof, and the baby was trapped inside. Amedeo could see her through the window, happy and unperturbed. He forced his fingers into an open channel between the doors and pulled. The frame straightened slightly but refused to release the door. "The trunk!" he shouted to Reina. "The tire tool. We'll pry it open."

Already the far windows had collapsed, and a steady flow of debris was filling up the car. It poured in like industrial sludge from a conveyor belt, the same undigested mire that Amedeo had seen gushing through the store. Now he couldn't help watch it cover the clutch and brake pedals beneath the steering wheel and begin its steady rise to the level of the seat. The back of the collapsing car was worse. Amedeo could see the baby's blanket being steadily consumed by dirt. He worked his fingers down to a lower hold, his face now on a level with the window and only inches from his daughter's face.

"Get a stone!" he screamed at Gabriel. "Break the glass in front and we'll reach around." But before either of them could move, the mountain intervened.

The far side of the car began to fold under the buildup of silt and slag. The roof sagged, and the frame gave out sounds like the groaning metal of a sinking ship. One of the tires blew out just before the entire suspension gave way, and the car dropped half a foot. The front windshield splintered just as suddenly, and then the back passenger window broke, leaving just enough of an opening to reach a baby if someone were fast enough. Reina was there, her arm already inside the car, her fingers already clutching the little arm when the boulder fell.

Then there was no sound.

Then something was exploding in the air. Perhaps it was the air itself because the pressure was all around them. And there was a blast of sand and grit upon their faces, but the sound itself never seemed to arrive. It was like a bomb without a noise. And when the boulder had found its equilibrium, it was simply there. Bigger than a house. There should be another word, Amedeo thought, for a stone this immense. That was all his mind could register at the moment his first life ended. Later, in the courtyard of the school, huddled beneath a blanket dragged from someone's shattered house, drunken Gabriel would say, "It was so big we did not see it as we drove by. I may have touched it when I got out of the car. Maybe I put my hand against it. Really, it did not fall any distance at all. It just teetered once and then laid down."

The window took Reina's arm, neatly, at the wrist. The glass and the collapsing metal frame worked like a guillotine. One moment the hand and the baby were there. In the next moment, they were gone. Reina could snatch away neither of them in time. There was a spray of blood, enough to splash back upon them. And at first she simply blinked. Finally, seconds later, she made a sound, although no one heard it. Reina barked. She made a coughing exhalation that expressed her surprise. It was Gabriel who seized the arm and tried to staunch the flow.

Amedeo was stunned into another world, contemplating the door handle in his hand and the sudden disappearance before his face. How could the great universal cogs and gears have moved so fast? So slowly? It seemed a problem worth bringing to a solution now that God had pulled back the curtain and allowed him to see the workings of calamity. It seemed worth the kind of laughter that turned a man inside out. The chrome handle he dropped into the dirt. He set his shoulder against the only conundrum he could see. Planted his feet and lifted. He lifted until the muscles knotted across his shoulders and the veins bulged in his neck. Until his feet were sliding back and Gabriel's cries were finally breaking through.

Gabriel was there shaking like a man just pulled from a freezing lake. His face was splattered with a mud that ran like tears, and he was shouting, gesturing in a way that Amedeo could not understand. Then he was trying to pull Amedeo away from the incomprehensible stone, but Gabriel had no strength. "... to do something!" Gabriel was screaming.

"Yes. I am." Amedeo was calm and steady in his concentration.

"... back to your senses. And help me get her down. I don't know how to stop the blood."

"Yes. I'll get her down." Amedeo turned his back and resumed his stance against the stone.

"No. No. Reina!" Gabriel was tugging at Amedeo's shoulder, but it was like trying to turn a bull. "Her hand is gone! She's sitting on the ledge. And. Her hand is gone."

"She's gone?" Amedeo asked.

"Listen to me! You've got to help. You've got to help me get her down."

Amedeo stood upright, looked deeply into Gabriel's face, and then patted his own with an open palm. The fingertips came away in red.

"Yes," Gabriel said. "She's over there. Where the ledge....it's giving way." He ran and waved his arm. Amedeo finally saw her, Reina, a bloody bag of clothes thrown beside the road.

He unbuckled his belt and pulled it from the loops, still moving slowly, as if this crumbling world were as safe and stable as the past. When he reached Reina, he made a cinch, drawing the leather tight until she cried out again and struggled to pull away. He wound more loops while Gabriel held her arm. It was grim and filthy work, and the bandage that they made from Gabriel's sleeve was hardly worth the time.

Together they lifted her and headed down-slope, sinking into the soft earth almost to their knees. They did not walk.

They waded. There was a steady flow of debris that rose at times to their knees and pushed them down and down into the village and into a chaos of bounding stones.

●

They thought the worst was over when the shaking stopped.

They pulled Reina from the muck and joined an old man herding his family toward the large gray building to the north and east of the village. No one spoke. No one asked their names. When they had covered half the distance, Amedeo could make out a walled terrace in front of the building and in front of the terrace a wide flight of granite steps. The style and scale were so out of place in a peasant village that he could not help but stop and look around. It was as if a building from some European capital had been lifted from its foundation and dropped into the mountains by mistake.

Amedeo helped a teenage boy lift a chest of drawers into a cart that was immediately wheeled away by a flock of children pulling and pushing at both ends. Farther along there was a man swinging his arm as if directing traffic and saying to everyone who passed by, "Go. Hurry. To the school. Do not stay here." He had a shotgun slung on a rope over one shoulder and spoke with a note of authority even though his face was creased with worry. He seemed to be searching the crowd even as the bodies surged around him. "Go on," he said. "Do not be caught in the open. The aftershocks will come. Go now. Hurry. All the way inside the school." The people went past him like salmon swimming upstream.

Finally a small boy slipped through the throng and threw his arms around one of the man's legs. The relief on both their faces took away the need to speak. The steady man kept waving, but with his free arm he reached down. Patted the quivering shoulders. Put all his effort into staying calm. "Do not stay here," he told them. "Don't be in the open when they come. The aftershocks. They are worse than all of this. Go. Go to the school. And stay inside. Go now. Hurry on. Go. Go."

The crowd streamed toward the north and the great gray façade. Amedeo stumbled among them, dazed, thinking that he should be carrying something too. On every side of him the people had their possessions in their hands. A box of tools, a cat, a sewing machine balanced on one shoulder, a cast-iron kettle stuffed full of clothes. Two boys went by leading a heifer. A woman had tied her household valuables inside a blanket of blue and gray. Children carried chickens. An old man clutching a leather satchel to his chest followed them, furtively looking left and right. There was a girl with cornhusk dolls.

Far below the village, on the wide valley floor, the younger men were stirring. The nearest ones had dropped their tools, gone charging into the back of an ancient pickup truck, one door still open, as the truck began its long ascent. Others in more distant fields were just receiving the alarm. They looked down at the trembling earth. Then immediately they looked up. The mountain was telegraphing its intent. So they too dropped their tools, wondering if already it was too late. They ran and ran. Another truck headed up the mountain. Soon there were only the men who'd been left behind, little more than specks in the farthest fields, shaking their arms and, apparently, shouting into the thin and tumultuous air.

In between convulsions the mountain had fallen back into a restless sleep. Its shape had changed. Now it looked like a husband who had lumbered home from the cantina, thrown his coat to the floor, and slumped himself into a chair. Minutes went by uncounted as people streamed toward safety. Others stood in the open spaces and stared upward as if they could read the mountain's intentions. Still others held their breath.

Finally the drunkard reasserted himself. The mountain groaned again and thundered, tearing huge crevices from east to west, dropping monoliths that had been shaken free in the first tremors. The loose fill had been sifted away, and now great boulders came in terrifying leaps, just like the little stones, but these new projectiles took entire houses when they bounded. The people screamed one collective scream at first and then babbled in panicked verses, some running with renewed energy, some still frozen as spectators of the wreck and ruin.

The northwestern wing of the school, stretching upslope into the flow of debris, took a wrenching impact from two megaliths that had been shaken loose and pushed along by the slag. They were like icebergs. Amedeo saw the collision and the great gray prow of the building collapsing, but the central mass of the structure held its shape, cleaving the flow to either side. Some of the roiling waste swamped the plaza and lesser buildings near the church. A wheezing wreck of a man, as gnarled and ancient as any of the uprooted trees, got jolted against Amedeo. They clasped hands, and Amedeo righted him. The old man would not release his hold.

"Stay with your neighbors," Amedeo said. "They'll take you to some place safe."

"My granddaughter," the old man said.

"Probably at the big building. You can look for her inside." Amedeo was shouting even louder now because the crowd in the street had grown so dense. "Go there. It's the safest place for you." Amedeo repeated, "The big building. Up there. You should go now," and then they were separated in the rush. He let himself be carried by the collective will, not thinking, not feeling beyond his instant animal reactions. Nearer the gray edifice they moved like a slow parade, some people pushing and shoving to climb the steps. Amedeo got turned by a sudden insistence at his elbow. It was the old man again, who'd hooked him with his cane.

"She's caught," he yelled. "My granddaughter, she can't get out. Please. Please."

It made Amedeo want to laugh. In the midst of everything that was happening, when people had ceased to be people and had become only animals to be slaughtered, there was still individuality. And here it was in the form of an old man and his childish arrogance. It was rudeness raised to the level of a joke, Amedeo thought. He wanted to wink in the old man's face. He wanted to laugh out his own unbelievable pain in single bloody syllables, and then wink once again saying, "Do you know what I left up there, old man? Up there on the road. Do you have any idea of what *I* left behind?"

"Please," the old man begged. "Please." He was crying and

confused, looking about with cloudy eyes as if searching for some words that may have fallen out of his pockets; but all he could think to say was "Please."

It was not enough. Nevertheless, Amedeo Muñoz took one step against the crowd and bent down to the old man's face in order to explain. It's impossible he wanted to say. I'm a stranger here. I don't know my way. I don't know ... anything. I can't carry you through a panicked mob. "I'm sorry," Amedeo shouted, taking one more step toward the retreating figure.

"Gracias. Gracias," the old man said.

"No. No. Listen to me. I'm sorry about your granddaughter. But I can't. Impossible. Your granddaughter's gone. I'm sorry." He pushed a burro and a boy aside to get closer to the man, to make him realize that it was impossible to make the sea of people part. Then Amedeo leaned a few steps farther into the tumult before he could grab the old man's arm. He had to fend away people rushing in the other direction. When the old man fell, Amedeo fought to lift him up, shoving angrily at a younger man who stepped into the space. In another moment Amedeo was fighting, swimming, bulling against the flow and still saying to the old man, "We'll never find her. It's not possible. You've got to understand. We'll never find her."

"Gracias," the old man said. "God will go with you. You are a good man. God will go with you all of your life."

Two streets over, where the cobblestones lay scattered, they found the part of her that was still above the ground. She was caught at an absurd angle, as if she'd been leaning forward when the earth closed around her legs. The old man cried out a name, but the woman didn't lift her head from the bundle of rags beneath her. Below the waist she was trapped in the street itself. The crevice that held her extended for sixty feet, but where it once had been a grotesque yawn, now it was a mouth that was grinding closed again. The bottom of the fissure seemed to be dropping away as more and more debris fell into the hole and disappeared. Amedeo began to dig with his hands. "A shovel! A hoe! Something to dig with. Get one. Now!"

But it was like shoveling through the fog. Every scoop was

refilled instantly, and he could not reach her buried legs. Half a
dozen times he tried to pull her free. It was useless. And the
old man had disappeared. No one stopped to help them. No
one even heard his cries, and all Amedeo could do was dig.
Finally Amedeo slipped his legs over the edge of the crevice
and dropped himself four feet below the surface of the street.
He laid himself down beside the woman and spoke soothing
words to her, digging his hand down as far as he could reach.
Soon he had her knee, but there was an obstruction holding it
and a slippery something that he recognized as blood. The
woman stirred and turned her head so that they were almost
lying now face to face. It was morning she seemed to think. It
was morning and she was waking up, blinking away the dust of
unpleasant dreams, and here he was, her sudden lover and her
reassurance that all was safe and well. Amedeo could read these
thoughts because he could see them in her face. It is as if they
had been this way forever, the two of them. She smiled at him.
Good morning, dear. And he knew that she was going to die.

The woman's face was unaccountably beautiful, marked
but unmarred by pain. The eyes were dark and deep,
unfocused but still trying for one single moment more to make
him real. Her smile was sad. She seemed to appreciate the
simple kindness of his effort. Good morning. And thank you
for what you are doing. It was a smile that was beyond her
body's dominion. Graceful. Almost amused. She blinked him
further into clarity, patted his face in a familiar way, and said to
him, "You have a funny nose." He loved the gentleness of her
touch. The sweet exhalation of her words. Yes, yes, he nodded
back to her, I have a funny nose. I do. The woman whispered,
speaking it seemed from a great distance away when she said,
"Can you save her?" But Amedeo realized that he shouldn't
answer. That it would be unkind.

He dug the dirt from around her waist and stood up,
tugging beneath her shoulders until he slipped and fell himself.
"Help me!" he called out, hoping for some passersby. "Stop!
Anybody! I need...." But no one stopped. He was alone with
the woman and stayed alone with her because they were paired
by some silly words and an intimacy more important than their

lives. He dug. He uncovered her hips and thighs, wrapping his arms around her as if they were making love, wedging his foot against something solid and pushing with all his remaining strength until another jolt buried them deeper in the same grave. He was suddenly down below her now, covered to his chest in loose fill and ashes. He swam up to grasp at cobblestones that looked like rotting teeth. Only when the crevice widened again could he claw free. A new storm of tumbling stones cleared the street even as he attempted to stand. And something that he did not see struck him hard in the ribs, bending him into a figure of pain.

The woman whispered something into the bundle of rags. Closed her eyes as if going to sleep. And he could sense her gradually slipping away. Then she was no longer breathing, and her upturned eyes had begun to fill with dust. Her body dropped a foot or more, no longer lovely or composed, but limp, obscene, like food being taken into a monstrous mouth. She dropped once more, and then she was gone. The blackness widened into a churning sinkhole, and he barely managed to back away. Standing was beyond his capabilities. He crabbed backward for ten or twenty feet, bumping into a stone foundation. He wiped his face with rags from the bundled pillow that he had saved.

Where was the old man he wondered. Where was the one who pulled me into this? Amedeo half expected to find him with a shovel wandering in some side street, but there was nothing. Everything was emptiness. Everyone who could flee had fled. The old man was dead or not dead according to the laws of chance. Everything, as far as he could see, was aftermath. Even the trembling of the earth had stopped. Amedeo pushed himself upright against the wall behind him and tried to gather his balance on his two unstable legs.

Without seeing another human being, alive or dead, Amedeo made it to the school, where the steps were inhabited by a babbling crowd, subdued but curious, like fishermen looking out to sea. None of them would venture into the street. They knew that the aftershocks could last for days. But the worst of the storm was over, and they wanted to survey the

ocean of wreckage and ruin. They looked at Amedeo without
ardor or interest. All the feeling had been shaken out of them.
He was simply another bit of flotsam being thrown upon their
shore.

He came plodding up to the granite steps, looking for
Reina or Gabriel. Recognizing no one, nothing. Pushed himself
farther up to the crowded terrace, searching faces. Finally he
found an open space where he could sit and rest. Dropped the
bundle that he hadn't realized he'd been carrying, and
something inside the bundle cried.

4

AMEDEO SLEPT ON THE TERRACE. When he awakened, the sun was shining and he wondered if he had slept for hours or for days. There were few people around him, and the space in front of the school no longer looked like the crowded deck of a ship. He pulled himself to his feet and for the first time tried to take in the whole of the scene spread out before him. He saw survivors picking through ruins, lifting sheets of tin or unearthing bodies or opening doors now tilted at absurd angles. From time to time he could hear a soft sobbing or a sudden wail near one of the piles of debris. For the most part, though, the people were quiet, more like doves than noisy crows. It was the children who were most unnerving. They carried bags, some of them, and they went like harvesters through the rows.

"What day is it?" Amedeo asked a passing man.

The man frowned and walked on, carrying his heavy trunk to a cart that was already overloaded.

"What day is it?" he asked a second man, who stopped and studied the unfamiliar face, the blood spattered shirt he wore.

"Who are you?" the second man asked. "Nobody here knows you or what you want."

"I just want to know what day it is. How long I've slept."

"August 3," the man told him. Then added, "1936." Laughed and walked away.

There were fires. Every forty or fifty feet was a blaze that someone was fueling with broken pieces of furniture or fractured window frames, but even the flames seemed subdued. They gave off a pall of black and heavy smoke that trickled into the valley like oil-smudge, never rising more than a few feet off the ground. Amedeo watched a man carrying the body of a dog by its hind leg. He slung the carcass onto one of the fires and returned to the rubble of his house. Another man and his sons finished loading their truck by lashing a mattress

over the heaping remains of their home and weaving the ropes
until they looked like the rigging of a ship. A woman and child
climbed into the cab; the boys found a place among the cargo,
and the father assumed the wheel. They said good-bye to no
one as the oldest boy finished with the ropes and pounded
twice on the roof of the cab. The truck churned its way
through stony ground.

Amedeo's bundle and what it contained were gone. There
was no pile of motley, no tattered blankets lying anywhere
near, and the girl he had asked to watch the bundle was also
gone. Maybe she had not heard him. Or maybe there had never
been a girl. Could he have imagined her and the wad of
blankets and the crying sound inside? Maybe someone threw
the bundle into one of the fires. Everything that had happened
to him, the randomness of it all, came back to him now with
the senseless obscenity of a dream. A second baby? It was too
much he reasoned. It was too much. And yet look around. Feel
the smoke. Taste the thickening despair. God was punishing all
of us he suspected. For what I have done, God was punishing
the innocent as well.

He retreated into the building behind him looking for
Gabriel and Reina, telling himself that he was not really fleeing
the stares of those few still huddled on the terrace. As he
passed inside, the daylight lost its mocking brightness. There
was a softer light being filtered through a huge roseate window
above the doors. Elaborate in its tracery and cut with a
jeweler's skill, it reminded him of European cathedrals. Even
without the colors of stained glass, the window was
dramatically out of place in a poor mountain village. It was a
masterpiece, framed by elaborate stonework and centered over
two stout wooden doors. The doors themselves were works of
art—heavy, carved bocote hung on massive wrought iron
hinges. The air inside smelled of floor wax and furniture
polish, as if a troop of custodians were expecting official
guests. Farther into the entry two staircases curved upward,
both of them blocked, absurdly, by velvet ropes linked to
polished brass rings set in the newel posts. And inlaid in the
floor, between the stairs, was a compass rose fashioned from

more hardwoods. Not even the damage caused by the earthquake could hide the ornate strangeness of the architecture. Not even the bodies of the victims. There were dozens of them lining the halls, some still alive.

Amedeo walked the hall surveying the damaged bodies and finding no familiar faces. At the north end of the building there was a pile of masonry, shattered glass, and twisted metal. The remnants of a stair hung from the second floor, and the upper floor itself sagged low enough to touch. Amedeo joined a group of men prying pieces of a body from the wreckage. They were warning each other to be careful, that there was no need to hurry any longer. No need to tempt the fates. It was the body of a child they are uncovering, and Amedeo stepped away for air.

When he was able to return to the stairwell, he helped the men shore up the second floor with beams from the debris, showing them how to cross-brace and how to buttress against load-bearing walls. He and a man named Tomas levered away the heaviest stones with difficulty, Amedeo grunting in pain from time to time. They sent a boy to climb down, all the way to the basement, calling out to those who might be trapped. There was nothing, the boy shouted back, only darkness and crumbled stone and twisted steel. He scrambled back up to the hole in the first floor, where Amedeo lifted him out by his arm. Eventually Amedeo walked farther on, looking for Reina and Gabriel. He examined faces in the south hall and—his eye couldn't help it—he noted where repairs were needed and where demolition was the only answer.

Back outside, looking over the south-facing wall of the terrace, he saw men who were already digging graves. There were eight of them working in pairs on the down-slope, adding a new row to the crosses and crude memorials. They joked quietly among themselves in between long intervals of silence, breaking rhythm only to pass a stoneware jug from grave to grave. Then they drank and continued flailing at the rock-hard earth. Amedeo watched them for a time. When he caught the eye of the nearest man, he called down to him, "What is this place? Can you tell me what it's called?"

The others looked up at Amedeo as if he were dumping out a chamber pot. When he called to them again, the youngest man, shirtless with an open vest, threw a shovel full of dirt and spat. "This right here? It's the dirt-wall hotel. Come on down, we're just finishing up your room."

"No, this building," Amedeo said. "Where I'm standing, what is it? Why is it here?"

"It's the school, can't you read?" All of them but the two oldest laughed out loud.

"A monument," interrupted the shortest man. "A monument to arrogance and pride." But he seemed to be talking more for the benefit of the others than for Amedeo. His contempt was clear.

"Read the plaque," the young one said. "Vasco Garza Camarillo. Governor of this state. A thief and a politician, but then I repeat myself, no? You are maybe a friend of his?"

When Amedeo shook his head, the old one added with slightly less hostility, "Born in this village. But I don't remember him. He left a long time ago. Then someone—the government I guess—built this building so he would not forget his own name. Built it to hold up his plaque. So that we the *horrura* would not forget to be grateful for ... something or other. I don't know. I forget."

The other men laughed, and all of them turned back to their digging.

"But it's a *school*. Is it not?"

"Oh, yes," said one of the down-slope diggers. "We even have a teacher. He came as part of the deal. But, you know what? We don't have enough kids to fill up two rooms, let alone an ark of stone."

"So it's an *empty* building?" Amedeo asked.

"No. No. The building is full," said the man in the vest. "Full of haughtiness and hot air. It just doesn't have any people in it, except when the earth shakes. But it does have electric lights."

"Not anymore," said his companion.

"I'm looking for two people," Amedeo called down. "A man and a woman, not from around here. The woman's hurt."

"Grab a shovel," someone said. "They'll show up here sooner or later."

He found a line of people plodding down a short hallway to the east and progressing through a doorway that apparently led them to a rear courtyard or to another terrace. Amedeo put himself into the parade and followed the men in front of him. There was another terrace where cooking fires and makeshift tables had been set up for the work crews. A woman put a tin plate into Amedeo's hands before he could ask his question. It was filled with steaming corn and rice, a few stewed pieces of chicken, and a thin marsh lake of juice. Hunger suddenly overwhelmed him, and he was shoveling with a tin spoon when he saw them at last.

Gabriel was seated, his back against the remnants of a wall. In one hand he had a bottle, which he lifted in half salute as Amedeo appeared. Reina lay beside him, unconscious. A hand-woven rug was beneath her body. A blanket and Gabriel's jacket covered her to her chin.

"They treated her hand with pitch," he slurred. "Like she was a pirate on a pirate ship. You know? Boiled it right up over there. Cut the hanging flesh quicker than…"

"Is she okay?"

"I don't know, quicker than … you could chop a chicken. I'd say it was about as quick. The chicken part. Then mopped it up with pitch. I'm surprised you didn't hear that part, Jesus. Then they wrapped it up with strips from someone's shirt."

"I'm sorry for you and for her," said Amedeo Muñoz.

"Amedeo, I am an educated man!"

"Here, you need something to eat," Amedeo said as he reached toward Gabriel. "Give me the bottle."

"An educated man!" Gabriel insisted. "I'm telling you, the sisters of Querétaro. They teach you how to hold a pen. Make the letters, every one of them. Every one!"

"You need to eat."

Gabriel reached up slowly and grasped the sleeve of Amedeo's shirt. "I know. I know. But where were you? Ah God, Amedeo, where were you when she cried out like that?"

"Eat. We can talk about it later."

From Amedeo's plate Gabriel took in several spoonfuls of corn and rice. While he chewed he studied the far horizon. After a time he said again, "Where were you?"

The carpenter shook his head and looked to the graveyard where a row of bodies lay in staggered disarray. "I was somewhere else."

"I know. That's why they call you that. Back at the hacienda. Because, even if you had been here."

"Eat more," Amedeo almost whispered. "You need to get some food in your belly."

"See? You see what I'm saying?! Give me a drink, by God."

"Finish your food and go to sleep. I'll get us out of here tomorrow," Muñoz promised.

"You haven't been listening. " The chauffeur was suddenly insistent, tugging the other's sleeve like a man dangling from a rope. "You see?! That is why they say you are a man of stone."

"Stay with Reina. Get some sleep."

"You haven't been listening to what I say. Amedeo!" The chauffeur put down the spoon and then dropped his voice into a whisper. "We *can't* go back. We can't ever go back again."

"I know, my friend." Amedeo patted the older man on the shoulder. "Now get some sleep. You'll be better tomorrow, I promise."

"I don't think so. Ah God, Amedeo. What have we done?"

Finally Gabriel nodded off without eating another bite. Amedeo took a long drink from the bottle and then poured the rest onto the terrace, watching it seep into the cracks. He rubbed his face hard with both hands, combing his fingers through his hair and massaging the back of his neck. His knees felt as if the bones had been knocked apart. His ribs ached. His hands and wrists were cut. He looked at them trying to remember what happened. When he sat down next to Gabriel, it took an extra effort. Every joint was sore. He was like an ancient man who had to close his eyes just to bend himself into a seat. The wall was a comfort and a mercy. Amedeo leaned back and let his breath leave him with a gentle groan. When he opened his eyes, there was a girl standing before him, fourteen or fifteen years old, barefooted, hair braided into a single shining queue. She was wearing a sash slung over one shoulder and heavy bundle at her hip, a tangle of cloth that he recognized immediately. But it was a baby that she lifted expertly from the rags and deposited in his lap. "No food," she said in fractured English. "No milk. *Mamá* say you have to keep. That she belong to you."

5

White smoke rose from the ground. It smelled of sulfur and burning fat. Some of the people believed that the lost village, the one beneath their feet, was on fire. Others said that it was steam being vented from the earth. Still others thought they were in hell. The family of Louisangel Ybarra refused to bury him beside his ancestors because the newly dug grave released a column of vapor twisting upward three times the height of a man. They took his body instead to the valley and laid him down in the dark soft soil beside his own plot of corn. On the day that Reina awakened she too saw the smoke from the earth through the clouded windows next to her bed. It was an hour before first light, and the white tendrils looked like souls ascending. She did not know where she was, did not remember the room or the bed or the high windows. Ah, but the lovely twining vapors reminded her of death, and she longed to go walking among them.

After four more days she could stand. She could walk a few steps. Thereafter Gabriel steered her down the hall twice a day, one arm around her waist, the other beneath her elbow. But her face was empty and the spirit had been drained away. Most of the time she slept. Sometimes, however, when she turned her head away from him, she simply stared at the glass, a flat transparency that mirrored the nothing of her thoughts.

Gabriel could not help but think it had all been his fault, driving the handsome car into catastrophe the way he did. He wondered if he should have waited for the señora when Muñoz told him to leave the hacienda. He wondered if he had helped to steal and murder a child. The enormity of what he had done and what he had seen came to him slowly, like the change of seasons; but he realized at last that Reina might have been telling him the truth. That they had no right to happiness.

One day, after a particularly dispiriting walk with Reina,

Gabriel stopped by the house where he had left the child, the real child, the one who had come alive out of the quake to haunt them. Muñoz had instructed him to find a woman who could keep the baby while he was traveling to Sangre de Cristo. He had given money to Gabriel and said he would bring more money when he returned. The Molineros, Hector and Adonia, had agreed to the arrangement. Their own house had not been damaged, and it was possible, Adonia said, that they had known the baby's mother, although who could say?

Gabriel couldn't remember all the questions they had had at first, and his head was aching as he knocked at their door. He could hear the baby crying inside the house, and he did not know how to answer their need to make sense out of what had happened. "A few days more," was all he could think to say. "The man you want to ask is Muñoz. He has money. And he will pay, I promise, for a few days more."

•

Nearly four weeks after the quake, Amedeo Muñoz returned to the village in the cab of a truck. With him was another stranger, a gringo named Matthew Jamison, who was the driver of the truck and the owner of a supply company in Sangre de Cristo. The truck itself was wide and gray, a GMC flatbed that resembled an aging elephant. It lumbered in by the valley road but could not climb the steep incline into the village because of its heavy load. It came bearing four and a half tons of building supplies and one small miracle, a brass-bound electric water pump that Muñoz carried with him up the hill and into the center of the crowd that had been watching the approach for more than half an hour.

After Amedeo spoke to the elders, the other villagers brushed aside his next words and wanted to know about the trickery. "What kind of name is this, Jamison?" they asked. "Did you bring us another scavenger from the north to profit from our misfortune? Or do you think you can just steal outright from those who have died?"

"He wants our money, yes? You and him together?"

"The two of you, you believe you can take what little we have and then just leave? After we have treated your friends like family? Vultures would be better for us and our children."

He let them talk. Some of them followed Muñoz to the steps in front of the school where they surrounded him with hostility and suspicion. Others watched the one called Jamison, who leaned against the grill of his truck smoking a cigarette. He was tall and thin, with the beginnings of a beard and a brown western hat tilted low over the eyes, like a natural thief.

"You think you are very clever," said a woman with anger wrinkling her brow. "You think those who were hurt will pay anything because we cannot leave." When Muñoz shook his head, she put her face close to his. "Of course you do! It was your plan to get back here before the government could organize its relief."

He waited until they exhausted the first of their frustration, until one or two in the crowd encouraged others to let him speak. Then he told them, "First, the government isn't going to come. Ever. You are too remote, too small, too high above the clouds. That is what I learned below. Second, that man down there, with the truck, he comes to the village of his own accord. He is a good man, but I have no dealings with him except for this." He lifted the small brass housing from his lap. "No one has to buy anything from him or from me. Although he has lumber, tools, and kerosene for those who want them."

"No one here needs tools," a voice said. "We can dig them from the store that was buried up there. On the road."

"Fine," Muñoz replied. "Dig away. Uncover your tools and build a city. I have already told you that I am not Jamison's man. He gave me a ride. I gave him an introduction. That's all. Third..."

"Third, what do you get out of it?" asked a man standing farther back in the street.

Muñoz waited again until the murmuring stopped. Even when the noise of the crowd died down, he waited some more, studying them and then casting his gaze out over the valley as if considering his answer. Finally he looked at the husband and wife who had been his harshest questioners. "I noticed one thing about your village before I left. That it used to have a waterfall. Up there." He pointed to the collapsed side of the mountain, the dry cove where water had once fallen over a hundred feet before streaming away toward the village. "And that now it doesn't have a waterfall. Or much of a stream."

"What of it?" someone asked.

"I noticed another thing too. That your spring is drying up. There's a ring of dry clay around it, and the water level is falling every day."

"What of it?" the same voice insisted. "When we find the water again, we will dig a well as we have done many times before. The shaking of the earth is a new thing for gringos, but it is not a new thing for us."

"Digging a new well," Muñoz said. "That sounds like a good plan to me. A reasonable thing to do. And maybe it will work out just fine, the way it has in the past. But if you do find water. If you do ... I'm betting that you find it below the old spring, not above. Maybe pretty far below the old spring. And when you do ..." he held the pump at the level of his chest, "*this* and the pipe on the back of that truck? They belong to me."

The people looked at each other. "What do you want?" whispered the angry woman.

"I need a place to live." Then he nodded toward the school. "In there. I'm a carpenter. I can fix a lot of what is wrong inside."

Some of them laughed.

This time he spoke over their laughing. "I also need a plot of land, out on the valley floor. I know some of the families have already left, and I could take over what they used to till."

The fat man in a striped serape stepped forward and spoke for the first time. "Your friend Gabriel he is a good man. We like him. You can make a place for him and the woman inside the school." The fat man smiled and looked back at the throng. "We hate the school. And the schoolmaster has run away faster than the lizards. As far as we are concerned, you can have the whole thing until the governor comes. As long as you understand that the water belongs to everyone. It comes to the fountain in the plaza, and it belongs to everyone. Yes?"

"What about the land?" asked Muñoz.

"First we see how you dig and how you lay the pipe. Then we talk about land."

•

For nearly a year the baby had no name.

She was small and brown, quiet and calm, but fretful around anyone outside of the family. With eyes set far apart and a mouth that hardly opened except for food, she seemed at first little more than a doll given to the older girls for sharing. While she was living with the Molineros, everyone called her Bebé and passed her around the way they did the orphan pup who yelped and licked. Elisenda, the oldest daughter, called her a serious child, one who would become a nun or perhaps one day a teacher for the school; but papa Hector remarked each time that he lifted her up how the plump legs would go pedaling or jumping in ways that would take her far from the village. He said this to the man named Muñoz who visited the Molineros from time to time and gave them gifts of money, an allowance he called it, for the care of the child. Muñoz would sit and stare into the wide-set eyes but would not take Bebé on his lap. "I could hurt her," was all he said. "I could drop her, and then what? This place doesn't need another ounce of pain."

"You need a wife," said daughter Elisenda. "You need a woman to drive away your dark thoughts." Then her skirt went twirling as she left the room, bare legs visible for the briefest instant and her hips awash in waves of pleated fabric. But when she returned from her imaginary errand, the man of stone was gone.

Over months the little one changed. Her face especially. At first it was as round and smooth as a peach. Later it was distinguished by a nose, a chin, a pair of ears that grew at comically different rates. At first she was a toddler who found her way beneath the wooden table and up the rungs of Hector's chair. Then—it seemed only a matter of weeks—she was a talker with a jumble of almost words. She became a favorite among the families who took their evening meals together when spring plowing kept the men out late. And then suddenly she was as active as the yellow pup, both of them busy, clumsy wreckers of order and rest and solitude. Thank heaven they had seen it before, Hector and Adonia, even the shyness that competed with her curiosity when Muñoz came to visit the family. She could walk now; she could hide her eyes behind her hands. Sometimes she edged herself into a corner and would not speak. Finally, on his last stopover at their house, Elisenda simply picked the baby up and set her in his lap.

Everyone was surprised, especially the carpenter who saw that this was hardly an infant any longer but rather a squirming fish, a jumping, grasping monkey who pulled herself close to his face. His spine stiffened. The muscles in his neck and shoulders cabled into heavy strands, and his arms made an iron wall above his lap until Elisenda put her own hand on his back and half-whispered to him, "She isn't going to fall. She likes you. Just hold her. Like this." Eli guided his hands. She patted the back of Amedeo Muñoz, removed a strand a hair that had accidentally fallen into his face. Her thick and scented hair, his hard and chiseled face.

The little one clutched at Muñoz's shirt and climbed with bare feet as if he were no more than a mound of clothing. "What does she want?" he asked.

But no one answered. They knew the reason that Hector had called Muñoz to their home. Adonia had said it would be easier this way.

By a curious trick of light the man saw himself reflected in both the baby's eyes. The little one patted his day-old beard, and then she took away the hand, pulling thumb and forefinger into her mouth. "She doesn't like it," the youngest Molinero said. "She thinks you ought to shave."

Muñoz nodded, gravely considering what the others took to be a joke. Then he leaned closer. The innocent face. The little mouth making syllables into nonsense words. And he said to her, "Do you remember me?"

The family, all of them, went quiet.

"Do you know me?" Amedeo Muñoz asked. "Do you remember who I am?"

"Yes, I think she does," Hector said at last. "I think she

remember something."

"But who is she?" Adonia asked. "What is her name? We've always wondered."

Whether Adonia meant something different from the words echoing inside his head, it was of no matter. Amedeo Muñoz said what he was thinking. He had been caught off guard by the woman's question, and the name just tumbled out. There it was, as irrevocable as lightning. And yet not one of the people in the room knew to be offended or surprised. It was only a name. He spoke it in front of them, making it real with his low and sincere voice. Gave it shape with his lips and perhaps did not even hear what he himself had said. But now it was there inside the house of Hector Molinero, almost visible. "Mía," he was saying. "Her name is Maria Anita. I can see it in her eyes."

"Good. Good." Hector smiled with some unknown victory and rushed on with an enthusiasm that he did not feel. To the baby he was saying, "I've often wondered who you were. And now we know, yes? A good name, a Christian name. It's a good name, Adonia, is it not? It's something we should have seen to long ago."

"Tell him," Adonia said.

Hector hesitated, and Adonia made a shooing motion with her hands sending the children into the little room with two beds. Only Elisenda stayed. From their visitor's lap she lifted the baby, smoothing the tiny dress with her hand and kissing the brow, the cheek. She stood behind Muñoz and glared at her parents like a young mother whose child had been insulted.

"So. We talk, you know. What I mean, we have been talking, the family that is, for a very long time now. About Zalcupan. Where we both have family, Adonia and I. We have stayed here long enough to help our neighbors, to pay our debt to those who suffer. It's not a decision we came to lightly."

"Some of the other families too," Adonia added quickly. "I know they think the same. It would be hard either way, staying here or trying to start anew. It would be hard, but at least there we have family. In Zalcupan. It's a town, about thirty kilometers away."

Muñoz ignored the woman but turned a focused stare upon the man. "This is a good place too," he said. "There's water now. Electric lights in several places. No one goes without food."

"Yes. All very good things. And no one who stays or goes is ungrateful to you. I have said this many times to the whole village, God knows, you got us through the bad winter," Hector said. Then he looked about the room as if searching for his next words. "You have a head for fixing things. And I don't want this to sound the way it's sounding because there never will be a good time for it, and I know, I *know*, my friend, how good you have been to this child and to this family."

"I have no more money except what I give to you. If that's what you're asking."

"No. No. God forbid." Hector turned next to his wife and raised his voice. "I told you! Did I not say already that this makes us look like thieves?!"

"We cannot take the baby," Adonia said.

Muñoz moved his head mechanically in her direction as the woman rushed on. "It was always a temporary arrangement. We agreed from the first, you and Hector and me. That it was a temporary solution. And you also said that you took responsibility when you pulled her from the earth. That *you* took responsibility for this child. You said those words yourself."

His face hardened. They'd seen it when he fought other men over stealing or diverting water. They recognized the voice he used just before he threw his fists. "So I did," he said.

Before anyone else could speak, Elisenda stepped before her parents. "I could stay behind," she told them. "Just for a little while. I could keep her until he..."

Adonia made a dismissive sound and flitted the back of her hand.

"I already keep her most of the time," Eli said.

"Don't be indecent," her mother said. "A girl alone in this house? People would do more than talk."

"I'm old enough to keep a house," Elisenda said.

"And yet not old enough to mind your words."

"I can do it," the girl insisted.

"No! You cannot." Adonia drew herself upright and turned a certain look upon her husband.

Hector Molinero knew that his wife was shaming him, that she was provoking him into speaking words which he did not want to speak. He could see it happening. His cheeks rushing into redness and the anger rising at his wife, at his foolish daughter, at the very presence of a stranger to witness this humiliation. The words, once spoken, he knew could never be recalled. And Elisenda was his favorite, the one who could touch his heart with just a glance, but now he could hear himself echoing the wife's last pronouncement and himself thundering, "You are old enough to be kept like a whore? Is that what you are saying to me?"

"I asked you before he came. And you didn't bellow then," Elisenda said.

Hector's face was purple now. "Is that what you are saying to your father? In your father's house? Is that what I hear you saying?"

The girl turned to Amedeo. "I could stay behind. I could keep Mía for you. I know how. I know all the things a woman knows."

Amedeo Muñoz looked at her, and suddenly he was in the avalanche again. He could feel the loose earth flowing like a river against his knees. He could almost hear Gabriel shouting again, but he couldn't understand the words. The bounding stones were flying past, some striking him in the back as he staggered under a bloody bundle that, this time, in his imagination, Amedeo had extracted from the car. The nightmare kept gobbling away at the present as he tried to shake it from his head. The details were recognizable but not real: a red-orange sky, a liquid car, a mushroom house. Shrieking trees that burned with pale green flames. He had to press against his head until he could see reality once again He could feel Elisenda's nearness to him. He could hear something desperate behind her promises and hope.

But the woman he had found in the crevice would not release her hold on him. She drew him back into the nightmarish vision as if singing a child to sleep. She was his forever wife, he remembered quite clearly now. There had been a skeletal priest, yes, in a mitred hat who'd happened to be passing by. There had been a priest who performed the marriage rite just as she embraced him and said "Have you always loved me?" He recalled now how he had been overcome by the beauty and depth of her eyes. And "Yes," he said. "Yes, I always have," as she slipped peacefully beneath the outline of Elisenda's face.

Amedeo tried to blink himself back to consciousness like a fighter who'd been hit from the side. He grasped the chairback that was in front of him, clenched his jaw, and struggled to keep himself within the room. He could see the parental fear on Adonia's face. It was the thing that brought him back into the room. The something that he could suddenly understand. That Elisenda did not know all that a woman knows.

So he took the baby from her and cradled it with one arm. When he took a step toward the door, Elisenda moved with him, clinging to his sleeve. She was beautiful and unaware. She was bound by what she saw in him, an outrageous strength that would lift her up and beyond her mother's life. But Amedeo loosened her hand and said to her, "No." And then more gently, "No. Do as your mother and father say."

He opened the door. He guessed that this was what they wanted him to do, Hector and Adonia. But it seemed still like a plan gone wrong. There would be no new family to raise the child. Only Reina now. So he plunged into the street and headed east, like a man taking to a cold and rushing current, one that would be pushing against him for miles. Harsh voices rose up behind the door that was closed after him. Harsh voices and the sound of a slap.

It was late in the afternoon, and other men were returning home as they had done for years. They were striding through the wreckage as if all of this had happened many times before. As if the rhythm never changed. The men were walking home with tools in hand, joking, or nattering or grumbling with the other men. The sun's great cycle was ending, and now it was time to be remembering beer or food or the embrace of women. Here was one who was pulling off his shirt and wiping down his face. And there was one lifting a boy to his shoulders, as happy as a boy or a man could be. They made way, all of them, for the one named Muñoz, who joined them as if he had lived in the village for years.

●

On the evening that Amedeo brought the child into the school and carried her unannounced into the one furnished room, Reina called him insane. When he first mentioned the baby's name, some days later, it took the very breath from her lungs. Gabriel said it was blasphemy, called it stealing from the dead. For a time they hardly spoke, the three of them. It was even more haunting, even more painful, that this baby looked like the original child, the one murdered by the mountain.

Reina cried at night. The baby cried. And what was there to do but pick her up and walk until they both were exhausted, just as she had done with Leala's child? Reina did it without emotion, walking aimlessly through the school at night like a ghost. During the day there was the busy litany of living, but at night it was another thing. The world receded, and the school became an island like one of the cloud-washed peaks of the upper range.

PART TWO
September, 1948

6

ON THE AFTERNOON that the man in the Stetson hat first visited them, Amedeo Muñoz fell behind in his repairs. Faraway thoughts clouded his mind. Even though the detective had been gone for hours, Amedeo was still preoccupied with the visit. Toward dusk, he helped Victor Pérez load firewood, but it wasn't until he and Victor shoved their rickety wheelbarrow of wood up to the cooking terrace that the immediacy of food and family came back to him. Like all of the men, Amedeo enjoyed the communal meals that were a part of harvest season. When he and Victor arrived, there were a dozen female figures moving about in an open space devoted to a smoky, sputtering grill and two serving tables.

Unmarried, unattached, and unaware of his limitations, young Victor waded into the hubbub with an armload of mesquite and a heart full of confidence. He offered to wed every woman on the terrace, to buy a herd of horses and a palatial hacienda in exchange for a single kiss. He wanted to make the old women young again, he said, and to make the young women rich, especially Angelina and Sarita, the two prettiest of the teenage girls.

"I would marry you tomorrow, my *amado* Victor, but I am waiting for a man," suggested an anonymous voice from the grill. "You know," offered another presence, "that when God punishes us, Victor, he gives us a child like you."

Amedeo Muñoz felt himself relax a bit at the familiarity of the scene.

His daughter Mía materialized within the group of women. She dusted her hands on her blouse and tugged at his shirt until he sat down. Then she threw herself into his lap. Amedeo

made a satisfying *oomph* and kept still, wrists on his knees and
eyes unfocused. After another minute he closed his eyes
entirely and listened to the women whose quiet laughter
comforted him. He felt the breathing of his daughter against
his chest and imagined her heart beating next to his, their
insistence upon each other for life.

"Do they really want Victor to go away?" Mía asked.

"No," he whispered. "They love Victor."

"Will they marry him?" Mía picked bits of dough from her
fingers and then wiped her hands one at a time on his shirt.

"Paloma, maybe. I think she looks at him sometimes when
he does not know."

"Did mama look at you when you were young?"

Amedeo opened one eye. "Ah! When I was young? Only a
daughter can break a man with words. Who do you think is
old, the man who lifts you to his shoulders with one arm?"

"Could you lift mama with... "

One of the older women stepped away from the others
and touched Mía on the cheek. With her right hand, she
brushed a strand of hair from Mía's face. "Come along, child.
You should help with the food." At the end of her left arm was
a stump where the hand had been severed by some calamity in
her past. She patted Mía with the rounded end of her arm and
guided her toward the table where the other women worked
with chilies and tomatoes and beans. To Amedeo Muñoz she
said, "We have to talk."

"Hmm." Amedeo did not at first stand up. "People who
have to talk, they never bring good news."

"And yet here you are, saying these same words for years,
and still putting yourself at the center of every problem. Walk
with me," said Reina de la Vega, "and see if Gabriel has sense
enough to come and eat."

The woman's eyes were dark and clear, marked by a depth
that was more than the accumulation of years. Her hair, gray
and black in equal measure, was pulled back behind her
shoulders though not braided or tied. Her high cheekbones
and copper skin suggested something more ancient than her
sixty years, perhaps that her ancestors were those who had

fought the *conquistadores*. Children of the village called her *Abuelita*, as did the men who respected her strength and the women who went to her when times were hard on their men. She wore silver bracelets on her right arm and a matching belt buckle at her waist. Bits of turquoise on a leather thong adorned her neck.

"What now?" Amedeo asked. "An electric refrigerating machine for your kitchen? Roll-up shades for every window? A new road up to the gates of Heaven, perhaps, one paved with silver and... "

"Herrera and his family," she interrupted. "They left this morning. And Malu Ibarra is talking to her man. She wants him to go where there is work."

"No one told me."

Reina made a contemptuous sound in the back of her throat. "No one wants to tell you. But the good people are leaving, Amedeo. It's the stragglers and scavengers who keep showing up. More mouths to feed. More fighting and drinking. There is nothing to keep the good ones here. This used to be a village, eight or nine hundred people before the mountain crumbled. Now we are two hundred, maybe a few more, though little more than a dumping ground."

"There are many good people still here," said Muñoz. "I'm talking to one of them."

Together they walked away from the chatter and the sizzle of the terrace, the woman steering Amedeo into the rear hall of the school and pointing upward. "We need water on the second floor. More electricity too. And a truck that doesn't break down on every trip to the market. We need more than one man can provide."

"There is more than one man here," Amedeo said. "And everyone works hard."

Reina held him by the shirt, just as the girl had done. "You know what I am saying."

Muñoz stopped, looked up at the second floor, and sighed. "We are back to that, are we?"

"Things are getting worse," she said. "Things that a man cannot build with his hands."

Amedeo Muñoz said nothing, but rather set his mouth into a straight line and looked away from *Abuelita*, who continued in a rush of words.

"That girl is twelve years old and can barely read and write. Now she is the only child her age since Llosa and his wife left. What do you think will become of a child like that from a place like this?"

He knew he should not reply, but Amedeo could not keep silent. "I read to her every night, and sometimes she reads to me. Very well. She reads very well I think."

"A whore or a peasant, Amedeo. That's what such girls become."

He turned a hard face to the woman and held her eyes. "I promise you. That will not happen."

"You cannot promise what you cannot know," she shot back.

"And so I should move on too? Take the girl and let the others fend for themselves? I think you know that I can't leave."

The woman wondered at such pronouncements. They came from his mouth as if he were king of a besieged realm, as if he had royal obligations that set him above others in the village; and now her own tone took on a sharpness as well. "You are a fool to think that we can live up here," she said, "like cave dwellers in an abandoned school. You could get a job somewhere in the north. A good carpenter can always find work."

"I had a job in the north," he said. "Perhaps you forgot."

"My name is Reina de la Vega, not *Abuelita* or *Abuela* or any other name. And I do not forget." Muñoz finally realized that it was not worry he was seeing in her face but fear. He could hear it in her voice, now suddenly lowered to a rasping whisper. "What I am trying to tell you," she said, "... is that he knows." She pressed her lips together and looked away.

Amedeo kept his own words steady. "News travels fast."

"I'm not talking about the man who came today. That was only his messenger. I'm talking about Alejandro Cruz. He knows you are here. And he knows the rest of us are here."

"We can't be sure of that."

As in most matters, Reina gave Amedeo Muñoz no deference and continued to press her point. "So you want to gamble with all of our lives?"

Still Amedeo did not betray the worry that had clouded his afternoon. "If he knew. *If.* If he knew he would have sent more than one man. Now. Let us try to finish the day without a panic."

They had walked through the hall as they talked and had made their way to the front terrace where a reclining form lay next to the crumbling stone wall. Amedeo squatted and shook the shoulder of the rumpled man. "Old friend, it is time to eat. Get up. Come with us. A fiesta. I promise." The figure seemed as frail as a scarecrow. Amedeo bunched the man's lapels into his fist and lifted him with one arm, steadying Gabriel with his free hand until the unshaven man was able to stand alone. Gabriel brushed at his long overcoat, leveled his shoulders, and sniffed. He was as thin as an undertaker, with the same sad eyes and economy of motion, yet he insisted to everyone that he was a happy man. Privileged to be alive.

Gabriel tilted himself in the direction of smoke and laughter. Moved forward without stumbling. Soon he could hear a woman's voice calling to Victor, something about the wild ponies in the valley being more useful, and eating less. Gabriel smiled. Reina herself was here beside him. The air was sweet. And, yes, there was still a pleasant shape to her hips, although she had a tongue, Reina did, as tart as the beautiful Sarita. But what man could ask for more? It was the ending of a good day. Soon it would be time to sleep again. But first, a bite of food, and then later, a sip of something strong.

●

On the evening of the detective's visit, Amedeo sat with Victor and Quentin and Gabriel on the cooking terrace at the back of the school. They added scraps of wood to the last of the fires, watching Victor's dog do tricks and comparing him to other dogs and other men that they had known. By ten o'clock Gabriel was asleep, and Victor and Quentin were fantasizing about life in the north. Amedeo rose up to make his final rounds before settling into his own bed, alone. He locked the front doors of the school and closed two of the windows that had been left open.

On his way back to the big room that he shared with Mía and Reina, he placed his hand against the wall every few paces. A habit that had not faded over the years. At Room 102 Amedeo opened the door and stepped into a soft light. Mía had forgotten to blow out the oil lamp next to his chair in the long outer quarter of the classroom.

Amedeo had built Reina's apartment and his own room and Mía's room out of scraps and scavenging, but the workmanship convinced people that he could save the village. Everyone marveled at his skill with tools. Soon the men were looking to him for advice, and after a time they came to him for their daily tasks. He was the master of practical solutions. When Mía cried herself to sleep, he took down the door of her room and put up a heavy blanket instead so that the little noises he made at the end of day could comfort her. It was a routine continued on the day that the detective came.

Amedeo took off his boots and eased back into his big chair. Some nights he slept so, without lying down on his cot at all. When he had a newspaper from the outside world, he read it in the evening, studying the details of every story as if for clues to a riddle he could not explain. But on this night there was nothing, just the meaningless numbers on Señor Gerald Manley's license plate. Amedeo closed his eyes and wished he could build a movie theatre, like the ones in California. Then he drew a deep breath and pushed himself further back in the chair.

A small voice from the other side of the curtain announced, "I'm not asleep."

"Yes, you are," he said.

After a few minutes the voice went on in a lower whisper, "I took *mama's* picture from your shelf."

Amedeo looked at the vacancy to his left where the silver-framed picture normally stood. "Why?" he asked.

"So we could talk."

Amedeo pulled himself out of the chair. "You're waking up *Abuelita* and everyone else who needs to sleep." He drew the curtain halfway across its rod and found Mía propped up in the bed, her face suddenly very grown up in the illusory moonlight.

"No we're not. She's snoring, like you," the girl said.

Amedeo rubbed his face with one hand. "It apparently does not please God that I should sleep at all, and so He sent you into my life. Here, get all the way under the covers before I lose my soul." He took the picture from her hand and polished away the fingerprints with his shirt. "Talk about what?" he asked.

"I don't know. She said we needed to have a talk. Me and you. *Abuelita* did."

"Ah." Amedeo sat on the stool and looked at the picture again as Mía squirmed beneath the blankets. He could see his own face vaguely mirrored upon the image of a woman holding her child. She had a smile as serene as the Virgin and thick black hair falling in waves over the infant's body. A christening blanket, a crucifix, a wedding ring.

"What is it?" she asked. "That we need to talk about?"

For a long time Amedeo did not answer. He knew Reina was trying to force an issue he did not want to face, and he waited for his annoyance to pass. He tucked the covers around Mía's feet. Brushed back her hair with his fingers and tried to tuck it behind her ear. He placed one of the dolls next to her on the pillow.

"I don't play with those anymore," she said. "I'm grown up now."

"I see. I think that is what someone was trying to tell me today."

Mía yawned but didn't take her eyes from Amedeo's. "You are always serious and funny and sad at the same time," she told him. "That's what people say. That no one ever knows what you mean."

He showed an unconvincing smile. "Go to sleep. Is that plain enough for a magpie like you?"

She turned away and closed her eyes. "But before that.

What were you going to say?"

Amedeo's words came out almost with a will of their own. "How would you like to go to a real school? With real teachers and children your own age? And a chance to be someone in the world?"

She yawned again. "No. It's better here."

"A real school could be good."

"Maybe someday, when you are old," she said.

Amedeo sat upright with a wider smile lifting his features. "Ah, so now I am a young man? While this afternoon I was old? I did not realize that daughters could move the hands of time so easily. Perhaps I need more sleep."

For another half hour they talked so, the words becoming, at last, not words at all but only a tuneless lullaby. When Mía finally drifted away, Amedeo Muñoz sat for a time longer on the stool, hands folded, head hanging forward on his chest. He appeared to be dozing, but after another while he stood and took himself outside to the broad front terrace of the school. The air was tinged with autumn, and the change of seasons suited him. The summer had been long and hot and hard, but early harvest and winter stores looked promising. And Reina was right of course. It was time to think of change. Amedeo paced and thought about what to do. Sudden changes were never good. They were what made the earth heave and buckle. Most troubling was the unexpected appearance of the stranger Manley. What did the man know, and why had he come to the village? This problem preyed on him more than any other. He would have to make a hard choice soon, but first he would have to talk with the one person who had never stopped digging into the past. He would have to climb upward to the old tunnel road and talk with the child murderer Jaasiel.

7

AFTER HE WASHED AND DRESSED, Amedeo lent his truck to a family named Torres and promised to join the harvesters in the afternoon. Then he left the village, climbing the rubble on the western side of the school and creating his own pathway upward, aiming toward a plateau several hundred yards higher and a half mile to the west. The slope was rocky, steep, and loose. He worked like a man wading a stream, picking his way through sliding rocks and hidden currents. Leaning into the slope, both hands at times touching the ground, he came to more stable footing. Then he went in a zigzag through the last of the debris, up to the clearing itself.

There the empty mouth of the tunnel was framed by broken timbers and a few of the boulders that had smashed them. The floor of the tunnel extended straight back into obscurity rather than sloping downward, and the opening itself was far too wide for a mine. Now, though, it was partially obstructed by one colossal stone.

Amedeo went to the mouth of the tunnel and called out a name. "Jaasiel! Jaasiel, you have a visitor!"

The person he sought was a man or a beast or a child, depending upon the tales that one heard. He was never seen entering the village, although he brought odd gifts for the villagers from time to time: a chain hoist on the steps of the school when a chain hoist had been needed, glass jars full of fruit for a widow on a winter morning, an envelope with eight wedding rings tied on a string for a young bride. "Don't worry," he had said to Amedeo once. "There is more. Half a town is buried up there. Where I live. Like a city of the dead. Come and see. Come, come."

The story of Jaasiel who had no last name was an unsettling mixture of horror and piety. In any retellings of his life, the proportions were never the same. To some who knew his past, he was no more than an escaped murderer. To others, he was a simple-minded saint. To still others, Jaasiel had merged with Juan Soldado, a folk hero among common soldiers and devout peasants. But for Amedeo Muñoz, the proper proportions made no difference. The indisputable fact was that Jaasiel posed a danger. He lurked wherever children were playing. He stole from the living as well as the dead. He crept into the village at night. The two men had fought many times; but the smaller, fiercer Amedeo could never drive away the creature he perceived as a threat. Always Jaasiel was within taunting distance of the school. Yet from time to time he called Amedeo his friend.

It was the tunnel that had become the obsession and the dwelling place of Jaasiel. He delved deeper, year by year, into the darkness. At first a few of the men helped with excavations. Still, the digging was never safe: even beams and buttresses could not always hold back the earth. And the human remains that they found from time to time? They were compacted into grotesque postures. Someone's pick or shovel would bite close and closer until the dirt would dribble away. Then there it would be, the next misshapen body, like a fossil in the wall. It was too much, the routine horror of this trade. And after a time Jaasiel worked alone.

"Jaasiel!" Amedeo called out, still at the mouth of the tunnel. "Jaasiel!"

But there was no reply.

Amedeo walked closer to the entrance and laid his hand against one of the timbers, taking the pulse of the mountain. He followed the light into the first hollow space where the air, even near the entrance, felt immediately thick and dry, the smell of the underground and some unidentifiable sweetness coming to him as soon as he crossed into shadow. A mammoth boulder formed the first sixty feet of the northern wall. Its solid reassurance told him that there had been no need for pillars or posts at this point, only a few timbers on the southern side and some beams to stay the ceiling. The floor was level for another fifty feet where it began a gentle curve, following the same path as the road that had once contoured the mountain.

Amedeo stepped farther into the shadows. He walked past the monolith and came upon the tunnel's first unreality, a discovery the villagers had made when they still thought there was something to be rescued on this slope. It was the partially crushed façade of a general store, its pale blue lettering in both English and Spanish. The building had been blown off its foundation by the onrushing earth and then pitched into the center of the road like a ship thrown inland by a storm. A chalkboard hanging by one corner from the fascia still had legible markings. Seed grain. Dry goods. Kerosene. Liniment. Rope. The door and window frames were still perfectly plumb, but the glass was missing, whether blasted into fragments by the landslide or taken intact for other repairs, he could not remember. All Amedeo could recall was that the merchant himself, a man he had never seen alive, had been pressed between the front wall of his store and the dirt that had filled every pocket of air around him.

The light in the tunnel grew dimmer on the other side of the store. At another distance it coalesced into a black disk, and Amedeo looked about for a lantern or one of the rag torches that workers had used in the years just past. There was a wheelbarrow tilted against a neat pile of paving stones. Several shovels and a pick lying crisscrossed beside it. A long-handled sledge hammer hanging from one of the beams, but there was nothing to make a light. He found instead a walking stick, probably a limb from one of the trees hauled up for lumber, and he used it to feel his way farther along. Amedeo looked back at the sunlit opening and saw the outer world becoming a small and remote uncertainty.

"Jaasiel!" he called.

And a voice answered him from the nearby dark. "What do you want of me?"

Amedeo turned toward the voice and waited. There was no further sound, no motion at all from the shadows, as if the voice had come from the walls themselves. The thick sweet smell of the remote darkness seemed as near to Amedeo as his next breath. "Show yourself," he said. "I am only here to talk."

A figure appeared. At first it resembled the silhouette of an upright bear, but then the form solidified into a human being. It shouldered a great mass of hair, almost a pyramid of curls and tangles, that hid its neck and merged into a beard. The face had unblinking, innocent eyes. The hands looked as if they could have sprouted claws. The man wore a ragged shirt of coarse cotton, tied neatly at the neck by a cotton string. The pants and sandals of a peasant. When he spoke, it was with a soft, deep voice but with the language and the manner of a child. "What do you want of me?" it repeated.

"Come closer. Stand where I can see you."

But the figure did not advance. It said, "You want to fight me with your fists. Because I make wooden posts and beams."

Amedeo kept his voice low and calm. "No. No, Jaasiel, I only want to talk. To ask you questions. About a man."

There was still enough light for Amedeo to see the giant squinting in concentration. After the words had settled in his mind, Jaasiel said, "There's no man here. The last one died a year ago, digging for gold coins and paper money. There's nothing now but dirt and pain."

"Jaasiel, listen to me. Did a man come to this place?"

"Yes, many people come," the giant replied.

"Many people? Here?"

"Outside. They leave me things. Flowers and food, on the stones. They say I am Juan Soldado and ask me to pray for them."

Amedeo slowed his speech more and showed his open hands. "I am asking about one man only. That's all I care about. A *gringo*. I am not here to fight you or to take anything away from your home. I just want to know about the man. When did he come to talk to you?"

The figure turned its head slightly as if listening to the past and opened its mouth but did not speak. After an interval it said, "A long time ago I think there was a priest. A very young one that they sent I think. That some people from the outside sent to me. This priest said for me not to take the things the people left. It was a blasphemy and wrong. For me not to pray like that, you know?"

"I don't mean the priest, Jaasiel. I mean another man. A *gringo* with a hat. In the past few days, or maybe before that, in the past month. Someone from the north."

"A *gringo*?" asked the giant.

"Yes. In a black hat like a cowboy. And did he come asking questions?"

"Gabriel you mean?"

Amedeo took a step forward and tried to make it sound as if he were addressing one of the men in the village. "No, a *gringo*. Think hard. We can be friends, Jaasiel. I can let you stay here and keep the gifts that the people bring to Juan Soldado. I just want to know about the man. Did you take him back into the darkness? Did he ask you something about a car?"

"I don't know," said Jaasiel.

"Think."

"No. I am pretty sure. There was no other man."

Amedeo Muñoz pushed a bit further. "I think there was, my friend. I think he asked you not to talk."

"Gabriel?"

The impatience that had been building in Amedeo almost spilled out in the form of words, but at last he controlled himself. There was no point in shouting. Jaasiel was either lying or not, but if he was being devious it was in the manner of a child. "No," Amedeo managed to say in an even tone. "This other man, I think you told him about something from the old times. Maybe something that you found. A piece of tin with numbers on it. From the bumper of a car. Is that what happened, Jaasiel? You showed him a painted piece of tin, with numbers, yellow and blue?"

Jaasiel remained as motionless as a stone. "No. There was no other man."

"Then I am going to need several torches," said Muñoz.

"What are you going to do?" Jaasiel shifted uneasily. "There's nothing here anymore. Nothing but a mountain of sorrow."

"I need you to take me back there," said Amedeo. "Into the darkness. As far as you can go."

●

The hermit Jaasiel, known to some as Juan Soldado, thought about what to do. Here before him in the tunnel was

Amedeo Muñoz, a man of many moods. Today he said, this Amedeo, that he did not want to fight; but all the world knew that sometimes his anger came at unexpected moments. It was best to keep a distance. Best to give him the light he wanted and to watch his every move. It was impossible to know what Amedeo meant by a gringo with a hat. Best to give him what he wanted and then to send him on his way.

"Over here," said Jaasiel. He showed Amedeo where he kept the lantern. Then he took for himself a torch thinking that he could use it as a club if the need arose.

They began by walking into the compacted darkness where the floor grew uneven. As the space between the walls began to narrow, the stony surfaces became more of a cave. Jaasiel could tell that Amedeo had never been this far inside. He looked nervously about, Amedeo did. And then after a time Amedeo asked him to take the lead.

"Give me the lantern," said Jaasiel.

"Okay, but light your torch and pass it to me."

They went beneath the roots of a tree, chopped flush with the curve of the ceiling so that it looked like a hand holding back the weight above them. Jaasiel lifted the lantern high to show how he had sculpted the roots. "See," he said, "the hand of God protects us. There are many things I can show. Many things. Farther down, just a little way, there's water flowing from a rock. Very beautiful. Very beautiful. It makes a little song. You'll see. We can stop and listen, because."

"Because?"

"... on the days that we are not enemies," said the giant, "we are friends. Is it not true?"

Amedeo thought about the absurdity of such a question and the childlike hope it seemed to express. He hesitated and then answered, "Yes. It is true," holding the torch low to the ground and following Jaasiel into the further dark.

They went down and left, toward what would have been the core of the mountain. The stones in the walls grew damp and cold to the touch. When Amedeo put out his hand, he felt a slick skin on the rock that reminded him of stagnant ponds. They picked their way around a stack of boulders that served as a fractured column and filled up half the passage. As he was squeezing past, the hermit stopped and laid his hand against Amedeo's chest. "Listen. Listen. Now? Can you hear it?"

"I hear. But I can't think that it is a happy sound. Running water and loose dirt, my friend, do not make a happy pairing."

"But see?" Jaasiel went on. "The road. The road starts again. Right here and for the rest of the way it's smooth and flat. Only one more room after the next one."

They crouched between the legs of a narrow arch and ducked into a circular chamber where water fell from a crevice high on one wall. It rippled across the granite slope like clear syrup until it dropped as a single transparent sheet into a natural basin. There it pooled and fell again, cascading among stones that divided it into multiple streamlets, all dropping again into a shallow lake that covered the passageway from wall to wall. There was a sandy shore on one side of the little lake, as smooth and undisturbed as a vacant beach. Amedeo wondered how far they had come along the path of the old road and how deep they had descended. Was this a finger of the stream that fed the village? It seemed impossible, and yet the flow among these jumbled stones was as steady as any surface stream. The torchlight made the water look bright and heavy, and when Amedeo waded into the pool, it looked as if he had been cut at the knees.

He moved toward the only other opening in the room, a low, dark cavity between two boulders on the far side. He stirred the sediment as he walked. He nudged a wave ahead of him, clouding the water for several yards around. Jaasiel made no attempt to follow; he placed his lantern upon an outcropping and then sat on an ottoman of stone. When Amedeo looked back at him, Jaasiel nodded toward the hole.

It only took Amedeo a moment to wade the pool, still he had the sense of disturbing something settled, something clean and pure, that grew murky and muddled as he progressed. The water inched above his knees. Filled his boots and made him shiver. He had the feeling of moving backward in time, groping with his feet where the bottom changed from sand to stone. He held the torch low in order to see the opening when the bottom dropped away. He went down suddenly to his shoulders, sculling with his free hand and struggling to regain his balance. The handle of his torch was under water, the flame only inches from extinction when he finally brought himself upright. He looked back at Jaasiel, who was smiling.

Had the pool been this deep when they first looked into it? Could the crystal waters have tricked his eyes that much? Yet here he was, the water lapping at his throat, sucking the vital heat from his body. Amedeo inched along, relieved that the bottom was holding firm. Wavelets rebounded from the wall and washed against his neck. He was shaking from the cold. He moved his hand up the handle of the torch and pushed it ahead of him as he waded. The unsteady flame and the undulating water made light and shadow interchangeable. He found himself squinting into the cavity ahead of him, fitting his head and shoulders around the crescent shape and hoisting the torch into another room.

For a moment he was pinned at the waist. A weak current tugged him on. He could feel his shirt ballooning, his pants pulling at his legs, but his body was too much flesh and bone. He held his breath. His body stiffened, making Amedeo's predicament tighter, more difficult to negotiate. With his left hand he reached below the surface feeling for shapes, fitting himself around the bulge and finally through the passage. He was into the next chamber, the current dissipating as quickly as a breeze. The room itself was wide and high suggesting a half dome or an entry to a farther cavern. But a gray colossus intruded. It was a boulder like no other, its enormous shoulders obscuring the true dimensions of the room.

Amedeo waded into the shallows. The prow and keel of the giant stone did not even touch the floor for fifteen feet, and the bulk of it rose up like a whaling ship that had been beached within the mountain. The flames played upon the water but their glow reached no higher than half the height of the monolith, which was, he realized, the absolute limit of the tunnel. Amedeo crouched on the narrow beach and studied the shadows, particularly a slight discoloration beneath the stone. Something had been crushed by the hull. It was what he had come to see. What he saw was a curved, streamlined shape in metal covered in the faintest veil of dust and still gleaming after all the years. Painted metal. An automobile the color of coffee and cream.

The car itself had been crumpled like paper, its axles driven into the earth by the weight of the stone. Only a portion of the trunk and the rear bumper were recognizable as manufactured things. But he knew them. Amedeo could hardly breathe. The air in the room pressed down on him, and he worked his way forward by inches, like a man whose legs were paralyzed. He dropped the torch, not caring if it went out, and forced himself past the first touch of polished metal to a place where he could reach the center of the rusted bumper, knowing, of course, what he would find. The license plate was gone. He laid his head against the trunk fender and tried to regain his breath.

"Jaasiel," he called into the void. "I need to know the truth."

And, incredibly, the hermit's voice came to him from the other room. It was soft and clear. It came flowing to him as easily as the water made its way through the funneled passage. Some cavernous acoustical trick he thought, and yet Jaasiel seemed not in the least surprised. "What truth?" he asked. "What truth do you need to hear?"

Amedeo rolled onto his back and closed his eyes, his face almost touching the underside of the stone. He imagined that the thing above him was delicately balanced. That any word he spoke might tip it forward. "Has anyone...*anyone* been into this room, the room where I am now?"

"Only you and I. I swear."

"But sometimes you go into the town for food, yes? Do you not? You take people things. And you talk to them sometimes about the things you find buried here in the cave?"

"Sometimes," the other allowed. "Sometimes I guess I do."

"But you swear to me that you gave the gringo nothing, not even the words from your lips?"

"Not even the words of the dead," said Jaasiel. "I swear. Not even when they speak to me. Like you."

8

THE OLD WOMEN went through the greenhouse with knives. Only a few of them used clippers. A sharp knife and a strong wrist made the work go faster. They cut to the end of each row where they dipped blades into a trough of bleach and flicked away any moisture by making the sign of the cross. Then they moved on to the next aisle of roses where darkness and the moist sweet fog of incubation hinted at memories of birth and babies and love too distant for words. Their hands were bleeding by the time they finished a single row. One of them called for Quentin to move the lights, but he lay sleeping in the seat of his truck. The grandmothers had to be satisfied with moonlight and stars like the younger women who were outside harvesting the carnations. It was still an hour before dawn, and the flowers had many miles ahead of them.

So the old women went shuffling into the far aisles, between wooden tables, searching for buds that had broken color and for straight stems that had grown past the marking string. These they cut and nestled in one arm. Some could carry bundles of eighty or a hundred flowers as gently as the Virgin nestled our new Lord. They deposited their flowers on the work table where the oldest grandmother stripped the lower stems. Cut off any side buds and wrapped them in newspaper. One dozen per bundle. A dozen bundles per box. Close by, Victor and Gitano Galván shoveled packed snow into the bottom of wax-coated boxes, upon which they laid a bed of newspaper and arranged the bundles. Then they closed the lids and stacked the boxes in the bed of Quentin's truck.

At five o'clock Amedeo came down from the school, silent, carrying Mía in his arms. He laid her in the seat of his own truck without waking her and felt his way back up the rocky steps to the greenhouse. "Quentin. Quentin!" He patted the boots hanging out of the window of the other truck. "Time

to go, *mi amigo.*" His words against the whispering background
sounded harsher than he intended, and several of the women
in the carnation rows looked up like deer caught foraging.

Amedeo went into the greenhouse, the one that he and
Victor had built from scavenged parts, hoping to raise
tomatoes for the market in Sangre de Cristo. The metal frame
they had taken from an abandoned mill in Zalcupan, and the
glass panes came from garbage dumps and vacant houses in
the same town. It was Victor who had built louvers and found
the big fan for circulating air, but it was three years before they
learned that flowers earned more money than food. That was
the way of the north. Now Amedeo took care to close the glass
door because every degree of temperature mattered. They were
as much trouble as children, the flowers. Yet the change
pleased him. Stepping into a house of roses was, for a moment,
like lying down next to Leala's hair.

"How many boxes?" he asked.

Old Ángelina did not look up from her wrapping and
spoke quietly, as if he had interrupted a mass, "Twenty-three,
maybe twenty-four."

"Tell Alvaro to make it twenty-three and to leave an empty
space next to the tailgate. How many loose blossoms do we
have?"

"Five boxes of roses. Who knows about the others?"

Amedeo touched her shoulder and offered the hint of a
smile. "Enough to pay for the gas. And maybe a silver comb
for your hair."

The old woman gave an annoyed wave of her hand. "This
isn't paradise if you haven't noticed. There's no future here.
You're a fool if you think there is."

"I'll bring the truck," he said. "Ask Victor to get me a
shovel, the scoop."

The women in the terraced rows stood up and looked with
widened eyes. A few of them took the moment to drop their
bundles into wheelbarrows, but they made no other sound. It
was dark, and they had only the headlights of Quentin's truck
and a very distant moon. They did not want to be inside with
Old Ángelina because it was easier with the carnations. Outside

it didn't matter if the buds were touching. And the rough-cut bundles could be tied together with string.

Amedeo went back to the school and this time returned with a battered suitcase which he fitted into the back of Quentin's truck. Then he went to his own truck, where he patted Mía's back and shook her gently, although she only turned her face into the crook of her arm. He untangled the hair veiling her eyes and patted the back of her neck. "Wake up, little pony. I have to fill your bed with roses." Then he backed the truck through Quentin's headlights, shoaling gravel on the steep embankment but nestling the bumper finally against the loading bin.

An even sweeter musk hung over the wooden stall. It was where they stored loose petals, open blossoms, and misshapen buds—any part of the flower that could not be counted among the long-stemmed beauties. Amedeo took the big scoop and began shoveling. The mongrel mixture of blooms would not suit the European perfume companies, but there was one local buyer who always took a load for a small sum.

The market in Sangre de Cristo would be opening soon, and they had a drive of more than three hours down the mountain and up the old coastal road. He shoveled with easy strokes, covering the bed of the truck in a few minutes and building a low mound in a few more. The buds fell where he tossed them, but the loose petals went flying like maple seed. After a while he told Mía to climb into the back of the truck and work the pile toward the corners.

"Use the broom," he said. "And try not to crush them. Slide your feet over the bed, like you are skating on a river of ice."

Soon she was wading among the blossoms, waist deep as the pile grew up the wooden rails of the truck. Amedeo thought of other children he had seen wading in the salty ocean, and he wondered if this child would ever be frightened by waves and what she would think when she first saw the great Gulf of California in a few hours. One or two scoops he emptied over her head, and she came up pursing her lips and blowing out her breath, wiping her face like a swimmer. He felt sorry for the other children, the ones who had only the ocean to wade.

He reached over the tailgate and lifted her down to the ground. "Run tell Quentin we are leaving now. I'll meet him at the little *bodega* close to the warehouse. And then tell Mother Ángelina you're going with me. We'll be back tomorrow."

He tamped the crest of his load with the back of the shovel, then stretched a blue tarp over the rails and began tying it tightly in place, allowing no gaps where wind could ruin their trip. When Mía came running in her good skirt and sweater, he was ready to go.

In another minute he had finished with the tarp and loaded himself into the cab. Then he drove away from the village and what little security the mountains provided, bouncing over the shallow ditch and onto the main road to Zalcupan. By the time they had passed the last road out of the valley, Mía was asleep again; and Amedeo wondered if she would ever forgive him for what he was about to do.

He did not notice the tiny red glow behind the windshield of a dust-covered sedan parked among the pinyons and tortilla of the valley floor. The driver had taken care to keep himself in the shade by day and in the shadows by night, studying the school itself and the village in general through a set of naval binoculars. He had been doing it for the past day and a half, and it was surprising what he could see at such a distance. Now that something was finally happening, he took a last drag on his cigarette and mashed it out in the overflowing ashtray, slapping the little drawer closed into the dusty dashboard and stretching his torso left and right before exiting the car. There was no need to hurry. The two loaded trucks with their billowing tarps were as slow as sailboats, and there was no turn-off for the twenty-five miles to Zalcupan. He relieved himself against the nearest tree, took off his shirt to shake away the dust, and then donned it once more with the care of a man dressing in uniform. He drank the last of the water from the jug in the back seat of his car, rubbed his nose as if trying to forestall a sneeze, and finally massaged his face until he felt somewhat alive. The first faint glow of morning was just reaching the eastern horizon.

The tall man folded himself back into the car with the slow deliberation of a mantis, stepping down on the clutch but then waiting another minute before starting the engine. At the first sounds of ignition he dropped the gearshift into first and eased his foot onto the accelerator. The smooth rumble of the engine reminded him of speedboats he had seen racing on Lake Tahoe. He admired their vicious efficiency, how they were as sleek and sure as javelins, parting the mirror lake like luxurious versions of the PT boats he had piloted in the Pacific. He let the car brush through the pinyons and straddle the main road before gathering speed. The engine took on a lower rumble as he shifted into second and third; and then from that moment everything, the job, the chase, the money, the car, all settled into one satisfying purr just before the rushing air drowned away all other noise.

He had not seen the girl in either truck, but he was sure she had climbed into the second one after she had changed clothes. And why bother with a suitcase if you weren't making some kind of run for it? He pressed his back against the seat, trying to stretch the stiffness out of his legs. If they were driving all the way to Sangre de Cristo, maybe a hundred and forty miles away on the Gulf of California, it would be a while before he could stand again. Finally, he reached across the jacket on the seat next to him and lowered his hand, very gently, upon the crown of his black Stetson hat, which he lifted and set upon his head with practiced ease.

●

Many miles later, after the road had descended into rolling hills and then finally brought itself to a level stretch, the sun appeared behind Amedeo's truck as a pink and yellow disk. It warmed the cab and from time to time brightened her face, but it was the birds that awoke her. Country wrens and sparrows in the uplands were giving way to parakeets and gulls along the coastal highway. Their calls were becoming less like songs and more like human conversation, the shouts and cries of many people gathered into one place. Mía squinted through one eye. She saw her feet in Amedeo's lap and felt his jacket rolled beneath her head. He drove with one hand on the wheel and the elbow of his other arm out the window. His sleeves were rolled up as always, a cigarette between two fingers. She watched the ash grow long and longer as the smoke swirled away, but the hand never rose to his lips. He was thinking about something in the distance. Finally the ash crumbled. He looked down at her slowly and without surprise, as if he had been watching her sleep for the whole trip. "Can you smell the ocean?" he asked. "Can you feel how the air is thick and warm?"

She wrinkled her nose and sat up straight. Flat fields of blossoms were scrolling by on either side: dahlias, poppies, marigolds, and daylilies in cultivated rows like vegetables. The colors seemed to blend into one of the extravagant patterns that came off of *Abuelita*'s loom.

They passed warehouses and fruit stands after a time, then a chaos of billboards and electric signs on the outskirts of Sangre de Cristo. Soon they turned off the main highway and joined a caravan of trucks like theirs headed toward the marketplace. Ahead of them were two much larger trucks with the names of farms lettered on the sides. There were a few cars with covered trailers and several with entire families packed inside, children leaning out of the windows and waving as if they were part of a parade. Mía wondered if everyone in the procession had come to sell flowers and how Amedeo could ever find Quentin amid such chaos.

When they had passed another block of storefronts, the flow of vehicles split into two streams, the larger one turning left toward the city plaza and Amedeo following the bigger trucks into the buyers' market. The line grew slower and slower until they stopped, and Mía was able to locate Quentin immediately at one of the covered sheds, where his truck was waiting to be unloaded. When it came his turn, he backed his red truck to a roller ramp where men began offloading his boxes before the flagman had told him to stop. In less than a minute the truck was cleared. Quentin received a slip of paper from the flagman's tablet and was then directed into a parking area.

"Hop out if you want to watch," said Amedeo. "But stay with Quentin. I have to go to the green tent for unloading."

Women in lavender aprons unpacked Quentin's roses from the waxed boxes, throwing damp newspaper to the concrete floor faster than sweepers could whisk it away. Other women wearing yellow gloves cut the stems to length and graded the buds, swishing them onto different conveyor belts according to color and shape and firmness. No one appeared to be speaking because of the fans, four big ones as wide as airplane propellers that were aimed downward from the metal scaffolding and roaring over any attempt at communication. Only the men on the loading dock seemed to be talking. Everyone else moved flowers. They moved them the way Quentin and Victor dealt cards on Saturday nights. Only a flicker and then they were gone.

Mía watched her roses as they were stripped and dropped into the stream. It was, she imagined, like watching fishermen unload their boats in the great harbor, the same sorting and scaling and packing in ice. Maybe the same destinations for the finest of the catch. From time to time one of the packers would hold out a stem at arm's length to judge its bend, but never could the great flowing stream itself be stopped. It could only be diverted into different channels. In a matter of minutes the boxes were emptied, and the flowers of their village had vanished into the torrent. Some of the red ones were being repackaged in green waxed paper sleeves; others were being arranged among fern fronds and getting bound with string; and still others were being thrown to the floor and swept toward a growing pile. Already there was a new truck being unloaded.

Everything streamed toward the ice-grinding machine at the end of the sorting shed, where two men shoveled continuously from its maw. The crushed ice went into the bottoms of new, coffin-like boxes, and a fresh layer of newspaper blanketed it. Then came a layer of roses in bunches of twelve, sorted by color and wrapped in green paper. The men staggered and stacked the bundles, covering them all with a shroud of sphagnum moss and more newspaper, stapling shut the box lid before moving on to the next box. The last man in line pasted a yellow shipping label on the top, and two pallbearers hurried the cargo into the back of canvas-covered trucks. One by one the trucks drove away. Some toward the airport, some toward the hotels and docks.

By the time Mía reached Quentin, his truck had already been re-loaded with the empty boxes they had carried down the mountain. Quentin was tying ropes through the railings, pulling with one foot on the bumper and grumbling when the boxes shifted. He gave Mía the slip of paper from his shirt pocket. "Take this to your papa. Down there, at the cashier. Then maybe we get some breakfast."

A tourist ship's horn sounded from far away, and the cathedral seemed to answer with its chimes. Mía went running to find her father, sandals slapping at her soles.

9

DETECTIVE MANLEY PARKED a block from the buyers' market. He fitted the notepad into his shirt pocket and left his hat on the front seat. No need to attract attention. The briefcase with the license plate and the pistol he locked in the trunk and then made himself part of the crowd moving toward the line of trucks. From a trash bin he pulled a sheaf of newspaper, folded it into quarters, and pretended to be studying grain prices as he walked. There were a number of Anglos in the market, many of them tourists wandering aimlessly, but also a few ranchers down from the north; and he walked close to these latter whenever a few were headed in his direction. It was proving to be difficult to locate the two trucks now that their tarps had been removed, so he drifted toward the cashier's station where a line of men with their narrow register receipts waited for cash payouts. Amedeo Muñoz was sixth in line. Manley waited until Muñoz was paid, then followed him back to the trucks.

And there was the girl. Just like that.

She was alive.

Hard to believe after all this time. Now, all he had to do was get her back across the border somehow, into the U.S., and then another six, maybe seven hundred miles up into California, which would take some planning. But no need to hurry yet. No need to provoke a confrontation. Locating her was the easy part. Now he needed to think. What else did he need to know?

There, tying down boxes in the bed of the red pickup was the boy with the knife, the one from the auditorium. The little girl was calling him Quentin. So here was another reason not hurry things, not to go off half-cocked. Because you could never tell what kind of craziness a teenager would pull.

The girl herself was tall and leggy for an eleven or twelve year old, her knees kicking out the hem of her skirt when she ran. Her eyes were as bright and black as her hair, while her face and arms seemed to be of a lighter shade of brown than either Muñoz or the kid who was tying down boxes. The detective wondered if she had been one of the children he had seen outside the school on the day he had first come up the path. He studied her face whenever she turned in his direction, and there was little doubt in his mind that she was the one: the nose, the eyes, the wide mouth and high cheekbones. Give her a few more years, he thought, and she would be a real knockout just like her mother Leala Cruz. Right now, though, she was here. That was all that counted.

Manley considered calling his client immediately. But no. Not yet. Cases like this, you needed all the information you could get. He didn't even have actual proof that this was the girl, although there could be little doubt about Muñoz. He was definitely hiding something. There was the suitcase he'd seen earlier, the one that Muñoz had stuffed into the bed of the second truck. But still, there was no need to jump in until he had absolute certainty. He had to be sure of her identity. What if this was just what it appeared to be, an innocent trip to market? You don't want to go to jail for being dumb.

Manley edged a bit closer to the man and the boy, turning his back to them as he stepped into one of the wide warehouse doors. By concentrating, he could hear snatches of their conversation, something about meeting at the cathedral. Muñoz seemed to be telling the boy where to park and then giving him some money for breakfast. In between sentences, Muñoz called to the girl, casually and without looking in her direction. Then he called "Mía!" twice more as if anxious to get away from the crowd. Manley took out the notepad, peeling back a dozen pages until he located the information he had copied from the birth certificate. Maria Anita Cruz y Sanchez. Probably Mía for short.

Born January 13, 1938. San Joaquin Hospital. Certificate # 38-0046. His note said that there was a footprint on the original document, which would be the only legal identification he could rely on. The Cruzes had shown him dozens of baby pictures, but what the hell good were they at this point?

Manley tried to think about his next step while listening to the teenager yammering at Muñoz, something about driving to the cathedral first so they could park within sight of each other. Muñoz saying okay, maybe that was a good idea. They finished with the boxes and climbed into their separate trucks.

Manley could see the cathedral's bell tower from where he stood. He guessed it was just a couple of blocks away. He could make it there on foot in about the same time it would take the other two to drive. So he stepped out into a group of ranchers who were headed in the general direction of his car, staying with them for fifty yards and then cutting to the other side of the street, crossing into the next block as the traffic light changed. He'd been lucky so far. So why not see if he could pick up a little more information?

When he got to the square, he found them immediately. They stuck out like American tourists because they were the only ones who weren't headed somewhere else. They were lost in conversation between the two parked trucks. On the other side of the plaza was the cathedral and the cathedral school, and behind a low stone wall there were schoolchildren playing on the enclosed lawn, their squeals and squawks drowning out any hope of overhearing the man and the girl. The mood between them had changed though. Manley could see the storm clouds even from where he stood. Something had happened on the short drive from commerce to cathedral. Now the kid named Quentin was saying a few hasty words to Muñoz, waving to the little girl, and edging the hell out of the picture like a thief. Manley saw him a moment later on the far side of the street, trying to put distance between himself and a conversation already going badly between Muñoz and the girl. Now Muñoz sat on the bumper of his truck with elbows on knees and head bowed. He made small gestures and looked to one side whenever the girl spoke to him. Once he tried to brush her hair away from her face, a clumsy mistake that she shook off like a spring colt.

This was not the close-up he had envisioned. Nearly everyone he had talked to in the past weeks had called Muñoz a hard man, a man with little patience for anyone who challenged him. That is what Manley had put in his notes. Now, though, he was seeing something entirely different. A criminal being hectored by a child. From time to time Muñoz tried to interject a few words, always in a low voice and with his eyes turned away; but the girl was having none of it, drowning anything he said in a torrent of indignation. The entire scene could have been comical if Manley had not been feeling a growing sense of unease. Something within this picture frame was not right.

Something in the background maybe? Something about the boy Quentin?

Manley looked toward the harbor and into each of the side streets, but the teenager was already out of sight. Where was the wrong detail? Was it the ancient Model T rattling down the street like an old man in a frock coat? Was it among the produce trucks belching exhaust? In the late-model Packard with a woman in the back seat alone? He focused on the playground behind the stone wall where the children had gone quiet and were now being ushered back into the school by two nuns. Then he shifted to the near side of the plaza and its cracked sidewalk bisected by sun and shade. There some men were carrying furniture into a storefront and a few women were transporting bundles on their heads. It took him almost a minute to find the source of his growing unease, and even then it did not register at first. It was a color that appeared, just as his mentor had predicted, in the upper left margin of his mental photograph. A color that did not belong in this part of Mexico.

Manley stared at the odd shade of green, an unnatural hue that had started out in a New York fashion magazine and ended up here, behind the grassy leaves of a nolina in a raised planter. Gradually the swatch metamorphosed into the stylized lines of a dress, fitted at the waist and broad at the shoulders, which was worn by a woman, maybe thirty-five years old, whose face, he felt sure, should not have been within seven hundred miles.

Now, he thought. Now, we've got a problem.

●

In the morning haze, from her principal's office near the cloister walk, Sister Patrice saw them, a man and a girl quarreling at the rear of a truck. It was evident, even through the nun's thick-lensed glasses, that the child was beautiful. Silken hair almost to her waist and the mixed blood of Europeans and tribal people in her face. Her bare arms were lighter than the deep mocha of the children she saw daily; and for an instant Sister Patrice worried that the girl might have been separated from one of the wealthy households or, worse, from tourist parents. But this one was clearly not afraid. She was angry, holding her arms straight at her sides and speaking over whatever the man was saying. Once or twice she made a further point by stamping her foot.

The man listened and tried to speak again, only to be interrupted again. And here, Sister Patrice thought, we have a sufficient history for humankind—a spoiled child who will not hear. Whatever sins this man would take with him into the next world, at least he did not hit the girl in public.

After a further exchange or two, both of them looked defeated. The girl sat slouched against the man on the bumper of the truck, her head touching his shoulder. They were not talking any longer. In another few minutes the man pulled himself up by one of the wooden stanchions over the tailgate, and from the back of the truck he lifted an old-fashioned suitcase. It was then that the little girl began to cry.

And it was at this same instant that a flood of recognition finally came to the old nun. She knew this man. She was certain of it. The set of his shoulders. The way that he carried his pain. In fact Amedeo Muñoz was in many ways the same as he had been as a boy, and Sister Patrice felt ashamed that she had not known him at first sight. Even if her eyes were failing, at least her memory was still sound. So she hurried to the chapel door when she saw the pair headed toward the cathedral.

Within a minute she was saying, all in a jumble of words, "God be with you, Amedeo, my child." It was a greeting, a blessing, a surprise. She could see that she startled him, but Sister Patrice stepped with ease into the embrace of the man who had taken down the suitcase. She patted his face and beamed with such joy that it looked like a grandmother's welcome. Amedeo Muñoz kissed her wrinkled hands and made one sad, failed attempt at a smile before gesturing toward the girl. "My daughter," he said. "We were hoping that...."

The nun stepped back. The one word, spoken so casually and without preface, had unbalanced her. Had brought the unhappiness of the quarrel directly to the doorstep of the church.

The girl looked to be eleven or twelve. Exactly the wrong age for Sister Patrice to reconcile with earlier, far unhappier memories.

Amedeo saw too late what was happening in the old woman's mind, but he could not protect her feelings. It was more important to protect the child, and so he pushed ahead saying, "Maria. Her name is Maria Anita. Muñoz." If it was a confession, it did not sound so. The words came out as something like a challenge.

"What have you done?" The nun whispered. "Come inside where you can explain what is happening here." To the girl herself Sister Patrice said nothing. Instead, she gave Amedeo a look that he had not seen in many years.

He set the suitcase just over the threshold but did not move out of the haze. "We were hoping that you could enroll her. For a time. Just until ... our own school, you know, can arrange ... for the teachers."

The nun recognized a lie when it fell dead at her feet.

"I can pay," Muñoz went on. "Whatever the cost."

Sister Patrice heard something behind these last words that softened her response. "We can talk. Inside. Whatever it is you are asking, you know I will help. But don't ask me to solve puzzles on the steps of the chapel."

"All I am asking is that you trust me," the man said. "The two of you, for a short time. Just until ... I can pull things together."

"The way that a mother loves her children is the way I love you, Amedeo. But," she tried to make it sound as if she were teasing him, "since a boy, you have never inspired trust."

Amedeo Muñoz lowered himself to his knees and said to the girl, "This is the right thing. And only for a little while." He put his arms around her waist and hugged the girl, setting his face next to hers and kissing her cheek while she barely lifted her arms in return. As he released her, the girl made a gesture so delicate and strange that hours later Sister Patrice believed she might have imagined the whole thing.

The child reached forth, with two fingers, like a priest giving benediction, and she touched the side of the man's face in a peculiar way as she withdrew. That was all she did. But the nun had never seen anything like this secret communication. It was a message of love and of loss that the girl wanted her father to carry to his grave. Here was a child with the sudden assurance of a woman, the poise almost of a medieval courtesan. For this treachery, she was saying to him. For this sharp and agonizing moment, I will find a way. I will make a path back to you. And then--I will break your heart.

After they watched him leave, the old woman and the girl walked together through the chapel, across to the cloisters, and down the stone steps into the place that was called the school. Several times the nun asked, "What is your age, child? Tell me exactly when you were born." But the girl was no more talkative than the man.

In the dormitory they found a vacant bed for her and a place for the suitcase that contained the sum of her possessions. Later in the day, when the other children were sent out for recreation, Sister Patrice came again and took Mía by the hand once more. "There is a special place," she said, "that I want to show you. A beautiful place, that I believe it will put your mind at rest."

This time they went into the great cathedral itself, which smelled of smoke and incense. They went next through a hall that reminded Mía of a centipede because it had so many rooms on either side. And from the hall they found their way to a stone walkway beneath the open sky, one leading to a corner of the courtyard and a single door set within the wall.

"The nuns," said Sister Patrice, "will come here to pray when they want to be alone with God. For many years it was nothing but a side yard for firewood and tools, a scrap of dry earth where compost was piled. But your father made it into this."

The girl went in willingly when the door was opened but stopped when the sudden sensation of white overpowered her. There were white flowers in so many shapes and combinations that a single word could not account for the coloration. At one end of the expanse was a kneeling bench and a small fountain in white stone. Another bench fronted an espaliered butterfly bush, its white blossoms hanging like grapes. On the far wall was a climbing rose dotted with quick painter's daubs of white. Two white hydrangeas bending under bouquets for a bride. And lilies in ovaled beds. White azaleas in groups of three. White dahlias and iris in choirs of ascending height. Stray white petals, like snowflakes, flecked an island of grass while a path of pine bark invited the visitor on a meandering course toward the fountain.

In all, the garden was no larger than one of the chapels along the cathedral's outer wall, but the open sky and the varying tiers of white gave the impression of a great space. And solitude. Mía felt a slight sympathy for the youngest nuns, the ones who needed refuge and escape. "He made this?" she asked.

"Yes. The bishop gave him permission, and he came here every week for several years. For a time, I honestly thought he would become a priest."

"Him?" She didn't pretend to smile, though the thought seemed ridiculous to Mía.

"Yes."

The girl shook her head and went farther along the path, inspecting the shades of ivory and snow and shell as if she needed to find the single glaring fault that would make the sister's story untrue. "Who looks after it today?" she asked.

"The gardener and some of the nuns."

"There's nothing to do here but walk around in circles."

The nun gave a low *mmm* and nodded. "And find things perhaps. Peace, for example. Answers. The voice of God."

"God doesn't talk to us anymore," the girl insisted.

"Maybe He is talking to you right this minute. Maybe He is talking to me. It's a puzzle, yes? A riddle whose answer changes. Isn't that why I brought you here?"

"It's just flowers," Mía said. "Anybody can plant flowers."

Sister Patrice pointed to a bed of bleeding hearts, low to the ground and starkly white. "The little stone, over there, with the name and the date. Like a headstone for a grave. Can you read it from here?"

"No. What is it?"

"He was always loyal to her, fiercely in love in a way that I cannot imagine. And it almost destroyed him, the grief he carried."

"A grave?"

Sister Patrice brought herself to the bench nearest her, sat with the heavy awkwardness of an old woman, and adjusted the white scapular of her habit. "No. There are no bones beneath this soil. Go and look. It's only a memorial stone. I had always assumed it was for the baby, lost in the quake; but here you are, as lively as any baby I've ever seen. And what does that tell us except that he intended it for your mother all along?"

"Mama?"

"He's not abandoning you, child. That I can promise. He will be as loyal to you, and as devoted, as he was to her."

"He made the stone for mama?"

"I believe he made the whole garden for her. As I said, it took him years. Whenever he came down from the mountain he worked here, sometimes for days at a time, sometimes for only a few hours. If you go and touch it with your hand, it will be his promise to you."

Mía walked across the island of grass and knelt in the pathway, brushing leaves from the letters and numbers. The stone was no more than a white plaque, nearly invisible among blossoms hanging from threadlike stems. Not a monument at all, but a white pillow embroidered with lace. "MARIA ANITA," it said. "1936."

The girl cocked her head to one side and then brushed some more as if expecting to bring forth other letters. Then she stopped, pondering.

"Your mother's name, yes?" the old nun asked. "You were named for her?"

"No," the girl finally said. "It's not my mother's name. It's only mine."

At first there was no anger in her at all, just humiliation. It was a feeling that she could not have explained in words except to say that it rose up from her knees and churned her stomach and rushed into her face like a flooding stream. It came wrapped in a grief so wide and deep that Mía could suddenly see herself, as if she were standing some distance away watching a child being beaten into the shape of sadness. She bowed her entire body forward, reaching her hands out and threading her fingers through the white flowers all the way down to roots and stems. Trying to hold herself to the earth. Realizing that the man had lied. And that the nun was lying now or else was no more than a doddering fool. Mía had no reason to know why her name had been carved into stone. She only knew it was not her mother's name and that the entire trip to Sangre de Cristo had been a lie. He had intended to bring her here all along.

When the anger itself rose up, it was almost a relief.

Mía closed her fingers around the soft stems and tore them from the ground. Even when Sister Patrice finally saw the child stand and begin ripping at the espalier, there was nothing an old woman could do. In a second the sculpted bush looked like a broken ladder. The same for the climbing rose, which Mía pulled away from the wall in a silent fury and left as tangled rope in the pathway. And the same for the branches and blooms on both sides of the garden. She went in silent, furious destruction away from the nun's pleading voice. To the heavy door still standing somewhat ajar. And from there, she ran.

10

SOMETHING ABOUT THE WOMAN in the green dress seemed disturbingly familiar. Now, after following Muñoz down the mountain and into Sangre de Cristo, a distance of nearly a hundred and forty miles, and after locating the girl herself and trailing the two trucks to the cathedral, detective Manley worried that he might be in danger of losing his quarry entirely.

He decided quickly that the kid would be safe with nuns. So Manley lit a cigarette and waited. He was almost sure now that he recognized the woman, but foliage partially obscured her face. Still, he could tell that she was Hispanic and that she was different from other women on the street. Her hair had been swept up and styled by a professional. She carried a pocketbook. And no one spoke to her or stared long at her expensive clothes. Perhaps the people respected the anguish on her face. She was looking toward the cathedral plaza where Muñoz and the child were having a difficult moment.

"Well, well," thought Manley. "Well, well, well."

As soon as Muñoz was greeted by the old nun, Manley sensed what was about to happen. The rich woman was going to throw herself into the mix, and Muñoz was going to bolt with the kid. Yes. There it was. The resolutely taken breath and the woman emerging from the shadows, marching directly toward the cathedral plaza. The detective had to step quickly to intercept her. Just before she reached the plaza itself, Manley caught the woman's arm and steered her toward palm trees growing on his side of the street.

"Imagine my surprise," he said.

She started to cry out, then recognized the face.

Manley was almost whispering. "Imagine my surprise after traveling all this distance, spending a great deal of my client's money, not to say several very uncomfortable nights in the cramped space of a dusty automobile ... only to discover, at the tail end of a difficult and time-consuming investigation, ... the wife of that very client. My, my, my."

The woman did not shout and tried not to make a spectacle, but she did not let herself be turned easily. "Let go of my arm."

"I mean, Mrs. Cruz, what is a humble wage-earning man such as myself to think?"

Leala Cruz straightened herself and tried to jerk her arm free. "If you stand in my way, if you stand one more second between me and my daughter, then I promise you more regret than you can imagine in a lifetime."

Manley raised one eyebrow. "Yes ma'am. I do believe you are sincere. But, you know what? Why don't we take a table down at that little café where we can talk for a minute and maybe not provoke a turn of events that nobody wants?" He kept his hand on her elbow and turned her, even more roughly, in the direction from which she'd come.

To her credit, she did not call out for help, not even when two policemen came shambling around the corner, chatting with shop owners and yawning their way into the late morning. The detective maneuvered the two of them across the street and held a chair for her when they reached the sidewalk tables. He put his back to the café, sitting so he could observe the woman and the plaza. He folded his hands on top of the table. Then sighed heavily. "Well, well, well. What an unexpected surprise. Mrs. Cruz. Whatever shall we find to talk about?"

The Cruz woman lifted her chin and looked away from Manley as if his presence were something she could barely tolerate. "Your flippancy is not appreciated. In fact, I believe we can consider your employment terminated as of this instant."

"Excuse me, ma'am. I don't mean to be rude. But I work for your husband, not you."

"If you work for my husband," she declared, "then you work for me."

Manley, now certain that he had prevented a catastrophe, took some of the confrontation out of his voice. "Why don't I order us a little something to drink? I gettin' the feeling that we started off on the wrong foot, and I can see by the way you keep looking toward the plaza that there's somebody you're anxious to meet. *But.* I just want you to consider the possibility that you might be making a very painful mistake if you go leaping without looking."

"I want my daughter back, Mr. Manley."

"Yes ma'am."

"Well then perhaps you *don't* understand. I've just seen my daughter for the first time since she was an infant. And I want her back." The words were hard and cold, but her face had begun to crumble.

"Yes ma'am. I understand that. I surely do. But I want you to think about this."

"I have been *thinking* for twelve years! Mr. Manley!" Leala Cruz broke down at last, not into the quaking sobs he expected, but into quiet tears that flowed from a deep river of pain.

"Yes ma'am. I don't know what to say back to that. But here's the thing. Are you listening to what I'm sayin'?" Manley waited for Mrs. Cruz to nod before he continued. "You and I are foreigners here." Manley tapped his index finger on the table as he spoke.

"You are a foreigner, Mr. Manley. I am the mother of a child who was taken from me."

"Just listen to me. Okay?"

"No!"

Manley spoke as slowly and intently as any hypnotist. "What do you think is gonna happen if you go knocking on the door of that cathedral and demanding one of the children, who, incidentally, you cannot prove belongs to you? Think about how that's going to go. Here you are marching up to the largest cathedral west of the Pasqural demanding that a child be taken from the protection of the church and, oh yes, maybe letting drop the fact that you intend to spirit her away to another country within the hour? I mean, let me ask, Mrs. Cruz, you got a birth certificate, a recent picture of the child? A few items of correspondence maybe? Do you have any kind of proof at all, other than a mother's sacred intuition, that that is your child? Because if you don't. Well, then I'd just like you to think about the kind of reception you might receive at that very wide and very thick and very Catholic door. That's all I'm trying to say. That's all. Now I do aim to put you back with your daughter. I do. But your way ain't the way."

When she spoke next, Leala Cruz sounded defeated but not yet ready to accept the detective's words. "I will give you any amount of money," she said.

A waiter appeared and smiled down at them. Manley told the waiter that he wanted *sand-witch-ez* plus beer for himself and a glass of wine for the lady. The waiter contorted his face and said something incomprehensible. Manley rubbed his eyebrows. "Look. *Cerveza*, okay? And a glass of *vino tinto* or *rojo* or whatever the hell you call it. *Uno vaso* of wine." Manley glanced across the table and said, "You know, Mrs. Cruz, somebody who could talk Spanish might prove useful here."

She was searching the plaza again from her seat.

Manley waved the waiter away. "Ma'am, it ain't a matter of money. But I can tell you a couple of things. First off, I'm trying to help you; I'm on your side. I guess you don't believe that, but there's definitely a wrong way of going about this, and you seem headed in that direction. Second, if you waited twelve years for a child who won't know you when you reach out to her, then you can maybe wait another day or two in order to do it right."

"You make that sound almost reasonable," she said.

"There's nothing reasonable about any of this, whatever this is. I'm just trying to keep it from spinning off into some kind of unnatural catastrophe. That's all I'm trying to do."

The beer and wine arrived, Manley nodding to the waiter while keeping his eyes focused on the end of the street and on the pickup truck that he had been following, it seemed, for days. "Please," he went on, gesturing toward her glass. "Let's just slow down for a minute. We got time. And I promise you that I will do right by you and your daughter."

"Have you spoken to my husband?" Leala Cruz was careful to keep a neutral expression on her face, but her voice was tremulous enough to suggest real anxiety behind her question.

"No ma'am, not in the past twenty-four hours," Manley allowed. "I did make a call on Tuesday night; and what I told your husband was, I'm guessing, the same things he told you. That I had located Muñoz. That I had spoken with him and showed him the license plate. That I had mentioned your missing daughter in the same conversation. And, that if there was any truth to our suspicions, I expected Muñoz to take the girl and run. I also told your husband that Muñoz made frequent market trips to Sangre de Cristo, which I believe accounts for your own presence here today. Incidentally, that's a pretty long drive for a lady who's used to a chauffeur; and I really wish Mr. Cruz had not shared that particular information."

"Because you think women are irrational."

He looked down and gave a single shake of his head. "No ma'am."

"Of course you do."

Without looking up again, Manley seemed to be speaking to himself as much as to the woman. "Well, let's just say that I know it's not a good idea to step between the mama bear and the baby bear. And that I'd walk a good ways to avoid doing that."

When she did not answer, Manley reached across the table and gently placed his hand under her jaw, turning her face away from the street. "Mrs. Cruz, he's not coming back to that truck for a while. And even if he did, and drove away into the mountains, that would be a good thing. You don't confront a man who's got a reputation for violence in a place where you can't predict what he's gonna do."

She did not answer.

"Now what I need you to do is go home to your husband. He needs you there."

It was the wrong thing to say, offensive in a manner that the detective could not understand; but Leala Cruz brought something new and cold into her voice when she replied. "My husband is dying, Mr. Manley. He has the same disease that killed President Roosevelt, and he has already been crippled by it to the point that he cannot walk or even breathe easily. In six months or a year I will not have a husband. But, by God, I will have a child."

"Yes ma'am. I'm not trying to keep that from happening."

"It certainly looks that way."

The detective offered a shrug. "You want to wait for that man Muñoz or, hell, if you just want to go shoot him on the spot, I guess I could help you. I got a Colt Peacemaker, a very fine revolver, back in my car which I could lend you. It's got a real smooth action. Pulls a little to the right at about thirty yards, but it would sure enough settle things, I guarantee you that."

"Don't patronize me."

"I'm not sure what that means," Manley said. "But maybe you'll let me tell you just one more little fact about your husband."

"I'm leaving." She tossed her napkin on the table and stood up.

Manley ignored her, suspecting that his next words would hold Mrs. Cruz in her place. "After I met ya'll for the first time and reviewed the case, I had what you might call a follow-up conversation with Mr. Cruz."

"Can you not hear, detective? I've had enough of your homespun wisdom. And you definitely are fired." She drew several bills from her pocketbook and dropped them onto the table.

"Yes ma'am. I just thought you ought to know this one remaining fact concerning your husband and Amedeo Muñoz, who, as I understand it, used to work at your hacienda. Am I remembering that right?"

She did not sit down, but she did not walk away. Rather, she continued searching through her pocketbook, took out a compact, and began refreshing her makeup. Finally she said, "I've got no idea what any of this has to do with...."

"You husband didn't hire me just to recover your daughter, Mrs. Cruz. He hired me to bring back Amedeo Muñoz. And if you could just be patient for a little while, I may have a way to do both."

●

Mía ran from the cathedral.

It was late afternoon, and the streets were emptying. There was no sign of Quentin, who might be the one person she could talk to. So Mía ran across the cobbles of the plaza and into a warren of streets that eventually grew crooked and coarse. She ran until the paving stones gave way to dirt and the lanes began to resemble pathways around her own school. At first the natural earth made her feel more secure. The cathedral was a bad place. Its bell tower, she knew, looked down onto the maze of rooftops for miles around; and, even though the sun had begun to sink, she knew that God and the sightless statues could follow her as long as the tower loomed.

Turning at last into a passage that was little wider than the ditches on either side, Mía shivered at the stench from human waste and rotting scraps. A burst of loud talk from men in a side street forced Mía farther into the lane, and she went stepping over puddles and piles of garbage that seemed alive with decay. An old woman sitting on a stool in a doorway smiled up at her, vast spaces between her teeth, and beckoned with her hand. "Come. Come," she said. "Inside, food and others just like you." Mía hurried on, almost running to the end of the alley.

Who would take her in now if not someone like this woman?

At the next corner Mía came upon a mongrel nosing through the feathers and offal of a slaughtered chicken. He yelped when she surprised him, not quite jumping back but rather cowering from the expected blow and edging away only a few feet, his head low to the ground, yellow teeth exposed in a silent snarl. The dog and the girl stared at each other until Mía put a fair distance between them. Then the animal straddled his prize and set to work.

Farther down the street a furtive movement drew her eye to another open door where she saw a one-room dwelling no more than four feet deep. Mía could make out a bed, a stove, a table, and a mound of clothes. A woman was on the bed, her face and hair suggesting years of slavish labor. Her few clothes were as filthy as rags in the street; and she was on her hands and knees, swaying slightly and gazing without interest into the ditch outside her door. Behind her a dark shadow, no larger than a boy, was thrusting itself into her while one or the other of them was making a huffing sound. Mía thought of the mating of dogs and cattle. But she saw no such energy here, and she felt shame in a way that she had never imagined.

She turned away from the narrow room and went more cautiously ahead, aware more than ever that she was lost. If she could only find her way to Quentin. If he would take her back to the village. If Quentin could stand up to Amedeo Muñoz. If. Then, she could have back most of her old life. And *Abuelita* would help. And Quentin could be strong, she was sure of it.

Finally Mía was able to turn herself in the direction of chimes. They led her through the city's darkest shoals until she found a real street, one with paving stones and a distant hint of light.

•

In another part of the city, Mía's hope and deliverer was himself searching for something that the tiny mountain village could not provide. Quentin was certain that the slow change of seasons was not for him and that Sangre de Cristo offered many exciting futures. But as day gave way to night, he found that the shops were closing their doors and that the streets were becoming as empty as furrowed rows. It was a dark and despairing thought. Perhaps the city was only a *carnaval* by day and a maze of emptiness at night. His entire trip, he was beginning to think, had been a loss.

Quentin had spent the late morning exploring the shops in the old quarter of town and watching fishermen cast their nets. In the afternoon he had befriended a girl named Iñes, or she had befriended him. He paid for beer and American hot dogs for the two of them, and they idled away the hours until it was late afternoon. Then she wanted money in order for him to stay the night; and Quentin felt ashamed at his poverty, at his degrading lack of paper money that should be snapped from a roll like turning the pages of a book. After Iñes, he wandered down to the harbor again, watching two of the tourist ships haul in their lines at dusk and then head south into open water.

Later, when it was fully night, he began drifting back toward the cathedral square thinking that maybe he would be a farmer all of his life.

Even Quentin's truck was alone, the only vehicle still in the plaza. A traffic light and one gas lamp outside the bank gave feeble illumination. He yawned as he checked the ropes and boxes on the back of his truck and then tightened two of the knots before coiling the remaining lengths into neat layers that he wedged behind the tailgate.

The city itself, he decided, was at times a grand calliope of color and sound, but the people and the parts did not fit each other. There was no seasonal order or rest. Only noise and directionless change. Only hurry and endless waiting for something that no one could name. He loved and hated the city in the same way that he loved and hated the beautiful Iñes. Still, he would be back when he had money. Because money was the reasonable thing, the only way to make sense of a city. Now, though, there was just the long and tedious drive ahead.

He needed coffee or cold mountain air blowing in his face. No, just coffee. Just black and bitter coffee. A bowl of it, steaming and strong enough to show the pure reflection of his face. Quentin groped through his pockets for any stray coin that would buy a sip of wakefulness, but there was nothing. When he reached for the door handle of his truck and pulled down, his stomach clutched, because something inside the cab had stirred.

Quentin came unexpectedly awake. He snatched open the door ready to confront a thief, an animal, an image from his own addled brain. But he found instead a bundle that someone had thrown through the window. At first he saw it as a roll of rejected flowers from the morning's sale and then the bundle seemed to become a pile of clothes, and in another instant it had gathered itself into a girl and had come flying at him with two tiny fists. She pounded his face and chest with such ferocity that he could barely recognize the voice behind the flailing.

"You knew what he was doing!" the voice was braying. "You knew all along what he was going to do! I hate you! As much as I hate him! I hate you both!" Her unbraided hair went swirling about her shoulders. Her fists struck the steering wheel and seat as often as they reached his face.

Quentin managed to ward off the last of it, gathering her wrists into one hand and then shoving her across the seat. "Mía?" he kept asking. "Mía?" as if the one word would be sufficient to bring her back to sanity. "It's me. What's wrong? What's wrong? Stop!"

The girl kicked his shoulder and knocked Quentin back against the partially opened door.

"It's me," he almost shouted. "It's Quentin. Settle down."

Finally he caught her wrists again and pulled himself all the way into the cab. Then he eased her hands down into her lap while making calming sounds. "Be easy now. Holy Christ, what are you even doing here? What's the matter with you?" He loosened his grip but kept one arm extended, the fingers of his hand spread wide. Patting the air. "Sweet Mary and Joseph. You need to tell me what's happening."

For a minute she seemed to relax. They both took breaths. Quentin glanced about the plaza to see if the flailing and shouting had attracted attention. No. The city square was calm. The streets were wide and free of traffic. He tried to think of a question that would bring some sense into the situation. When he turned in her direction, she caught his chest directly with her heel, then kicked with both legs until he had fallen back out of reach. Quentin came up shaking his head like a rodeo cowboy who'd been thrown to the ground.

"God Ah-mighty, girl! You knocked the breath outta.... Jesus! I can see your underpants when you do that. You need to calm down."

She kicked again.

"Come on, now! Come on! Quit! Tell me what's happening."

"I hate you!"

"Okay! I figured that out." He rearranged himself just outside of the cab, holding the door open and reaching to the ground. "You knocked my hat off and pretty near ruined my shirt. Look at that. It's torn. What's happening with you? What is it that you think I did?"

"Take me back," she said.

"Take you back where? And why? What has somebody done to you?"

Mía did not look at him when she answered. "The school. I want to go home. I want to go back to the village now."

"Amedeo's not here?"

Her voice lost all intensity. "I don't care."

"I mean, he's not here? Like a question." When she didn't answer, Quentin fitted himself behind the steering wheel and closed the driver's door. He'd heard the girl say that she didn't care, and now he felt her hand on his shoulder, maybe hitting him again; but the blow was so light that the wrongness had to be something else. But what?

When he heard her crying he felt he should reach out to her, but a mistake now, he knew, would be worse than doing nothing. He had to think. Where was Amedeo? For a time Quentin studied his own reflection in the windshield, and for another time he looked at Mía as she gathered her own hair and clothes into some kind of order. What was the right thing to do? What was he supposed to say? A man should have the right words and a sense of the right direction at such a moment, but everything he could think of seemed wrong. Finally he came to a conclusion. Or maybe to a mistake. But it was all he could think to do.

"Are you hungry?" Quentin asked.

"Yes."

"Well. Maybe *Abuelita* will have something when we get there."

He started the motor and backed into the street. Before they reached the coastal highway she was unaccountably leaning against him, already asleep. Only once on the long trip back into the mountains did she rouse herself into half wakefulness and shake his arm.

"What?" he said.

She muttered something incomprehensible, a few words spilling out of her dream, before falling back into a deeper sleep. To Quentin it sounded as if she'd said "Are you strong enough? Can you stand up to him?"

11

AMEDEO LOADED THE TRUCK with care. He put the two wooden crates of chickens next to the cab so the wind would not buffet them. The sacks of wheat flour he wedged into a corner. One spool of barbed wire and another of rope were laid flat and held in place by bags of sugar. The copper pipe went along the side. And so with every item. He found its proper place and fitted it into the load like a man building stone by stone. In the end, the store clerk asked him if he needed a shoehorn to get salt blocks in there next to the tailgate. No, said Amedeo Muñoz. But he would appreciate some credit for a couple of weeks or until his next trip to Sangre de Cristo.

Amedeo gave the clerk all of the money in his pockets and then signed his name in a brown ledger next to a regiment of figures. Without exchanging pleasantries, he stepped back into the gray morning and steadied himself for the drive into the mountains. The new morning air was heavy with clouds drifting in from the ocean. They were not like mountain clouds. Here they seemed to muffle sound and blur the vision. Sometimes the whole lower world seemed hazy and indistinct. He thought about waiting for the sun to burn away the fog but then decided he would be driving away from the problem. May as well leave now.

He nodded his respects to the congregation of old fellows at the front of the store. Then took his hat from the nail next to the screen door, noticing a figure that was crossing the street in their direction. Amedeo squinted and made out a woman dressed in lavender or gray. She walked with a purpose and a poise that was evident to all of the men, drawing the old ones out of their ruminations. Even before she emerged fully from the mist, her beauty, somehow, preceded her. With his mind still in another place, Amedeo edged out of her path and reached for the door handle of his truck. When she struck his face, he took a step backwards but did not flinch.

One of the old men rocking on the hard-packed earth gave a loud *whoa* and then cackled, lifting both feet and then stomping down, as if he had been listening to a radio comedy. All of the other old men decided to laugh as well. They rocked and hooted, touching one another on the shoulder and remembering raucous days. "Now that right there, muchachos! That right there, that one! Let me tell you something, that one was no slap!" said the shrillest of them. "Whup! That's the way you bring a man back to his senses."

"The way you back a bull into his stall," said another. "With your open hand. Like this. The way I used to do it." He waved his crooked arm in the air to demonstrate.

Amedeo did not show surprise, and he did not even look into the woman's face. Without any haste at all he raised one hand to his nose and then checked his fingertips for blood. When she swung silently, more viciously, a second time, he caught her arm. This was the moment he had been trying to visualize, and dreading, for more than a decade. Here she was before him at last and, as he could have predicted, he found himself empty of any reasonable response. There was only a flood of guilt and shame.

"Leala," he managed to say.

"What have you done?!"

"Leala."

"What have you done with my child?!" She struggled without loosening her hands from his grip.

He waited, but the words that he needed did not materialize. Finally he heard himself saying, "I did the best that I could do. I did the only right thing I knew how to do."

The old men began to mutter their disappointment. Still, the woman she had a fine figure, no? And the women who dress rich, who walk in the most excellent vaquera boots and put up the hair with fine combs, they deserve all a man has in the way of patience and appreciation. That is the price we pay for their beauty. Is that not true?

Leala Cruz found little that she remembered in the face before her. There was gray throughout his hair, little flecks of it in his eyebrows and scattered throughout the stubble of his jaw. His skin was tanned and creased with worry in a way that she had never seen. It was, she decided, a face that had rarely smiled in the years since she had known it, but there was an underlying strength that she had once loved. A small pale scar had raised itself on his right cheek, and another scar, this one two inches long, followed the curve of his eyebrow. So it was only the mouth that was the same, a solemn line that remained straight and closed.

"Oh God, what have you done with my child?" she repeated, meaning something different this time.

"There is a cathedral," he said. "In the center of the town. Your child is there." The words were coming from his mouth of their own accord. He had not thought to say them. He only wanted to stop her pain and his humiliation. They were like bandages, these words, like clean rags to lay over an open wound.

"I know. I know. I know. All of it! I saw you, and I saw her. I almost threw myself at the doors after they were closed. It was the detective who stopped me."

Amedeo released her hand and gestured toward the truck. "Manley? If he's around then we should not be talking here."

"Tell me that my daughter is safe."

Before he answered, Amedeo considered what to say. Anything he revealed to Leala could change all their futures, and so he went forward cautiously, with a minimum of words. "She is safe. That I can assure you."

"That's not enough."

Amedeo sighed. "She is tall and beautiful ... and safe. And happy until I brought her here."

"You have a gift for causing pain," said Leala Cruz.

Amedeo knew she deserved more than he was giving, and reluctantly he opened the door to the past a bit more. "She walks with her back straight, like she was born to ride a horse. She sings and laughs in the mornings and believes that she is too old for dolls or playing with younger children. She had never seen the ocean until yesterday. Never heard a harsh word spoken in her direction. She has a sorrel pony that follows her like a dog, and she has grown up among good people who call her Mía, as her mother wished. And I swear to you that no child has ever been so rich or so loved."

"And yet you swore to me also that we would be together, the three of us."

He said nothing.

Leala's initial anger, feeding on itself since she had seen him at the cathedral, began to give way to another necessity, the need for some rational explanation, some commonsensical narrative that would explain the missing years. "Tell me what happened, Amedeo. For God's sake, tell me why my life has been hell and why I have not heard a single syllable from the people I trusted most."

"The earth fell apart, Leala. And it made us small again."

He walked her to the other side of the truck, held open the door for her and nodded when she hesitated. Finally, she slipped into the cab. He got behind the wheel and tried to say some decent thing. He asked about her husband.

She said that Alejandro was worse. That the disease was slowly taking his life, but they had developed a sort of friendship in recent years. And she could not leave him to die alone.

He nodded again as if he understood.

"And Reina?" Leala asked. "What has become of Reina de la Vega, the loyal nursemaid and friend?" She could not keep the hard feelings out of the last few words.

"She lives with us. In a school. Up there." He gestured in the direction of the mountains. "She lost her hand in ... an accident, years ago. The children call her *Abuelita*."

"The children?"

"Yes, many of them. Although ... not so many now."

"Amedeo, what kind of man says things like this? You live in a school. You have many children, although not so many. You drive every week or every two weeks to a market town, but you cannot use a telephone or write a letter to the mother of one of your many children."

"Leala, there was an earthquake. People died."

"That is what you have to say to me? Now? Today?"

"No. No, I'm trying to explain that people do what they have to do. There was no help, Leala. None. People screaming underneath a roar of thunder that you have never heard. There was nowhere for us to run but to a broken school. And then it was a year before the first outsiders came. No one thought there was a village left that was worth a name."

"And yet ... you survived?" She made it sound as if he had conspired.

"I did. The people took us in. And I helped to keep them alive."

"And so, in your second year, Amedeo—or in your third and fourth years, living in the village with no name with your many wives—did you give a thought to the woman who carried your baby in her womb?"

Amedeo Muñoz could not keep pace with her accusations. "I do not have many wives," he finally said. "I have no children but your child, and at night I still think only of you. But during the day I fight to survive. Every day. There is no rest. You have food brought to you, Leala. You have fine clothes in your closets. You have wine in your cellar and art on your walls. In our village, we have food when we grow it. We have fire when we have wood. And only then. A telephone? It is a thing I have not used in ten years."

"When did it become 'our' village?" she continued.

"The moment that the people took us in."

It began to rain in fat, syrupy droplets and then soon in a steady patter. It was a torrent before he could drive back to the market and park under one of the awnings in the deserted lot. He got out of the cab and unfolded a tarp, stretching it over the supplies from corner to corner. As he worked the tie-downs beneath one sideboard, he felt her tugging the canvas just across from him and fitting it around the irregular shapes. In spite of her wealth, even in spite of her anger, she was still the daughter of a working hacienda. He knotted off the tie-down and crossed to her side, putting his hands beside hers. Pulling the rope and the canvas tight. "Like this," he said. "Like you're cinching a saddle."

"I can do it myself."

He took away his hands. "That's exactly what *she* would say," he told her.

That statement purchased a kind of peace between them, a temporary truce. Still, he recognized what they had become. It invoked a word that had never passed his lips and that had hardly ever entered his thoughts. They were divorced. Never married, they were nevertheless destined to battle over the child like a bitter husband and wife. The whole business would have a cruel ending for both of them. Amedeo tried to think of words that would make circumstances better, but words were not his tools. Finally, from some distance that Leala could not comprehend, he simply said, "She's twelve years old," as if it were a miracle.

Together they finished covering the supplies and then sat in the cab waiting for the rain to diminish. Nothing else passed between them for a long and uncomfortable time until she said, "That day that you left, the four of you, I thought we were beginning a new life. And then to hear nothing.... It was like being trapped on a sinking ship. I lost my child, Amedeo. I lost my child and endured that loss with an ache so deep I had to look at it for years from the corners of my eyes. I can't be with you. Ever again. I can't trust you ever again. And I certainly can't forgive you."

"I know," he said. "I don't expect it."

Leala thought that Amedeo Muñoz was giving her none of the story that she needed. It was the way of men, was it not, always bargaining for what they can never have? Finally she offered him one concession. "I'll do you the one kindness, Amedeo, that you would not do for me. --I'll let you see her grow up. You will never be within reach of her again, I promise you that; but you could come north. You could see her marry. You could know that she would inherit a fortune."

From some emptiness inside of him Amedeo Muñoz said, "No. I can't."

It was a pronouncement so indecent, so shockingly absurd, that Leala could not at first believe he had spoken the words. "Who *are* you, that you could say such a thing! What kind of darkness clouds your mind? "

"I am tied to where I am, just as you are."

Leala felt a paradoxical sense of relief. There was no longer any point in arguing with whatever man Amedeo Muñoz had become. When she spoke again, she sounded bitterly amused. "You don't honestly believe you can keep her, do you? Are you that insane? Alejandro Cruz will hire an army of men like Manley. Believe me, he will do more than take away the name of a tiny village. He will erase it from the earth."

Amedeo leaned forward and started the engine once more, easing the gear shift lever into first and revving the motor gradually into the weight it would have to pull. "I know," he said.

"You don't sound afraid."

"I'm not." He took a bandana from his pocket and wiped at the condensation on the windshield, then handed it to her so she could clear her side. "I think the rain is beginning to slacken now. I doubt it'll blow under the tarp." He turned the truck into the street and drove west, toward the cathedral plaza.

"Where on earth do you imagine you can go?" she finally asked.

"You said you wanted your child. I'm taking you to her."

They drove the few blocks and stopped close to the cathedral. They got out together and ran through the rain to the same chapel entrance that Sister Patrice had opened into a new life for Mía. Once inside the door, Leala held back long enough for him to turn and take in the full image of her. "Don't expect me to thank you for my daughter," was all she said.

It was Amedeo who first heard the approaching voices but Leala who recognized the accent. It was a voice that came echoing ahead of steady, patient bootsteps. And it was saying, "Well, well, well, imagine my surprise. For a second time."

12

Jaasiel heard the music before he saw the colored lights. Lumbering to the edge of his clearing, he wondered at the scene below. The villagers, all of them it seemed, had gathered in the streets around the school. Some were dancing, and others tended fires where great slabs of meat were roasting. He could smell the alluring, spice-heavy smoke even at this distance. He could see them making music while children ran in and out of the shadows. There were candles in many of the windows; and candles, he remembered from childhood, were an invitation.

He found the path with no trouble, making his way through the loose shale down to the darkest of the streets where he would not be seen. For a long time he lingered in shadows, taking in the smell of beef and beer and women wearing flowers. He could sit and smell. Maybe that would be enough. He could see the colors and taste the odors. Could feel the musky women on his skin, like whores in San Mateo. A woman would be nice, a young one. So he sat beneath a window that burned no candle and waited for what the night might bring.

When the fireworks began, Jaasiel almost ran away. The first one was a star that exploded directly over his head. It scorched the eyes and chased away every shred of darkness, only to be followed by *pop-pop-pop* and a cascade of sparkling yellow. The overpowering smell of death. But he could not drag himself from beneath the spectacle in the sky; green circles and red meteors and blue horses' tails that hung over him like a sign from God.

By the time the barrage had ended, he found himself among people moving in no particular direction. They bumped and brushed by his body, sometimes staring up at his great height by never challenging his presence. They smelled like chilies and ripening fruit. And they finally gathered around a boy and a girl who seemed to be the center of all the celebration. The girl wore a white dress with a white veil that had been turned back to reveal smiling eyes and painted lips. The boy had on a black bolero jacket with white embroidering.

While happy faces eddied around the couple, Jaasiel moved along the edge of the crowd itself, staying always within reach of the shadows. Four men were playing *mariachi*; and, from time to time, people would lay flowers or small presents at the feet of the couple

Farther down the street, where the sidewalk stopped, someone had strung colored lights between the rooftops. A man sat outside the first house cranking a hand generator that was wired to the strands above. His wife sat a steaming plate on the table beside him and demanded that he eat. "A child could do that," she said. "A child or a bull like that one." She waved the back of her hand at Jaasiel. "No need for you to sit all night like you're playing music. You were a fool to put those things up."

The man took several substantial bites of food and several long draughts from a tumbler. While he ate, the lights dimmed, a few of them tinkling as the breeze rose and fell. There were still lanterns and candles enough to make faces visible, but the color had vanished from the night and with it the feeling that had drawn Jaasiel down from his dark dwelling place. The man at the generator ate with the slow rumination of a cow, looking all the more ridiculous because of the filthy rag that his wife had tucked beneath his chin. When he finished eating, he smoothed back his hair with both hands, drained the tumbler with a belch, and threw the cloth contemptuously at the ground. Then he leaned forward. The mechanical box whirred. And the lights magnified his smile a hundredfold.

Up above the bride and groom, on the level of the terrace, older women carried bowls and platters from somewhere inside the school to makeshift tables at the bottom of the steps. Jaasiel recognized some of the faces. The woman with one arm was there, yes; but others seemed to have driven up from Zalcupan or from one of the farther towns. There were trucks parked all along the valley road, even one or two cars that had made it up to the gentle slope near the greenhouses.

Jaasiel finished the beer that someone had offered him, dropping the bottle where he stood. Another someone handed him another beer, and no one asked his name or stared too long at his shapeless clothes. They seemed intimidated by his immense size. Jaasiel let the irresistible flow of bodies take him through a cascade of laughter and song, depositing him at last near a whiskey barrel where he found a cup that had been dropped upon the ground. When some women encouraged him to take his first portion, Jaasiel reached all the way down to his elbow and came up dripping. The tiny congregation roared with laughter, all except the owner of the barrel. He shoved at Jaasiel, but only propelled himself backward. This time the revelers roared as one, joyously clapping Jaasiel on the back and mocking the entrepreneur. Again, again. They wanted him to dip again, all the way to the bottom of the barrel. And when the whiskey man came charging back with money, money pouring from his lips, Jaasiel gave him nothing but the back of his hand. There was no containing the drinkers then. They swarmed the sloshing barrel. Jaasiel himself was pushed to the back of the crowd, and after a moment of dizzy confusion he made his way nearer to the cooking fires and music.

He'd walked less than a block when two of the whiskey dealer's friends came at him, one with a knife, the other with a hammer. They called him an ape and a mental defective. The tall one with the knife slashed at his face while the hammer man swung at his knees. Jaasiel kicked once and pounded twice with his fist. As the two men began lifting themselves from the ground, he threw one through a wooden door and the other down the stone steps leading to a stream. Still not a soul had raised an alarm or ordered him to leave.

Soon he was at the terrace where everyone was watching the one named Quentin play his guitar. A woman danced before him, her arms going rhythmically over her head and then down over her body in patterns that suggested both embrace and surrender. Her hips and feet made the music into a story. When Quentin changed the rhythm, she changed with him, making herself a spectacle more alluring than the music. Other dancers gathered, some of them clapping in time and others simply giving themselves up to the melody. All of them were women, young and beautiful. In the outer circle was the child Mía, barefoot and attentive.

Jaasiel sat himself down next to Gabriel, the drunkard who never seemed to leave the terrace. Neither of them spoke at first. Gabriel gave the other man a slow blink and leaned away for a moment as if looking up at a mountain. Then he made a soft belch and reached the bottle over to Jaasiel without further comment on the man's great size. They remained together for a while, letting the atmosphere of happiness warm them as the night air grew cooler. Finally the old drunk pointed with the bottle to a half-burned effigy hanging from a tree. "The *rey feo* who does not burn," he said.

"Who is it?" Jaasiel wanted to know.

A drum and trumpet had joined the gathering below, and the old man used a name that did not quite rise above the music.

Jaasiel was still puzzled. "What does it mean?" he shouted.

"*Quema del mal humor.* The burning of ill humor. Before every *carnaval.* At Lent."

"This is Lent?" the other said.

Gabriel himself was momentarily confused. But after a clarifying pause he shouted back. "No. No. It's just something they do, a joke, at Lent. A joke. They name an unpopular leader and burn his image so that fun can begin. The signal that fun can be set free. Blowing off steam. You know, before the serious.... "

"This is not the Lent?" asked the giant.

"No. No, in the spring. In the spring. Have a drink with me. It's a celebrated, a wedding celebrated, almost. Victor and that girl, I don't know her name. We don't even celebrate Lent. That's the thing. That's why they joked him. Over there. In the tree."

"The *rey feo?*"

Gabriel nodded extravagantly. "Except he wouldn't burn. Stuffed him with wet straw or something."

The giant nodded as well. "He wouldn't burn."

"That's his daughter. Down there. Without her sandals."

"Ah."

"It's a secret." Gabriel patted his lips with all four fingers of one hand. "Nobody knows her name either."

"Is it Mía? Is that her name?"

A momentary horror crept over the drunkard's face, but whatever prompted it faded away after another drink or two. He leaned into Jaasiel's ear. "That's what they call her." The two men passed the bottle back and forth several more times, and their conversation slowed, as if each one were carefully considering his thoughts before putting them into words. "Me, I only drove the car, you see. It filled up, just like that. And I ran back. But there was nothing you could do."

"Filled up?" Jaasiel was more than puzzled. The drink had muddled his mind.

"Dirt," Gabriel went on. "Rocks and dirt. Her mother, gone, I mean, left behind I suppose. It was over just like that. In a flash."

"They burn her in a tree too?"

"The mother? No. No. No. You are a fool. It's a different thing that I'm telling you now. A whole different thing."

They sat and listened to the musicians. Quentin, the one with the guitar, stood up and strolled into the crowd of women, playing first for this woman and then for another as the crowd closed around him. He stopped in front of Mía, and his face lifted when he recognized her. He turned the body of the guitar toward her and seamlessly began a new tune which brought an appreciative "ahhh!" from the crowd. They made room for her to dance; but Mía could not take her eyes from Quentin, who appeared to her for the first time as something other than a friend. It was a sudden and strange feeling, this realization that Quentin, even after her outburst in the cab of his truck, was speaking to her now with his music as if she were the only one who mattered to him in the jostling crowd.

Mía felt that all the people were reading her thoughts, that the music was fading away, its rhythm lost in the huge canopy of night. She tried to sway in time to the former songs, but it was no use. The clapping around her sounded like galloping horses. It was the first dancer who saved her, the beautiful Sarita who had danced for Quentin with her whole body. Sarita stepped into the open space and put her hands on Mía's hips, moving the two of them back into the tempo and drawing appreciative whistles and cheers from the men. The light of the fire made Sarita's face shine. Quentin gave a huge smile and bowed toward Mía and Sarita as he played. It was a triumph that raised Mía's spirit into the sky.

But then she realized what had really happened. The space at the center of the crowd had widened and moved in a new direction. Sarita had done it with her beauty, and the crowd had followed like beasts. Now Sarita was dancing with Quentin once more, her hands touching his face as whistles and cries of joy rose into the air.

Mia backed away from the center of the dancing, her face a pretense of joy that she no longer felt. She went to the steps and sat, watching the colors in the street, as silent and solitary as Gabriel, who slumped on the steps above her. The other girls her age were helping to carry food or dashing happily from scene to scene. No one but Quentin knew that she had run away from the cathedral school. And, when she looked again, she saw that not even Gabriel was alone: he had a friend, sharing his bottle and his wild tales.

The man beside Gabriel slipped down a step. After a few minutes he pointed toward the highest hump of the ridge above them. "I live up there," he said to Mía, "where it is quiet and cool."

She looked into his face, saw the childlike innocence even before she noticed his great size. For an instant she was afraid. Then she saw how he struggled to make words.

"I live up there." He pointed toward the mountain. "Where it is quiet."

"Why? Why do you live up there?" she wanted to know.

"Your papa. He doesn't want me around," the man said. "He says that I can't come into the village."

"Why?"

"Because...." After a long and thoughtful interlude, a new look gathered itself upon the giant's face. "Because," he whispered, "I know the secret of your name."

•

The truck made its way along the valley road, its headlights cutting only a sliver from the night. Inside the cab there was no longer any conversation. The woman had ceased trying to fight her way back into their shared past. In the face of her anger, Amedeo had little to offer in the way of answers. After they entered the deeper darkness of the valley itself, he drove with both hands on the wheel and did not glance in her direction. She sat watching him from the far edge of the seat, remembering him as a young man and wondering what had hardened his face.

Amedeo had wanted to leave her behind in the town, but Leala would not stay and would not ride with Manley and would not listen to any further talk of delay. She'd become adamant as soon as the detective had discovered the two of them at the cathedral and had reported on what he'd learned. That Mía was no longer in Sangre de Cristo. That she had been seen with a young man in a faded red pickup truck and that they had left together.

Now the truck and the car slowed where the valley road veered east and where another road, hardly more than a cleared path, led north. Amedeo pushed in the clutch and let his truck coast to a stop. There was an unexpected glow above them in the village. A deeper worry etched his face. "What is it?" Leala wanted to know. "A fire?" But he only muttered to himself and downshifted to first, taking them at an even slower pace up the slope until they came to a clearing where several trucks and unfamiliar cars were already parked.

Manley brought his own car to a stop next to Amedeo's truck but did not get out. His face flared momentarily as he lit a cigarette, and he leaned back against the seat. From the darkness inside the car he spoke to Leala. "We'll leave tomorrow," he said. "Or maybe the next day. As soon as Mr. Cruz makes the arrangements."

Amedeo did not wait for an explanation. "We walk the rest of the way," he said to Leala, and took the path leading upward.

The music came to them like gusts of rain, soft and

soothing at one instant, racketing down like hail the next. They made their way through a colonnade of pines and then along a stone path that gradually assumed the character of a stairway. Leala felt his hand guiding her at several turns and let herself be helped even though she wanted to shove him away. She reached the street level first and stopped, taking in the spectacle with a kind of disbelief that caused her to turn and stare down at him. The village was not like anything she had been led to believe. "I don't want any more of your lies," she said. "I just want my daughter. Where would she be in the midst of ... this? Whatever this is."

Amedeo studied the flood of color and sound. Leala saw him draw in a breath and let it out, but she did not wait for him to invent an explanation. She plunged into the tumult, slowing her stride only when the people began to make way, pulling back from her on both sides and staring. One child, her face awash with wonder, reached out to touch the fabric of Leala's skirt. The girl's mother pulled her back cautiously, as if taking her baby out of the path of a tigress.

When the path closed again, Leala let Amedeo take her hand, which he did with an unceremonious grab as he began to make a way for them through the crowd. He brought her to the steps of a huge edifice unlike anything else in the village, a school it seemed, but more like a ruined palace than any usable building. There was a courtyard with a low wall falling to rubble in some places, broken windows in the collapsed northern wing, and wide cathedral doors that had been propped open with stones. She noted that Amedeo greeted no one. Took himself to the bottom of the steps and then began examining faces in the crowd as if taking roll. A woman coming down the steps with a steaming bowl turned and went back in the opposite direction. One or two men lowered their musical instruments.

Amedeo took out his pocket watch, pressed the stem, and the cover popped open. He studied the silver hands and then spoke in a soft voice to a stocky man in a blue shirt. "Plenty of time for an early start tomorrow. Am I right, Tomas?"

Leala could see that the stocky man was suddenly afraid.

"Amedeo," the man said. He stopped himself, looking about for help from the bystanders. Someone behind the man spoke in a whisper and urged him forward. "Amedeo, please," the stocky man said. "Do not be angry."

"Did I speak to you in anger?"

The man named Tomas hesitated. "It's just.... We never seem to step aside from work. Every day, like animals. I think that once or twice we need to--."

"I see." Amedeo turned away from the crowd and began climbing the steps to the courtyard of the school. It was Tomas again who stopped him.

"Forgive me, my friend. I think that you do not. I mean, I think that you do not see what an ordinary man sees." There was nodding and some mumbling of assent.

"I believe I do." Amedeo lifted his eyes toward the effigy still hanging from a low limb.

"Amedeo, please. A joke, a harmless laugh," said the man. "Victor and Paloma, we have been joking them all night with much, much worse. No one here gives you disrespect."

"Ah. Victor and Paloma. They have each other now. I am glad. But tell me, Tomas, do they have food for the coming months? Plenty of wood for the winter, do they? That surprises me, because I thought supplies were low." Some of the people lowered their heads. A few edged back away from the stocky man as Amedeo continued. "And yet, here I see a village. No, in fact, I believe I see a village and the half of another village burning most of our dried wood in the street. Eating most of what we have gathered. Spending what we have saved."

The fat man pursed his lips, as if holding back that he really wanted to say. "We can get by without beef but not without happiness or hope, Amedeo. We think that sometimes you forget, perhaps, to embrace ... good things."

Amedeo was sorting through the crowd, looking for the one face that could take the edge from his voice. Finally he found her father back, next to *Abuelita*, clinging now as if she were as afraid as any of the men. Back and forth her eyes were darting, from Amedeo to the woman standing on the next step below him. Amedeo tried to relax his shoulders and to put some conciliation into his voice. "Victor and Paloma, they have a place to live already? A door to shut ... so that their happiness does not run away?"

Tomas took it the wrong way. "We are your friends. No one doubts that but you. We follow your orders every day. But even God allows the people to sing."

"Then let God find them a--."

"Amedeo!" Tomas was close enough now to put his hand on the other's arm. "Do not say such things. Please. Do not make the people afraid of you."

Leala felt a sympathy for the crowd. Already she had seen enough to know the way they lived, to understand the gamble they made on each harvest and the grim winter wait until spring. The people were not just afraid of Amedeo. They were afraid that he was right. But, no, it was more than that. Leala could see that the man named Tomas was wrong. Amedeo Muñoz was not angry. He was troubled. She could see it in his eyes and, with some allowance for their time apart, she could hear it in his voice. Some tiny measure of Leala's own anger faded then, and she took a step closer to his side.

"I think they expect me to introduce you," he said aloud. Leala's face colored and she looked away, not knowing how to react. It was the same when he spoke again. At first he said the word softly to himself, and then he shouted a name. "Victor!" Was it genuine anger this time? The shout was strong enough to stop the phonograph's wobbling chords, and Leala tensed. Amedeo waited until a slender boy in jeans and bolero jacket came forth. The boy named Victor left his bride within the circle of her sisters, but Amedeo motioned her forward too, and the people made a path for her. "Paloma," he said. "Stand here."

Amedeo took a step down, reaching into his pocket, this time to withdraw a set of keys. "Victor, is this your wife? Have you bound your life to hers?" The boy nodded. Then Amedeo nodded. "Well ..." he put his left hand on the boy's shoulder, turning him to face the crowd, "congratulations. Go with God, and with your beautiful bride."

There was a roar of approval and a thunderous applause. The trumpeter raised his horn and signaled to the other musicians, but he was quieted by Amedeo's upraised hand. "Wait. There's one thing more." The gaiety ceased as if someone had switched off a radio. Amedeo reached over Victor's shoulder and dropped the keys into Victor's hand. "Don't forget to unload the truck. As soon as you are able. Tomorrow morning."

The crowd exploded with laughter, and the trumpeter at last had his moment of glory. Whatever was said next did not rise above the tumult. Amedeo found the woman's hand again, taking it more gently this time and leading her into the jostling throng, toward the back where, unlike the others close to her, Reina de la Vega shivered as if pursued by ghosts. And where the girl known as Maria Anita stared in wonder and incomprehension.

The reunion that Reina had so longed for was happening now at the wrong place and at a profoundly wrong time. Leala's sudden appearance was like the earthquake itself, a disaster that would change all of their lives. It had caught Reina without a story. What could she say to the woman who had lost her only child? How could she explain why all of them had let Leala suffer for twelve years? There was no supple lie that could pardon such cruelty. Reina thought of blaming Muñoz and his mad crusade to save the village. She even thought of telling the truth, but that was far more cruel. Instead, she chose a lie that had been gathering credence for years. She stood behind the child and smiled. And, in the fleeting instant, it saved her.

Leala found her child by following Amedeo's eyes. There, first of all, was Reina, older and taller than the other women, more severe about the mouth and distinguished by the silver in her necklace and in her hair. And then there was Leala's own child, standing before Reina in such beauty that it took the breath from Leala's mouth.

Reina was saying something formal, something timorous and weak, as she brought Leala into a dutiful hug. But Leala was hearing nothing, not even seeing the disfigurement of

Reina's arm. There was only a flood of emotion that had overtaken her and the realization that there was little from Reina that she needed to hear. She needed the touch of her child. She needed to fall to her knees and open her arms. It was not until she had stepped back from Reina's stiff embrace that Leala realized how utterly her imagination had failed. It was no infant in front of her. It was a budding young woman, incredulous and suddenly shy.

Leala was struggling to find her own words, any reassuring phrase that could ease her into her daughter's life. Why had she not thought of what to say? And why did the child look so shocked? I am her mother Leala thought. She is a part of my body and soul. Why is she not hearing me? Even as these thoughts rushed upon her, another disturbing something began to make its slow way to the surface of Leala's mind. Something about Reina's ceaseless babble. And another something about her husband Alejandro, his unpleasant habit of seeing deceit behind any soothing words. But Leala pushed the older woman further from her thoughts and wordlessly reached out to touch the beautiful child's face. That, too, proved to be wrong.

Mía did not rush into her mother's arms.

It was too much, everything that had filled this day. It was too much for Mía to absorb or to comprehend. Here was her miracle, the mother she had dreamed of, stepping out of the silver frame. And yet here too was the man who had left her at the cathedral. She hated him. How could she trust his sudden appearance with the mother she so longed to see? Then suddenly Amedeo Muñoz was kneeling beside her, saying, "Mía. There is someone I would like for you to meet." And it was too much and happening far too fast. And when Mía looked up again, Reina de la Vega had disappeared into the crowd.

Leala instinctively searched the girl's face, hoping to find some reflection of her own features. Perhaps the aquiline nose. Perhaps the full lips and sensual mouth, which, true to her father's blood, remained firmly closed. And the shoulders, and the way she held herself? There in those slight shoulders was the mark of pride inherited from her grandmother. And yet.

The villagers could not have found a better disguise. The blouse that Mía wore was at least one size too large for her. Its embroidery, at one time bright and skillfully displayed, had faded into threadbare obscurity. Her skirt, filthy at the hem, stained by ashes and God only knew what else, had to be cinched at the waist and held in place by a man's belt. A princess now nearly indistinguishable from peasants.

The girl studied Leala just as intently. Then, at the moment that the woman reached out again, Mía bolted, dashing up the granite stairs and into the depths of the school.

"Mía!" Amedeo took a step in her direction.

But Leala held on to his shirt. "I am a stranger to her. And this is not the way any of us imagined that we would meet."

"She's as wild as that pony. And just as disobedient."

"Yet you love her more than your own life, Amedeo Muñoz. That much is clear. Your friend Tomas would have done well to let her speak for him. She has a rope around your neck already."

"I'll go find her," he said.

"No. We have time. Manley will not disturb us tonight and maybe not tomorrow. He has to wait for Alejandro to send his dogs. Tomorrow or the next day, then we will have to decide what to do. But tonight.... Why don't you show me where you live, and where my daughter lives." She took his arm almost naturally, still angry and confused, but willing to walk with him for an hour, maybe two, after seeing the hold that her daughter had upon his whole being. It was even possible, Leala conceded to herself, that Amedeo Muñoz had been telling some small portion of the truth.

The two walked until they reached the plaza where the collapsing side of the mountain had finally come to rest. Amedeo revealed the sweep of the damage and showed her the young trees just now taking hold in the debris. Pointed out the fields of stone and the cleared terraces. The greenhouses. The seven haunted streets and the five that were almost spared by the quake. "When you go beyond that street, there, with the blue door, it is like Pompeii. I have seen the pictures. The broken walls. The open windows and doors. Dogs lying dead beside children. The buried waterfall. They say that fire and heat are worse than the shaking earth, but those at Pompeii died in minutes. Here, for some of them, it took days."

They returned through the arcade of lights, where children jumped through a maze they had drawn in chalk on the paving stones. At the corner a heavyset man sat grinding at a generator as if the giant music box of the village, with all of its *carnaval* creations and its twirling, splendiferous energy, depended upon him alone. He nodded gravely at Amedeo, who, rather than walking on, stopped and turned back again, pointing upward to the lights. "Thank you," he said. "Thank you for that." The man's wife appeared in the doorway and after an appraising stare came forth to stand behind her husband. She tapped her husband's shoulder, and the man stood, hoisting his suspenders and waiting expectantly.

At last Amedeo removed his hat. "Carmelo Herrera Ramírez and wife Rosabla, may I present to you ... Leala Anita Sanchez de Cruz, my guest. And the mother of Maria Anita ... Cruz ... y ... Sanchez. My daughter." He bowed slightly and took the woman in the direction of the school. The man and his wife stood without speaking, their mouths agape.

Amedeo intended to show Leala where and how they lived, but they were stopped again as they approached the upper wing of the school and its bouldered ruins. It was Mía materializing from the darkness and putting herself in their path. For the first time the three of them were alone. Music had lured the dancers farther down the street. The drinkers and talkers had settled into their spots. And the children were falling asleep or slowly returning to their families. Only the man and the woman and the child stood far away from the rest. Mía had something in her hands, and they waited for her to speak. Instead, she lifted it into the candlelight from the windows and put it into the woman's hands. It was a picture set within a silver frame, hardly more than a snapshot, showing a woman with thick cascades of hair that fell all the way to the child that she held in her arms.

"It's you," Mía said. "Isn't it? I knew that you weren't dead. I felt it, even when he said you were in heaven. I knew that you would come." She threw herself into the woman's arms and did not let go.

For a long time they stayed as they were, the girl breathing in the wonder of the moment, the woman kneeling just enough that she might touch and see the face, the hair, the thin strong arms that held her fast. The moon took itself behind a cloud, and there it lingered for a time until it came forth again with a pale light that seemed to transform the framed picture into a moving image. How young and carefree the woman appeared as she turned her face from the camera and brought it close to her child. And how happy and plump the baby seemed, reaching with tiny hands and turning into the heavy breast. And how beautiful the christening gown, long and billowing in the moonlight rather than moldering among sheets of tissue paper, inside of a mahogany chest, hundreds of miles away.

Leala stood up and spoke with a first hint of kindness to the man named Amedeo Muñoz. "Please go," she said. "For a while. Do not say that life is complicated or that a men are coming tomorrow or that we cannot share this life. Just go. For a little while. And let me be with my daughter, Amedeo. Then, I will pray a blessing for you on the day that you die, even if I cannot forgive you for what you have done. She can bring me to the place where you live later."

Amedeo nodded.

13

ON THE MORNING AFTER THE FIESTA, some children playing in the old gymnasium found a piece of paper folded beneath a pair of shoes. Since they had not been schooled in the reading of words, they showed this paper to Mía, who examined the letters and then took the note back into the gymnasium, placing it on the floor where it had been found, beneath the shoes and next to the chair. None of the children considered showing this paper to any of the adults. It was not wise since they were never allowed to play in the gymnasium. It had been shaken years before and was no longer safe. So it had become one of the forbidden places, like the collapsed staircase in the north hall. Dust covered the floor of the gymnasium, and now little tracks laid down by bare feet looked as if field mice had worn a path.

The man himself hung from a long and twisty rope.

Mía bumped the shiny black shoes as she replaced the note, making the body swing to and fro while spinning in a slow pirouette. It looked sad and yet somehow dignified, like an old man dancing alone. The children were hypnotized by the sight, a frail pendulum in a black suit with a red-striped tie, the only man in the village wearing leather shoes instead of boots or sandals. Why had he been so sad? His face was turned down, one cheek touching his shoulder, the eyes softly closed like the pictures of Jesus that *Abuelita* had cut from magazines. A handkerchief in the breast pocket of his suit. His hair oiled and gray and parted with meticulous care. Why had he dressed so well, like someone who did not belong in the village at all?

It was the father of the boy named Donzel who made all of the commotion. He was shoveling ashes into a wheelbarrow and scattering them over a flat terraced garden where he hoped to grow strawberries in the coming year. Trekking back to one of the ash piles, he made out a silhouette in one window of the old gymnasium. It reminded him of something he had seen

forty years before when the law was a vague and distant
presence.

The father of the boy named Donzel ran to the door of
the gymnasium and then halfway across the floor, where he
was stopped by the insistent attention of a fly. It lit upon his
lips. It inquired at the corners of his mouth. And the father of
Donzel, who normally would not have been disturbed by a fly
or even a horned beetle, spat and thrashed his hands. When he
turned, the children saw such a look on his face that they
scattered; and so in the end it was the man's wife and not the
man himself who came into the gymnasium and picked up the
note for a second time. "My Dear Friend Amedeo," it began.

My Dear Friend Amedeo,

*I believe you are surprised that I may write at all. But I was
taken through four level of grade by the Sisters of Querétaro.
Believe me I know how to behave in a school although maybe not
so much on this day though I should not make the joke. And
may God Take away my sin and Forgive me for the path I
choose.*

*Amedeo I can no longer carry the weight of what I know for
I am not a man of stone like you. So please to sit with me for a
while before you lay me in the ground and if possible have here a
priest to pray for my soul. I know that you are loyal to your child
and that God will hear me when I pray for blessings onto you and
onto her. This is what I have done. I could not bear thinking of
Leala what we did that day and then after that day. I could not
bear it after seeing her.*

*Almost two month ago I use the money I save and bus to her
in California and see her at the stable where she go to ride. I talk
to her but Alejandro he did not see me. I already mail her the
plate from the car before I realize it would not be enough. Jaasiel
he found it for me for money and I told her that her child was
alive Amedeo. Please forgive me. Yet it almost make her mad
with grief and pain because I would not tell her more. Not even
where we were living now only making it worse. So in the end I
keep faith with you my friend. I am sorry to you and to her.*

Now on this day I see that what I do is perhaps wrong and perhaps right but there is pain either way. Amedeo you must tell her the truth and you must not tell her the truth. You must do and you must not do at the same time. See I cannot know what to say even as I write on this paper except for my sorrow and shame. In this only did I betray you I told her that her child was well the worst sin of my life. Then I return to here. What is a man to do? Because like you I cannot leave I am bound to this place. So may God be merciful to me a fool.

Gabriel Garcia López Covas

Amedeo himself cut the rope, cradling Gabriel until a table could be brought. Then four young men, as grave as soldiers in formation, carried him outside where they found a suitable space beneath a cypress bough. No one had ever seen such a thing, and no one knew what to say. It was *Abuelita* who broke the stillness, giving such a cry when she saw him that it hurt the hearts of all who stood nearby. She struck at her own face and breast until fat Tomas had to hold her arms, and then she cried in words that were stretched so long they ceased to be anything but a single wounded sound. This was a man, the other women said, who had stored up love in someone's heart. Now see what pours out in return. All of her pretense of disapproval, all of her fussiness about his ways, had been but a thin disguise. *Abuelita* had loved him from the depths of her soul.

The new bride, Paloma, came in bare feet, standing outside the circle of women who were the practiced ministers of death. Bring a tub of cold clear water said one of them. A cloth, a towel for drying him. We can do it here in the shade beneath the trees. But in the end no one touched the corpse—she would not allow it—except for the one he had known as Reina de la Vega when they were both young. Amedeo stood nearby speaking to the men about cedar boards and nails. They went quietly to the storeroom for saws and hammers and planes. One by one the women followed through the school and to their scattered errands, some to convey the news and some to prepare a meal and some to consider fabric for the veiling of the dead.

After a time there was only *Abuelita* and the pale figure upon the table. She talked to him now more quietly than the way she used to talk, untying his shoes with her one hand and placing them side by side on a flat stone. Next she removed the red striped tie with slow difficulty, folding it as carefully as she could and laying it across the shoes. The buttons of his shirt and his old-fashioned collar were impossible to do. Her fingers were still stiff and swollen from morning pain. Her hand shaking. She found herself bending forward by degrees until her face was touching his chest and she was sobbing once more; it was then that Paloma, who had not walked far away with the others, came to her side. The girl removed the shawl that she had thrown about her shoulders and folded it into a pillow that she eased behind his head. She went to the opposite side of the table where she finished with the buttons and helped to take off the coat and shirt as one. "Someday my Victor," she said through tears, "I will love him even more than this."

The old woman shook her head. "That is not possible, child. But you will blessed if you try."

They washed the body with slow and gentle strokes, taking care to rinse the hair in front and back, scrubbing the soles of the feet, and talking, from time to time, about the reckless pride and vanity of men. At the end of an hour they had dressed Gabriel again in his best clothes, the laces of his shoes a bit straighter than before. The buttons of his shirt perfectly aligned. Paloma folded the handkerchief with care and then asked what more there was to do.

"Some more chairs, little one. Over here and over there. Have the men bring them down from the room on the second floor. When the others come, we will need to talk and keep him company."

"What else?" Paloma asked.

"In the little room where he has his cot, on the shelf beneath the mirror, he keeps a bottle of lotion for after he shaves. Bring it. And the rosary under his pillow. And maybe the Roman coins from the tin box on his chest. For luck. And

Amedeo. Tell him I wish to speak."

Paloma went to find Amedeo first.

The other men, when they had finished the cedar coffin, sent their best carpenter to the place where Gabriel rested. The carpenter's name was Stefano; and first he made the sign of the cross as he told his friend good-bye, admiring the suit and then thanking him for the many adventurous tales they had shared on the evening terrace. Next he led *Abuelita* by the hand back to the terrace itself, the men parting for her as she approached. The ones polishing the wood with beeswax stopped their work, stepping back for her inspection. She put her hand inside where the sweet smell lingered and where the joints were smooth. "Like a single piece of wood," Stefano said to her. "Like a box for jewels and precious things." They brought the lid, already finished and coved, for her to examine. She touched its edge, forcing a smile and a nod. Her lack of interest in such boxes, her true feeling for wood and for nails, would have hurt their pride and dishonored her Gabriel. So she smiled and gave them a nod. It was all she had to give.

Old Ángelina had saved yards of cloth for the making of cheese, as delicate as a spider's web. The women cut it into lengths and used it to veil the corpse. By early afternoon all the men had come up from the fields and made a slow procession past the table, hat in hand, to give a fond remembrance or a word of praise for the fine black suit and the handsome tie. Then they took a plate of beans and sat, each one with his family, in the cooling breeze. Some listened to talk of years gone by, how Gabriel had been a chauffeur for a wealthy man; and others offered stories about the passing seasons. Only Amedeo stayed away, carrying out the task that he had assigned himself.

On a hillside beneath the school, among rows of standing stones and swaths of prairie grass, he worked. He used a shovel at first, little clouds of dust blowing upslope as he dug; then he used a pick when he reached hardpan. The excavated earth grew slowly into a corpse-long mound and then into a rounded hill, little rivulets sliding back into the hole when he did not pitch high enough. The boy Quentin joined him when the hardpan turned to stony gruel. They worked without their shirts and took turns with pick and shovel, not pausing until Sabina brought a gourd of water and a plate of beans.

"You are striking sparks with the pick there are so many stones," she said.

They looked up at her from the waist-deep trench. "Only another foot or two," Amedeo told her.

"The earth does not welcome someone who seeks his own salvation," the girl declared.

Amedeo stood up after another swing of the pick. "The earth welcomes anyone, Sabina."

"Still, this is consecrated ground, no?"

"At one time I suppose it was. And then, my young friend, the earth made a new hill and a new cemetery," Amedeo nodded toward the mountain, "from up there."

"Still, it is consecrated ground."

He pried loose a skillet of stony ground. "We will lay him here as *Abuelita* wishes."

The girl addressed Quentin this time. "You are not afraid of what the priest will say? If one comes."

But it was again Amedeo who answered. "If one comes, we will worry then. But tomorrow we lay him here."

Sabina left to report all that was said by the man who set himself above the church.

Amedeo and Quentin ate from the same plate, sharing back and forth. They spread their shirts over the loose fill and laid back like dead men themselves. They talked in low tones about the ways of death and how long it was before a man turned himself to dust and then from dust to stone. Amedeo remembered the old ways of his own village, how the family would sit three nights while mourners came from miles around. But not so much anymore.

"Still, this is a good place," Quentin said. "For my own grave, I want the head higher than the feet so I can look out and see. The valley. The mountains. I like to see those trees you plant from seed each fall. The maples from Japan."

"You are seventeen, too young to be thinking of your own grave."

"When you die, we will plant you in the grove beneath the valley wall. Is that what you want?"

Amedeo did not answer at first. He reached for his shirt and wiped sweat from his face. "What I want? On the day that I die, I want a beautiful woman to shed tears for me. I want my friends to carry me on their shoulders with respect, maybe place me here beside old Gabriel. And I want God to say to me that my task is done. But on the day following, I want--."

"A load of flowers on your grave. A load of manure on your fields. New window glass for the school. A new radiator for the truck. New fencepost for the corral." Quentin was delighted with his list and prepared to continue, but Amedeo interrupted.

"Yes. Precisely. I want you all to go about your lives."

Quentin believed that Amedeo was sincere but could not believe he would leave the villagers in peace. "Ha. With you in the grave, we sleep for three days."

"Fine," Amedeo agreed.

"And the beautiful woman, will she surprise us like *Abuelita*?" Quentin raised his eyebrows as if he expected a serious answer.

Amedeo liked the boy too much to rebuke him with any conviction. "Don't be disrespectful," he said.

So they continued digging for a while. And when they had reached the depth of their shoulders, they squared the edges and the walls. Then they tamped the floor, leaving a slight incline as Quentin had suggested. When they both were satisfied, Amedeo gave Quentin a boost to help him climb out of the grave. Then Quentin pulled the older man back to the surface of the earth. It was mid-afternoon by the time that they had finished and gone their separate ways.

14

AMEDEO WALKED ALONE to the valley wall, and there he thought about the words that Reina had used during the long night of sitting beside the coffin. She had told everyone that Gabriel had no pride. That the truly poor cannot afford it. As the sitters nodded, she went on to say that his death was not a sin, only a sacrifice. And then from her place in the darkness Reina de la Vega said, without a hint of bitterness, "I am talking to you, Amedeo Muñoz, whose pride has brought us all to this dry well." No one spoke again for many minutes.

Now, in the aftermath of burial, Amedeo stood at the lichen covered wall brooding upon the rocks below, puzzling over the words in Gabriel's note. What choices did he have now? When a hawk appeared in the morning sun, Amedeo tried to imagine himself at such a height, perfectly still amid the turbulence and far from the concerns of men. What was it like, the wind that rushed like water? Was it cold and sweet, or hot and sour like the air above a flame?

He was taken by a sudden impulse, not so much a thought as a reckless curiosity, an urge to know what it would be like to hurl himself into the sky. His feet seemed to move independently of his conscious mind, taking him closer to the wall itself. His legs leaned him into the waist-high barrier and there, just inches from his face, the great heavens opened and invited him to soar or to plummet as his spirit willed. Amedeo wondered what would happen if he spread his arms and put himself into the wind. He leaned farther and considered the stones at the foot of the wall. From this height they looked like bits of sculpture that had fallen to the artist's floor. He lifted his eyes in the other direction and then heard someone behind him.

It was Leala, still dressed as she had been two days before. Now, though, she looked more like a villager than the wife of a wealthy man. Her fine skirt had accumulated enough dust to turn the lavender into gray. The matching vest had been discarded for a borrowed shawl. And her hair had been brushed back and loosely braided. When she spoke to him, she sounded empty of everything except exhaustion. "I wish it had been you instead of Gabriel. That would have been better for us all. Wouldn't it? And right now I wish I were a man strong enough to shove you out into the air and watch you fall. I think that would give me some degree of peace."

She came close to the wall and looked cautiously over the edge just as he had done. It was several hundred feet to the ground, and Leala was obviously afraid, but she was compelled by something more durable than fear. "Reina was wrong," she went on. "Your arrogance doesn't rise high enough to be called pride. It's always been just another form of greed."

He thought of all the possible things she could mean. He thought of Sister Patrice and Reina, who had asked 'What have you done?' with the same notes of defeat and sadness. "I did the only thing I knew to do," he told her. "I've already told you this."

"A rather poor excuse for the way your daughter lives. Wouldn't you say? Perhaps Reina can give me the whole story. As I recall, she was never a friend of yours. Perhaps Alejandro and I will bring her back to the hacienda, give her a moment to recover, and then ask her about the only thing you knew to do."

Amedeo tried to look into her face, but she would not acknowledge him. When he tried to put reason into his voice, she turned away entirely. "The earth fell away beneath us, Leala. And before the wailing stopped, I made my way to Sangre de Cristo. It took me three days, walking for most of the time, getting a few short rides as well. When I reached the cathedral, where we had agreed to meet, I waited. And when you did not come...."

"You went back to the mountains rather than give our daughter a home or to do any other sensible thing for her. So I'll ask you again, as I asked you two days ago—could you not pick up a telephone, even once, in twelve years? I needed to know—any mother needs to know—that our child was safe!"

He put his hand to her shoulder and turned her toward him. "First you said she was not mine. Now you say that she is."

Her sudden vehemence, springing from what had been a melancholy tone, surprised him more than the slap at his loaded truck. Leala did not shout, but she threw herself into the words she said next. "You *made* her yours! You stole her in twenty different ways!"

Amedeo was just as fast and just as heated with a reply. "And I am telling you again that I raised a child. Our child, if you are to be believed. I have carried her on my shoulders from the valley floor to the top of the stone steps. I have cooked her food, mended her clothes, plowed her fields. I have repaired her truck. I have cleared the streets of her village, rebuilt her school, pumped her water, built her furniture. I have told her stories. I have fought the ones who would steal from her. I have made her laugh. I have wiped her tears away. Every day, Leala, I have done these things. And I did not falter once. I did not bend or break, no matter what the weight. That is what I have done."

Leala stepped close enough to him to whisper. "And I am telling you, again, that it was not enough."

"You are so angry you don't know what you say."

"I have a right to be angry! Don't you dare try to talk away my anger! "

Amedeo did not back away, but he did try to control his voice. It was the closest he could come to making a concession. "You have never been able to see beyond your own way of seeing. For God's sake, woman, what is it that you want from me at this unhappy moment? What is it that can't wait for a man to take a single breath?"

"My child. I want my child," Leala said. She wrapped the shawl more tightly around her shoulders and let the interval of silence grow between them. When she spoke again, it was with less force and with more of her original exhaustion. "I truly did not come out here to fight with you. After seeing the way you live…. I just want my child, Amedeo. I just want her back. Is that so hard for you to understand?"

"Of course not. The rich want everything. As they always do." He started to walk away from the overlook.

"Wait," she said. "Amedeo, I am sorry for what you have endured. And for poor Gabriel. And for the suffering of these people. I truly am. But there's no love for you anywhere in my heart. I simply came to tell you--."

"You cannot have her," he suddenly interjected.

"--to tell you goodbye." Leala had not acknowledged his interruption and had not paused in her speaking. "And to tell you that he is coming now, Manley, with policemen, from a second car."

Immediately he wanted to know, "Where is she? Where is Mía?! Where did you tell her to go?"

"Amedeo, it's time for all of this to be over. We don't have long to talk, and you know that Alejandro can purchase three policemen or three hundred, however many it will take."

Amedeo looked back along the street that followed the contour of the mountain. "Did she go with the other children, or did you send her where Manley could find her?"

"You're not listening to me," Leala said. "You never are. Amedeo, this life is over for Mía. Those men are here to take her to her real home and to a new life. A better life. For you I am not sorry, but I am very sure Mr. Manley has everything he needs to...."

"He's got no proof!" At last he bellowed, the force of Amedeo's words echoing from some far valley wall.

Leala spoke very quietly in return. "They don't need proof! They don't need anything. They have guns."

Leala's tears were giving way finally to bitter amazement. "My God. You're just realizing, aren't you? After all of this. You built a castle around her that you can't keep from falling down." While Amedeo scanned the terraces and steps, she brought her oracle's pronouncement closer and closer. "Now the families are leaving you, one by one. Even the thieves and murderers will be following them. And one day soon you will be the ruler of broken glass and empty streets. That's what it is, isn't it? Out there in the world you are nobody, but here in the land of dreams you are king. It's simple arrogance after all."

Suddenly the truth of Gabriel's letter came to him. My Dear Friend Amedeo, it had said. I am not a man of stone like you.

Amedeo decided at last to tell Leala the story that she did not know. But as he opened his mouth to speak, he caught sight of someone he recognized leaving the school, someone climbing upward across a rocky and dangerous slope, in a direction that she should not go. Amedeo closed his lips. Turned his back on the woman. And ran.

15

ON THE MORNING AFTER the funeral, Mía felt the eyes of many people upon her as she took an orange from the outside kitchen and went to the big stairs inside the school where she sat peeling it and eating the slices. A swath of sunlight fell through the open doors and landed at her feet. Busy silhouettes crossed and recrossed in front of her. From where she sat it was like watching a moving picture. The village was trying to recover some of its normal routine after days of turbulence and confusion and pain. She watched the people come and go, focusing at last upon two figures in the distance near the valley wall. A man and a woman in deep discussion.

Mía did not notice the other man, the one who had come up from the street toward her, until his shadow fell over her face. She closed one eye and squinted into the light that surrounded him.

"Hi there," the man said. "I don't think we've officially met."

She had seen him before of course, on the day that the dogs had bayed at him and Gabriel had pointed into the school. He wore the same coat and hat; but he seemed taller now, and his boots made a clep-clepping sound as he crossed the floor. When he reached the bottom step, he went down on one knee and nodded as if introducing himself. "I'm a friend of your mama's. You might say I work for her, and your daddy. My name is Manley."

With a whole orange slice in her mouth, the words came out in a slurry of hopeless garble. "You don't work here."

"No ma'am, I don't." He produced a business card from some inner pocket and presented it to her. While Mía studied the name and moved her lips over the other words, the man turned his back so that he could sit on one of the lower steps and face the same direction she was facing. "You ever find yourself in need of a private investigation, well, then I'd be happy to oblige."

Mía didn't know what to say. She felt sure that the man was teasing her, but he spoke in such a slow, serious voice, keeping his face away from hers, that she could not be sure. Finally she decided to say "thank you" and handed back the card, reaching it over his shoulder, because it looked expensive.

"No ma'am, that's for you to keep," the detective said. Can't ever tell when you might need it. You're the one they call Mía, right? Kind of a nickname or something for Maria? That's what I was told."

"Yes," she said while still giving most of her attention to the peel.

"Glad to meet you." Manley turned partly in her direction and offered his hand. Again Mía could not tell if he was joking. She put her hand in his and let him move them both up and down several times. Then he turned his back toward the door, rested both elbows on his knees, and sighed. He said nothing more and seemed to be content watching the village bring itself back to life.

Mía could not decide if she was supposed to talk next or if she could just leave. She tore off another slice of orange and put all of it in her mouth. After she had chewed for a time, she said, "Why are you here?"

"Me?" He raised the fingers of both hands and then dropped them back into his lap. "I'm just waitin' I suppose. Probably going to be driving you and your mama in a little while."

"Where?" she wanted to know.

"Oh." The words sounded surprised and yet somehow rehearsed at the same time. "You mean she hasn't talked to you about that yet?"

"About what?" Mía stopped chewing and tried to imagine what her mother and father were talking about at the valley wall.

"Well," Manley went on, "it's probably not my place, you know, to be lettin' on about private family matters and so forth."

Now she wanted to know all that the detective knew.

While Mía could not hear the faraway words of her parents, she could see that their conversation was not going well. And she needed the detective to speak to her directly. "Driving away?" she asked. "From here?"

"Oh my. There I go spilling the beans. I guess your daddy's gonna be hot at me about that. Maybe I just shouldn't have said anything at all."

Mía thought back to her fit of rage in the secret garden, back to her running away into the town and getting lost. Amedeo had not yet said a word about either. Was he sending her away again because he was so angry? Was he sending them both away, her mother and her, at the moment they could be together and happy? Why had he been so distant and sad since Leala came with him into the village? Mía tried to think of happy answers, but suddenly there were only questions tumbling over each other in her mind. "What did he say to you, my papa?"

Manley turned now and faced her, a momentary confusion lifting his features. "Oh, you think that he ... that man out there ... ? Ah, hell. I shouldn't have said anything at all. Look, sweetie, I'm as sorry as I can be about the whole...."

"What do you mean?" Mía laid the orange aside and slid down to where she could see Manley's face.

"Why, nothing. I don't mean a thing." The detective stood up and dusted his pants with the hat. "I guess I better go see what they've decided about the, you know, the whole thing."

The girl stood up as well. "What did you mean? What are they deciding?!"

Manley rubbed his face as if pondering one of the great unanswerable questions of life. "I don't know," he said. "It's got to be a pretty big shock, your mother showing up and all. I mean, did he tell you that she had died a long time ago, or did you just not talk about it yet? Don't that strike you as a little strange? Every child has got a natural curiosity about where they come from. Like, if it was me, I would have been wondering."

"Wondering what?" Mía said.

"Well. If you weren't *born* here, then how did you get here

in the first place? But I guess that's not for me to wonder
about." He walked back out to the terrace where he gave a
loud whistle and then motioned with his arm for some unseen
person to begin the long climb up.

Mía felt the light and dark spaces tightening around her.
Amedeo had only told her that her mother was in heaven, not
that she had lived some place beyond the village. It was not a
possibility that Mía had ever considered, and yet now all of the
impossible details of a fairy tale began to swirl and collide in
her mind. As she followed Manley onto the terrace, she moved
her legs with slow stiffness, like *Abuelita* in the early morning.
The detective had momentarily disappeared, but she no longer
needed him and did not look for his shadow or shape amid the
sudden confusion of her world. All of her other questions had
condensed themselves into the one big question that she was
afraid to ask. She turned instead toward the plaza and found
the path that led upward, though the rocky landscape and
among the stunted trees. It was the only direction she knew to
take.

She did not see Amedeo in the distance suddenly breaking
away from her mother and beginning to run in her direction.
Nor did she see the policemen climbing sluggishly toward the
school, nor the children who played ball in the street. She
could see only the face of the innocent man, the one who
stood taller than any man in the village and who so struggled
with words on the night of the fiesta. The man Amedeo would
not allow into the village. The one who had sat beside Gabriel
and then slipped down one step to say to her, "I know the
secret of your name."

●

She took to the slopes like a deer, her sandals barely
leaving marks at all. Only a pebble or two went bounding as
she climbed. Only a trickle of sand went sluicing into the air.
When she slipped, she caught the trunk of a low-growing
juniper and pulled herself through a loose rivulet of grit and
powder. Still she did not pause to look behind or to
acknowledge the name that he called out from below. "Mía!"
he was shouting. "Mía!" As if the sound of that one word

could keep her from finding the truth.

Why should she waste a backward glance when all he wanted was to keep her from her mother's world? She leaned into the ascent now, using her hands and her feet to scramble where his heavy frame could not go. The narrow plateau loomed directly above her, and beyond it lay the dark opening of the tunnel where the children were not allowed. And why? Because of his rules. Because of one of his bullying rules that he gave without explanation. Because, she realized, he did not want people to know the truth or even where to find it.

Mía reached the edge of the clearing, stood up, and looked back through time. The valley, the village, and all the human effort at living had been shrunk and laid in dizzying perspective at her feet. For a moment her anger and confusion receded. From this elevation even the aftermath of earthquakes seemed sane and beautiful. Even the patchwork repairs of human beings seemed part of nature's plan. The panorama was more than beautiful. It was fearful and magnificent in a way that had no words. Mía brought herself to the edge of a precipitous drop and became as still as one of the stone sentinels in the distance.

She looked down at her mother, still in the narrow street below the church and just now starting to run, her skirt flapping against her legs, her voice rising like a cry from the past. Even at this distance Mía could hear her calling out, first from simple surprise and then with growing alarm as Amedeo did not answer. "What? What is it?! Amedeo!" He was far ahead of her of course. Ignoring her. Of course. Mía watched him until the revulsion began to creep back up from her knees and assert itself once more. She watched him lose his balance among the boulders. Watched him trip over his own carelessness while climbing and calling her name. Everything he did slowed him down. He came wading the shale like a man whose pockets were filled with stones.

She turned her back and walked to the timbered arch.

Mía stood just outside the opening and listened for any welcoming sound. "¿Hola?" she said into the darkness. Then, stepping over a line made by the first shadows, she peered as

far back as she could see and said again, "*Hola*. Are you there?"
But no echo or answer came to her. In fact, after the first few
feet of the entrance, much of the interior space was filled by an
egg-shaped boulder that seemed to block off any possibility of
a passage. She put her hand against its cool surface and
followed its long curving balustrade to the left, into the
mountain and into the gathering gloom. She found that she
had entered an emptiness that was far larger and more
haunting than the boulder itself. It was a tunnel indeed,
stretching back along the level path of a perfectly recognizable
road that had been swept clean, at least for the first hundred
feet, by the hand of some patient custodian.

"Are you here?" she said. "I can't see you. And he's
coming to...."

From some remote bend in the corridor she heard a
familiar and comforting sound, the scratching of a kitchen
match, followed by a fizz and a flare. At first it was as faint as a
candle, but the pungency of sulfur came to her, and the torch
that he lit fluttered only a few feet from where she stood. It
gave a yellow and wavering light beneath a tendril of soot, the
oily rags barely able to sustain a flame. Mía stepped near
enough to feel the warmth against her skin, but still she could
not see him, the slow and soft-spoken giant who had promised
her a name. She let her eyes adjust to this new world, and what
she discovered first was a part of the old world in a dreadfully
wrong place. A front porch.

Her face was within inches of it, the first step almost at her
shoulder height and leading to the ruin of a general store or a
bodega it seemed, with signs in faded blue lettering. And a cash
register sprung open on the floor. She could see all the way to
the back wall of the little building, see the empty shelves and
the fill of dirt left behind by the excavators; and the absurdity
of such a thing struck her as a dream. It was as if someone had
squeezed the little store, intact, off of its foundation and
deposited it in the center of a road, the one door and the four
windows still perfectly framed, the roof cracked and sagging
beneath dry sludge and stone. From a distance it would have
looked like a dollhouse; yet here it was, inside of a mountain,

with a sign hanging below the roof, as ordinary as last week, listing the prices of seed corn, kerosene, rope, and wire.

"This way," said the gentle voice. "A little farther along."

He was there at the edge of the dark, a ragged mound of a man with a cloth tied around his neck and fingerless gloves on both of his hands. The shirt, or vest if that's what it was, lay open to his waist; and his pants, held up with a drawstring, seemed made of the same coarse material, a gray tatter that ended at his calves and blended with the color of the walls. He lit another torch and leaned down from a great height to study her face.

His eyes were squinted into dark slits as he kept trying to magnify her into something understandable. They went up and down her body while he tilted his head to one side, studying his memory of where he had seen her before. She was the girl from the fiesta. The reborn daughter of his enemy Muñoz. Offering herself to him.

Mía studied him as well, worrying now about his altered appearance. The subtle distortions of a normal face that had been magnified by his size. There seemed at once too much flesh for the covering of his frame and yet at the same time there was a hardness beneath, as if someone had mashed dough over the features of a rock.

"I know you," he said. "I could smell you. From back there. What do you bring to Juan Soldado?"

"I don't know what you mean. They say your name is Jaasiel, and people are afraid of you. So no one comes here because...."

"Many people come!" he intoned. "They bring gifts. Because they want miracles and visions."

"I just want ... what you said to me," Mía told him. "On the steps of the school."

"I remember you," he allowed.

"Then tell me who I am. You said to come to you. You said you knew the secret of my name. That's what you told me on the steps."

"You want what they all have wanted, yes?" He set his lips together as if resting them after a long and difficult speech.

Moved his jaw as if chewing. He took heavy, bovine breaths through his nose and wiped sweat from one side of his face.

"I want you to tell me. Before he comes."

"Yes. Yes." He touched her hair.

"Just tell me."

"I know," said Jaasiel. "But first, let me look at you. I have to be very sure." He put his finger beneath her chin and tilted her face into the light. He took her hand and raised it from her side as if expecting her to pirouette. He moistened his lips twice with the tip of his tongue, then drew the back of his own hand along the underside of her arm, and down her back, and across the curve of her hip. "Yes," he said. "Yes, I know that you're the one. The one that I saw." He brought his hand down to her thigh and took one of the folds of her skirt into his fingers, lifting it away from her leg. He inspected the shape of her inside the clinging cloth.

Mía felt a flush in her cheeks. She stepped back. "No! You said you would tell me!"

"I said that I would tell you something? I don't remember now. But there are things I can tell and show you, yes, if you come with me," he said.

"Just tell me now! You said you knew my name!"

"Yes, maybe. A secret, yes. But first.... " Jaasiel made a beckoning motion with one of his hands. "Lift up your skirt for me. Just enough. Just enough to see, that's all. To let me see."

She turned and began to run.

"It's what you brought to me, isn't it? Well, I can tell you something, because I saw you die. And I saw you born! Back when the earth was shaking. I did. I was always here!"

His voice receded, but the urgency of it, the pleading, desperate need came through to her in a way that she could not explain. It was the voice of a child. Mía slowed her retreat, keeping herself out of the torchlight and headed toward the whiter glow of day, but when her hands touched the monolith once more, she stopped, struck by something helpless in his tone. He had no idea he was saying something wrong. The utter insanity was itself sincere. "I found a woman once!" he was shouting now. "In the wall. I did. Skin as soft as deer, and her eyes open all the way. Like she was looking straight into me, from the wall, a little bit farther along. Down there." He pointed. Mía could see his silhouette.

This time she did not reply but rather looked toward the still distant opening as if expecting an answer from outside. When she looked back at Jaasiel, he was reaching out his hand and motioning her toward him with small and intimate gestures. "Come. Come. I can show you what you want to know. A little bit farther along. I can make a light."

He was so sincere that she almost went to him, imaging the rage if her father found her now. She had seen Amedeo fight other men who defied him, watched him take food from those who did not work. Wasn't it true, what the women said, that he was a king who endured no disobedience, a tyrant who punished the rebellious first? And the children who were afraid of him? Could they all be wrong? Maybe the ragged man was not so dangerous. Maybe his mind was just jumbled and slow. And maybe if she stayed out of his reach she could make him tell her more until his rambling thoughts brought him round to the words she needed for him to say.

But suddenly he was there, his huge hand gripping her wrist so hard that she felt grains of sand biting into her flesh. When she kicked and tried to jerk away, he simply lifted her from the floor. Now with his warm, slow breath washing over her face, he spoke with a different tone. "You are nobody," he said. "And Amedeo should never have allowed you here. He brought this upon himself."

●

Leala knew nothing of the mountain, only that it had sent rocks crashing into the village years ago and that many had died. The devastation was still evident after a decade or more, and so was the danger of rockslides. It was why she tried to stop Amedeo. She called to him as he went charging through the rubble, chasing Mía higher and higher into danger. What had provoked such an outburst, bellowing her name as he did, shouting at her the way he would shout at a runaway dog?

As he stumbled among the boulders, Leala almost cheered

for the girl. And why? Because his daughter was far beyond his reach and now far beyond his words. Mía was standing at the lip of a small plateau, looking down on him and then walking away almost casually. Amedeo kept climbing with undiminished effort. When he did pause to turn around, he was still shouting, this time at Leala and the few curious villagers gathering in the nearest street. "Get Quentin or Ordóñez!" he roared. "Find one of them, and get him here now!"

There was no use trying to stop him. Leala followed upward, hoping to calm the scene before he lost the girl entirely. By the time she reached the grassy patch of flowers, the stretch of blue flax and salvia, Leala could make out an opening in the side of the mountain. A bit of her anxiety returned, and Leala hurried. It was not what she had expected at this height, but surely the child would know not to venture outside the shaft of light that marked the entrance.

Leala could not keep herself from calling out. After she gained the plateau, she went to the curve of the great boulder, surprised by the porous ceiling and the sprinkling of light. "Mía, sweetheart," she said. "Come to me. Come to the sound of my voice. I'm holding out my hand." From farther down the widening corridor, somewhere out of sight, she heard men working. "Mía, darling, don't be afraid. Just come this way and we'll go down together. I have a surprise for you. We've come to take you home." The splintering of wood now. The grunt of a man who had fallen and the rasp of a weight being dragged through the dirt.

"Amedeo! Bring her to me!" Leala waited in the sudden silence.

She was answered by a high-pitched scream, then another silence, the girl's cry cut short by a muffled something that impelled Leala forward. She ran without thought away from the surety of the boulder and into the insanity of the next chamber where two figures struggled in silence, one of them as thick as a bull and as tall as the timbers holding back the mountain. A torch had been thrown to the floor and was now sputtering out its life and making shadows against the walls. A heavy dust cloud rose up like smoke. Leala could feel it settling on her face, obscuring her sight. And it was the low, continuous coughing that turned her in the right direction. There at last was Mía, transfixed within a frame of thick timbers, holding her arm as if it had been broken.

The smaller man had launched himself at the larger one, driving a shoulder into his stomach and hurling them both against the wall. The impact made a dull echo, as if the wall were partially hollow. Rubble fell to the floor, and a halo of gray dust expanded around the two entangled figures. As Amedeo loosed his grip, the big man slumped but did not collapse. He went instead to one knee and then slowly pushed himself upright. Amedeo punched with precision, the blows landing with furious strength, striking the brow, the chin, the nose, the eyes, faster than Jaasiel could defend himself. Already there was an open slash above one eye and a steady trickle that ran like sweat. As Jaasiel rose, he swung with his other hand, a fist the size of a maul, and knocked Amedeo into the shadows. Then he pulled himself fully upright, wiping at the eye socket and contemplating blood. He seemed to be puzzled but not hurt.

Amedeo charged again. Neither of them spoke. Neither of them looked to the woman or to the girl. They simply fought, Amedeo boxing and finding his mark with nearly every blow, the other swinging his arms like a bear. Jaasiel no longer backed away, but rather stalked forward, knocking the smaller man off balance each time he struck and then reaching out with his massive hands. Amedeo hardly bothered to dodge, pounding at ribs when he could not reach the face, striking the same targets repeatedly until, at last, the giant stumbled again. Amedeo kicked at one leg, and the ragged man fell to both knees, lifting up his hands this time as if he had been blinded by the sun.

From the edge of the chamber Leala could see that even on his knees Jaasiel was nearly as tall as his foe and that his only protection was his great strength. Though Amedeo had been blooded and hurt, still he worked with cold and ruthless effect. It was like a man beating a child, until finally Leala could stand the cruelty no longer and called out, "Stop it! Stop! Do you want her to see this? Do you want her to watch you killing a man?!"

Amedeo stopped. He looked at Leala and his daughter. He opened his fists and looked at the split and gory knuckles. Found himself breathing too hard to speak and twisting his torso away from the pain in his ribs. Waiting for any words to float back into his mind so that he could answer the sickening look on her face. Leala pulled the girl toward her and started to walk away while Amedeo tried to think of any syllable that could stop them. He made a noise that rose up from his heart but came out like pain. When he tried to speak again, he felt a sound so near to him that it turned his head, an explosion that expanded inward until there was nothing but blackness. Then Jaasiel was upon him, and someone was screaming from far away.

Amedeo lay on his back, feeling the warmth spread across his face and watching, as from a remote distance, the great fists hammering down on him. There was no pain, only a dull sense of impact. He thought of Reina, how she would hang a rug on a line and thump it with the handle of a broom. How she would do it in the mornings, slowly and methodically on each side. He admired her cleanliness. He admired her grace. And for a moment he thought he was being killed by a woman, strict and severe, who had for years been the only mother to his child.

Someone said, "Quentin."

He heard a faint but familiar child's voice saying the name Quentin, and suddenly Amedeo was able to breathe again. The weight was lifted from his chest. He sucked in the sweetness, swallowing dust as eagerly as life-giving air. Then when he coughed, the first of a shuddering cascade, a fierce and jagged pain went ripping through his upper body. Amedeo sat up, moved his head slowly from left to right. Tried to locate himself inside the darkening room. He heard scuffling sounds to his left, punches thrown and returned, then one heavy *whompf,* like a sack of grain dropped from a man's shoulder.

He shook his head again and saw the boy. Quentin was lying in a heap, a drizzle of dirt falling from the wall above him.

"You. And me," the giant was saying to Amedeo now. "We are the same, eh?"

"No," said Muñoz. "We are not the same." And Amedeo, now exhausted and bleeding, levered himself upright and began as before, battering his giant opponent as if he were breaking down a wall. He could hear Quentin coughing himself back into consciousness and could see with quick glances that Quentin was trying to stand up by using the handle of a nearby sledge hammer. But it was a mistake for Amedeo to look away from his adversary. When Jaasiel's great fist landed, it was as if he had been struck by a train. Amedeo's body fell in upon itself, and he closed his eyes feeling an almost pleasant sense of sleep. He was tired beyond any fatigue or ache at the end of day. He was tired of living. When he was driven into the wall, the impact was no more to him than falling into bed. Perhaps there would be pleasant dreams on the other side.

Jaasiel hoisted Amedeo and wrapped his arms where he could tighten the hold with ease. He had heard of giant snakes that killed this way, of monstrous sea creatures that did the same, pulling their enemies close and taking away their air. It was the right way for Muñoz to die, who held on to everything like one of the *hacendados*. And so Jaasiel squeezed. He shook, hoping for resistance. He whispered to the unhearing ear, "You think you can pound me down? As easily as that? Well, I think you may be wrong."

This time Jaasiel saw the boy coming, saw him take up the hammer like a weary man gathering his tools for work. There was dirt matted on the side of his face where he had fallen. A long rip that separated one sleeve from his shirt. An open, seeping scab beneath his eye. He came at Jaasiel with his head tilted, the hammer held close to his chest. When he swung, he did not aim for the giant at all.

There came a solid, reverberating boom as he connected with one of the vertical timbers along the passage. The log moved six inches out of alignment, and the header above it twisted. The falling stones and dirt sounded like hail. The header groaned. Quentin put the full arc of his reach into his next effort, striking the timber flush and low. It kicked left. The header catapulted away, and the weight of the ceiling fell like thunder. There was no crumbling, no slow disintegration or avalanche. Only a blast and a sudden shaft of light. The dust itself looked like the roiling waste of war. Alarmed voices from the outside world came to Quentin, but he could not judge their direction. It was not a ringing in his ears, but a constant tone that confused him. He seemed to be alive and yet buried in dry muck and slag. He swam, strangely, downward and rolled onto what had once been the smooth surface of a road.

There he grappled for a shovel, the short-handled spade that he was sure he had seen when picking up the sledge hammer. When the other voices reached him, he had already thrown himself at the mound of debris. "Dig!" he said back to them. "Dig!"

PART THREE
September, 1948

16

SIX MEN CARRIED Amedeo Muñoz from the mountain to the school. There, in the room he himself had renovated, they laid Muñoz on a cot where, beneath the comings and goings of those who visited him, Amedeo dreamed that he was trapped. He dreamed at first that he was walking in a street and that the earth was shaking beneath his feet. Then that he was lying in a crevice that had split the street like a red laceration. Beside him was a woman and her bundle of rags. Stones were raining from the sky. People up above—he could see snatches of them, their flashing legs, their discarded baggage—they were falling down, they were scrambling up, they were running like animals stampeded by fire. In his dream the woman in the crevice was calm because she was trapped and dying. The earth chewed at her legs. It swallowed her to her waist. And as he dug beneath her with his hands, he put his face next to hers, as close as if they were man and wife. Her smile was sad. She patted his face with her hand and said, "You have a funny nose."

During the daylight hours people visited the sunlit room where Amedeo lay. There was neighborly concern of course, a great show of food and beverages arriving from many hands. But there was hardly any grief. How could the people grieve someone they did not love? He was a tyrant, the women said, who worked their husbands like slaves, even if it was to save all of their lives.

Still, a few were surprised by their own alarm, even by their affection for Amedeo. They were the men he drove so hard, particularly the ones who'd carried his battered body from the tunnel. This, they said, is proper, keeping vigil on the steps of the school. Not allowing him to die alone like a dog. Because he is our friend.

And the girl herself attended him. And her *abuelita*, the woman with one hand. Together they washed him, bandaged him in linen strips. After two days the villagers felt free to breathe again. The story would have no grand conclusion. He lived. That's all. The men retreated from their vigil, pulling carts and driving trucks back to harvesting on the valley floor. The boy Quentin went with them, and there was talk of giving him his own plot of land in the spring. There was joking and storytelling that treated Quentin as equal to any family man. But the girl Mía sat by her father's cot each day waiting for the first fluttering of his eyes. Who knows what is really in her heart, the gossips said. She is as wild as one of the boys and as flighty as the wind.

On the evening of the second day he moaned and moved his legs. Reina said he was dreaming but the girl, who knew him better, said that he was fighting his way back up. He coughed and spasmed inside the cough. He drew up his knees reflexively and would not be still enough to lie upon his back. They let him shift onto his side, but the pain still pulled wrinkles and crows' feet into his face. There was talk of a trip to Zalcupan for laudanum or something from a pharmacy. But best to wait: the trip would take half a day, and already another night was coming on. Rutilio brought him whiskey, which Amedeo Muñoz took without opening his eyes. In the morning, when he finally acknowledged the light, the girl had gone for breakfast and Reina was there staring out the window at a light drizzle, ignoring the book in her lap. When he stirred, she turned the same look, the same distance, upon him and did not speak.

"Ah. Clean sheets," he said. "They must have told you I was going to die."

When she saw that he could speak, she told him, "We have to talk. They're going to take the girl away."

"Not even a good morning? Not even a how do you feel?"

"Listen to me," Reina said. "Do you understand what I am telling you?"

"Mmm."

Reina had never cared for Muñoz and his arrogance. His

peasant's affair with Leala had been the start of all their misfortunes. Of course she had known about it almost from the first; everyone at the hacienda with half an eye had known about their affair. Leala and her laborer were reckless lovers, and for an instant Reina's reservoir of anger overflowed. "I can't help but believe it was you who brought us to this place. And that it was you who kept us here. So you will forgive me if I don't weep over your pain."

"You have always been free to leave," he managed to reply. "Perhaps your master Don Alejandro would have arranged a celebration for your safe return." It was enough of a speech to exhaust him, and he closed his eyes again.

Reina softened her look as well as her voice. "He would have been no more tyrannical than you," she murmured.

"Ah." He seemed almost amused. "I see. We don't intend to spare each other's feelings."

"I care nothing for your feelings," she went on. "I care only about the girl."

"Good." Amedeo opened his eyes and gave the hint of a smile. "Then set me up a bit higher so I can see. And water would be nice. A cup of water. Then talk. You and I. We need to reach an understanding."

Reina went to the head of the bed and leaned near to him, lifting one of Amedeo's arms over her own shoulders and putting the stump of her arm as far as she could reach around his body. When she hauled him up, he spat out air like a man who could no longer hold his breath. She seemed almost satisfied to be this close to the pain, watching it work its way across his face. Then he fell back against the pillow. She brought him the cup of water, which he took with one hand, steadying it before he raised it to his lips. She watched him drink. Then took away the cup.

"Did you hear what I was telling you?" Reina said. "They're going to be taking the girl away. Today or tomorrow. I don't know what they plan for me."

"Plan? They don't have a plan for you, Reina. You have always thought you were one of the family; but to them you are an afterthought, a piece of luggage. A Guatemalan." Amedeo pushed himself higher in the bed and waited for his breath to catch up to his words. "If they take you back, it will be to ease Mía's transition into a new life. That's all. So let me ask you this. Did you talk before she left, you and Leala? Did you talk at all about what happened?"

Reina put an unreadable look on her face but did nothing to hide her sarcasm. "And say to her what precisely? That she could discard us all like husks and silks? That I am trapped, like you and the girl herself, inside of your monstrous lie? No. That information somehow didn't make its way into our conversation."

Amedeo actually nodded. "Then why are you here with me now?"

For a long time Reina did not answer him. Rather, she stared at the distant mountains and at the approaching rain, just as she had been doing when he awakened. She was quiet for so long that Amedeo realized she wasn't seeing him at all. Finally she said. "Because there's a possibility now that the girl can have a livable life. That we can accomplish something good, even if it is untrue."

"What do you mean?" asked Amedeo.

"You can tell one more lie," Reina said. "Or at least half of a truth, enough to give her a chance. Tell her that you're not really her father. And that Alejandro is. Make her believe it is so."

"I can't do that," he said.

"Are you that vain, that you would throw away the one good chance that fate has dropped in front of us? Perhaps you don't remember what I've already told you. A whore or a peasant, Amedeo, that is what such girls become. Just tell her that much of the truth. That you're not her real father. Then let her imagination carry her into a new life. She'll believe whatever Leala tells her."

He turned his face and knotted the sheet in one of his hands. His chin dimpled, and dark creases turned to crevices of grief. Still, he did not cry out. He only whispered, "I can't say that. It would kill me if those words came from my mouth."

Reina watched until his pain subsided. She found it oddly comforting to see the mechanical Muñoz suddenly humanized, and after a time she spoke more gently to him. She closed the door and began an urgent negotiation, telling him that they had little time but, still, a way to influence what was happening. They could be allies, the two of them, if not exactly friends. They could still make a difference in what was happening. He listened impassively. When she finished talking, he neither agreed nor disagreed with the things she had proposed. But by then it was too late for further talk. The girl herself was back, opening the door without a thought of interrupting. And then there she was, rushing to the bed and wrapping her arms around his bandaged chest.

"I'm sorry," she was saying to him. "I'm sorry. I'm sorry I ran away."

"Were you hurt?" is all he said at first.

"No. *You* were hurt," she told him.

And he tried to make her smile. "Ah, then that explains it. This tightness in my chest."

"I'm sorry," she repeated.

"No. I'm learning what every father learns, I think." He tried to find some way to show that he was joking, but the effort of a smile wearied him and his eyes drew closed once more.

Mía didn't understand all that he was murmuring, and there was too much that she had to say, too many questions all jumbled with her feelings, that she barely had time to think. Barely acknowledged Reina, from the doorway, who was telling Mía now that Amedeo Muñoz had something he wished to say.

Then he was patting her hand and reaching up to touch her hair and asking her to keep a promise. And Maria Anita Muñoz, who in the slow accumulation of the moment did not understand what she was saying other than yes and yes to anything that emerged from his lips, who, before the words were fully formed, was promising that she would stay with her mother for a while. Promising the injured man that she would give this new life in the north a chance.

Reina, already in the hallway, made a slight nod in Amedeo's direction and then left the two of them alone.

●

10:00 A.M. at the valley wall.

Detective Manley stood in the light rain and wondered at the accumulation of sorrow. He took off his hat and shook it, running his sleeve over the upturned sides of the brim. Letting the rain on his face bring him back from too much thinking. Besides, for a man who had been raised on the edge of the Sonora, this looked like a little patch of paradise, wasn't that a fact? He concluded that he would have to come back someday. In happier times. Then he ran two fingers around the inside of the crown out of habit and eased the hat back in place, tilting it a bit to favor his right eye. Because, bub, you don't ever look a bad situation straight on. Best to come at it from the side.

On his way to the school his boots made a sound that reminded him of horses in the street. There were old people standing in doorways watching the rain, reverently. As quiet and still as their ancestors. Looking at him, when he nodded, as if he came from another time and place. One barefooted child brought the only animation to the scene. She tried to catch the rain and eat it from her hands. Two houses farther along there was a wet dog outside the door, curled into a perfect U, who moved only his eyebrows when Manley passed. Up to the steps of the school he went, whistling the two uniforms off their asses and out of their three-day stupor. He needed them for decoration. To make the whole thing look official.

Muñoz was dressed and sitting up. He looked pale, like a suddenly smaller image of himself, and he was eating sliced fruit from a wooden bowl. When Manley and the two hirelings walked in, Muñoz moved his eyebrows like the dog outside. Manley sighed, walked over to the windows as if he had come to appreciate the view. "The way I heard it," he said, "you come out on the *good* end. And, boy, if that's true, the other fella must have been in a world of pain. Cause, I'm telling you, you don't look ready for your next rodeo."

"What do you want?" said Amedeo Muñoz.

"Well. I'm just making the rounds. Checking up on all the patients you might say. How you feeling?"

"What do you really want?"

Manley winced, put a dramatically pained expression on

his face, and ambled toward the window. "Now here we go, getting off on the wrong foot again. Me trying to be friendly and you acting like your regular self as near as I can figure out. I'm just trying to slow things down. Keep it easy. Personable. You know what I mean? I don't see a reason in the whole wide world why me and you can't be on the same side when all this is done and over with."

"When what is done?" asked Amedeo.

"Well." Manley turned and faced the man in the bed. "That's what we got to talk about. Did I ever give you one of my cards? I got one here somewhere, telephone number and everything. You ought to keep one with you, cause you can never tell when you might need somebody with my special set of skills. I can find most anything."

"I haven't lost anything," the other observed. "I don't have much to lose."

"Turns out, that's not entirely the case, although this whole thing has taken a good deal more paperwork than any of us figured. And by paper I mean pesos, a whole dang truckload of 'em, you know what I'm sayin'?"

"No," said Muñoz.

"You got a chair or anything around here?" the detective went on. "Or do people just stand up the whole time when they come to see you? Cause I thought I saw a chair that first day, when I came by to check on you, and Miz de la Vega was pretty concerned I can tell you that."

The injured man adjusted himself in the bed. "Second floor," he said. "Two rooms down from the stairs. On the left. It's full of chairs."

Manley shook his head once, as if he could not believe the injustice in the room. "You're just not in a friendly mood, are you? Hell, Amedeo, you been as chary and uncharitable as a Presbyterian banker ever since I met you. That's not the way we treat people back home."

Muñoz nodded at the two hirelings just edging into the room. They had guns, but they moved like spineless coyotes eyeing a wounded wolf. Amedeo regarded them with contempt. To Manley he said, "I didn't bring soldiers into your home."

"Them? They're not soldiers!" Manley sounded indignant.

"Who are they?"

The detective drew a breath and then gave an embarrassed smile. "Well, you got me there. I think their names are something like Juan Carlos and, hell, I forget. I think they might be deputy marshals or some such. I heard somebody say the word *federales*. They seem to respond to that, but they don't speak much English. Tell you the truth, I got no idea how it works down here, and I haven't heard 'em say more than ten words since we met. But I'll tell you one thing. That's one humdinger of a uniform. You gotta give 'em that."

"Where is Leala?"

"Mrs. Cruz? Dear Lord, Amedeo, your mind is all over the place. You sure you didn't get, you know, tapped on the noggin a little too hard?"

"Where is she?" Munoz said.

"Well, she had to go on back home. We had quite a little discussion about that. But I'll tell you the same thing I--."

"Where is she?" Amedeo demanded.

Manley lowered his head, took a long moment, and then looked at the uniformed men as if he could not believe his bad luck and the necessity for such immortal patience. The men stirred, expecting orders. Manley patted the air with one hand, calming them back into lassitude. Finally he said, "I told you. She had to go home. Her husband, I guess you might say, sent for her. This is not all that difficult to understand."

"We need to talk."

The detective brought himself to the side of the bed and held up a single finger. "Wait a second. Do you mean we, like me and you? Or do you mean we, like you and her? Because I can see that you're wanting me to skip the social part and get right to the point."

"What is the point?" Amedeo said. "Why are you here now?"

"All right then. I got just one question. Do you feel well enough to travel?"

"I suppose," said the man in the bed.

"Good! Cause then you under arrest for kidnapping." Manley drew the handcuffs from beneath his coat and flicked them shut so smoothly that the wooden bowl did not waver in Amedeo's hand. "I mean that's the main point. Kidnapping's the big one, but there's a bunch of miscellaneous charges thrown in too. It's all down on the papers that we got as a result of spreading around them pesos I was telling you about. You fellas still got the papers, doncha? Heck, I forgot they don't speak legalese. But anyway, don't worry about it. It's pretty near as official as you can get. "

Amedeo set the bowl on a little table next to the cot. He had to use both hands. "Why are you doing this?"

"It's like I told the lady. I don't work for you."

"You're not a bad man," Amedeo continued. "You could say that we ran away."

"There you go with that we stuff again. Who you talking about now? You and that little spitfire of a girl? Cause if it is, then you really *don't* understand who I'm working for. *Jesus*, Amedeo, you one hardheaded son of a bitch, you know that?" Manley lifted his prisoner by the elbow and steadied him while Amedeo slipped into his boots. Then he made hand motions to the other two men while he spoke. "You all take him down to the first car and sit tight. I'm gonna go see if I can find that girl."

When Amedeo spoke again, he kept a calm and conversational tone. "Mía. Why didn't she go with her mother?"

Detective Gerald Manley patted down the prisoner's shirt and jeans. "I thought I explained all that. You can't just go dragging a kid across the border without the right kind of paperwork. And it took us a few days to paper the right guy. But don't you worry. She's going across like a princess."

"What about Reina?" Amedeo asked.

"Miz de la Vega? Well, a' course she'll be going along, to keep things all proper and peaceful for the girl. And, besides that, I think Mrs. Cruz might have a question or two for her. You know, about what must have happened after she trusted her baby girl to the one person in the world that she thought she could trust."

17

THEY ARRIVED IN SEPARATE CARS, Reina and the girl in the first vehicle with a silent driver and a woman from Manley's San Antonio office. Amedeo Muñoz came in the second car with two guards and Manley himself at the wheel.

After twelve years, the cottonwoods along the drive to the hacienda had grown into mature giants, their interlocking branches forming a spectacular passage of quaking leaves. It was like floating through a tunnel. Amedeo looked up at the canopy, already yellow with autumnal gold and admitting shafts of sunlight that seemed to be spiraling to the ground. The broad heart-shaped leaves did not flutter. Rather, they twirled on their leathery stems, dry-rattling with the eerie rhythm of *chapayeka* dancers.

Both cars parked beneath the old pepper tree, now thick and gnarled, its roots like arthritic fingers reaching into the soil. There were clay pots of bougainvillea and ivied topiary around the fountain, low hedges and flower beds lining the walkway. When Manley rang the electric bell, the travelers gathered behind him. A maid opened the door and forced a smile. Manley asked for Señor Cruz. "Of course," she said. "May I tell him this is par-taining?"

Manley handed her a card.

They waited in the inner courtyard, an atrium that served as a conservatory and a grand entry into the living quarters of the hacienda. The open roof made the courtyard appear as if a part of the outdoors had been brought inside. There were marble steps leading up to a great room that opened before them like a stage. The whole space was wider, fuller, and more lavish than Reina remembered it. She felt her own world begin to narrow and darken. The girl, Reina gradually concluded, might turn out to be her only protection. One of the guards unlocked Amedeo's handcuffs and slipped them into his own pocket. The other one put his hand at Amedeo's elbow. The maid came back and said, "Please to follow me." But before the others stepped into the great room, Manley gestured for the guards to wait behind with Amedeo. He held his hat in one hand and prepared a humble smile. Then he placed the hat at Mía's back and ushered her into the warm light. His clients were already waiting.

"Mr. and Mrs. Cruz," he said, "may I present your daughter."

Leala rushed forward, sobbing, laughing, reaching out with both arms. They hugged; Mía held her mother politely and recalled her own strange promise to Amedeo Muñoz, that she must learn to live in her mother's world. At least for a time. That is the phrase that came into her mind and eased her anxiety. She would stay here, with her mother, at least for a while.

Leala, on the other hand, grasped the girl with a desperation that made her hands tremble. She touched Mía's face, wiped at her own tears, and hugged again. No one said a word until Leala's juddering breath settled and she began a sentence which was overwhelmed once more by emotion. Finally she managed to say, "My child. I've spent every hour remembering you. Every hour since the day you were born." Leala tried to show a smile, but her face broke again into a surge of tears. "I'm just so grateful. So happy." Now Mía lifted her arms into a full embrace and gave herself to the flood of emotion. She buried her face against Leala and said the word over and over. "Mama," she said. "Mama. Mama." While Leala stroked her hair and whispered calming sounds.

Watching the moment unfold, Amedeo thought *This is my punishment. Nothing Alejandro can do to me later can be worse than this.* He had heard that there were people in the world who sent their children away at a much younger age, to be schooled and raised by strangers; and yet Amedeo could scarcely believe that anyone did so voluntarily. Here was Mía crossing over into her new world, and the loss inside of him was worse than any pain he had ever felt. Nevertheless, Amedeo kept his face as blank as stone. He knew he was being watched by a man who would read any flicker of emotion and use it when it came their time to talk.

At last Leala let go of the child and acknowledged Manley, to whom she gave a nod of thanks. It was only then that she found Reina, a pale, skeletal figure standing apart from the others in the shadow of the doorway. The older woman wore a full black skirt and a black riding jacket over a ruffled white blouse, as if she had dressed formally for a return to bygone times. One sleeve of the jacket ended in a vacancy which Reina kept next to her hip. Leala gave a formal smile, one that preserved the distance between the two women. "Reina," said Señora Cruz in a neutral tone. "Welcome home."

Amedeo, still standing with the guards just outside the great room, thought that he saw Reina give a small dip, like a curtsey, and say "Yes, Señora." There was a coldness that Leala could not hide; and everyone, including the child, noticed it. Leala herself sensed the tension of the moment and gave another smile, as if she had briefly forgotten her manners. Then she took the two brisk steps which allowed her to embrace the older woman with barely a hint of strain. It was then that the girl visibly relaxed.

The man in the wheelchair sat apart from everyone, watching with an intensity that he could not disguise. He was fascinated by Reina and her stump of an arm, which made her briefly interesting, but he cared nothing for her fate. Let Leala keep her or cast her aside. Then of course Manley deserved his little moment, strutting about on the stage as he was. The detective put himself on the edge of the satin-covered loveseat, elbows on knees, spinning his hat in little circles as he thought of what to say. Before he could bring himself to the right subject, though, he was startled by a voice that he both recognized and also found disconcertingly altered. It was a soft voice that seemed suddenly artificial, as if projected from a gramophone or from a radio trying to pick up a distant station. It was a calm voice, polite and gentlemanly, touched only by the slightest of accents. "Would you like a drink, Mr. Manley? Is there anything I can offer you?" said Alejandro Cruz.

"Well. I'd be much obliged." Manley relaxed a bit and sat back.

"Whiskey, I believe?" inquired the man in the wheelchair.

"Yes sir. That would be mighty fine."

"And your friends?" asked Cruz.

"No sir, they won't be requiring anything."

"I see. How has your day been so far, Mr. Manley? Mine has been most excellent. Most excellent indeed."

Cruz looked as if he had been put together with sticks. All of his joints were set at right angles, conforming him to the shape of his chair and to the whim of his disease. Only the wrists worked naturally. The fingers themselves moved intermittently; and the left hand hardly moved at all, nestling in his lap for the most part and becoming unclenched only when he concentrated. It was the right hand that he used to counterfeit normalcy. The man's upper body leaned forward, suggesting that he was always about to ask a question. The air went in through his mouth, an audible effort that was followed by a few spoken words or a slow leak from the nostrils. Already he had been swallowed by the disease, and now he sat looking out through eyes that had seen the approaching shadow. He wore brown linen trousers and a white shirt. Onyx cufflinks were his only ornamentation. Still, some hints of his former self remained. There was no doubt he had been a handsome man. His face was animated and strong. His smile was still convincing. But the bedroom slippers gave him away. The slippers, and the fact that he had to move one leg with his hands.

Leala brought the girl a few steps closer to her husband but still kept the both of them some eight feet away. "Alejandro," she managed to say. "Your daughter."

Mía tried not to stare. She had never seen a chair with metal wheels or a man who had been crushed by the invisible weight of disease. He seemed to be suffering with every breath and at the same time shamed by the grotesque turnings of his body. She thought of twisted apples drying in the sun, and tried to look past him until he spoke. The voice was hardly more than a whisper, but it was soft and sincere, emerging from some place deep inside of him that Mía could imagine was his heart. She thought it was the kindest voice she had ever heard.

It was saying, "Please don't be afraid. That would break
my heart. You don't have to look, but I hope you don't mind if
I look at you, just for a moment. Because you are the most
beautiful daughter that a man could possess." As he said these
last words, Alejandro Cruz stole a glance at the man standing
between two of Manley's guards in the courtyard. He added a
slight smile which, after a moment, he turned upon the girl.

Mía felt the sincerity of his smile, and her first impulse was
to give Alejandro a hug; but her mother was holding her back,
both hands on Mía's shoulders and pressing just enough to
indicate they had reached a boundary that neither of them
should cross. The man winked at Mía, as if forgiving some
mistake or perhaps sharing a family secret. "In fact," he said to
her, "after you have a look around, I'm hoping you decide to
stay with us for a while. Your mother and I would like that
very much."

Mía thought again of her promise to Amedeo Muñoz and
how grave he had sounded when they talked. And now,
nothing but kindness from the man in front of her. With some
apprehension she asked him, "I can decide?"

"Of course," said the crippled man. "Reina will be here,
just as she was before. Your mother will be here. Your room
will be next to Reina's, as it was. Your school, your new
friends, are all here at the hacienda."

"Alejandro, you're going too fast. Give her a chance."
Leala combed Mía's hair with her fingers, making soothing
motions as she lifted stray strands from the oval of her face.

"Yes. Yes. I'm sorry. I'm tripping over myself, aren't I?"
The man laughed as if embarrassed by his own humor. "Well.
Mía. I hope you become comfortable here, because everything
you see is for you. Everything. And we have Mr. Manley to
thank for his dedicated service to our family."

"Thank you," Mía said to Manley, unsure of how the
words had been pulled from her mouth but sensing that this
was the first of many thank-yous to come. It was not that the
man in the chair had ordered her to say anything at all. Rather,
he had left an uncomfortable space behind his spoken words,

then sat watching her, waiting to see if she would fill the emptiness. And she had done his will. Alejandro Cruz had made it as simple as putting on a coat.

Manley set his drink on the butler's table beside his seat. "You're most welcome, young lady. Mr. Cruz. Mrs. Cruz. That about all you need from me?"

"One or two more details," said Alejandro. "If you could give me just a few more minutes of your time. --Mía, I hear you are quite the horsewoman. And that you're an excellent rider. Is that true? That you like horses?"

The girl started to tell him about her pony, but at some point the man in the chair had gently inserted himself into the telling and redirected her attention to a terrace on the other side of glass doors. And from the terrace, he indicated, there was a path that led to an entire stable that she might like to see. In fact, Alejandro Cruz went on, maybe your mother and Reina would like to show you themselves. Get them to walk you through the stables, suggested Alejandro. And see if you can pick out the horse that belongs to you.

Everyone waited until the women left. Then the man in the chair rolled himself to the center of the great room where he could see directly into the courtyard. He looked at Amedeo Muñoz, smiling as if they were two friends who had just met after many years. He let the silence build until Manley stood up and offered a packet that Alejandro took without opening.

"This is the, ah, paperwork. Back-dated and signed by two doctors," Manley said. "Both from San Juaquin Hospital in Bakersfield. And both of them were there in 1936, so it'll look legit if anybody checks. The blood tests will show that he can't possibly be the father, in case you might need that someday."

"Hmm. Thank you."

"Well," said Manley. "I don't guess I need to introduce--"

Alejandro raised one hand and silenced the detective in mid-sentence. Then steered himself closer to Amedeo, nodding appreciatively and speaking with unexpected animation. "This man, detective, is someone I admire."

"Really?" Manley did not sound convinced.

"Do you realize that, during his lifetime, he has never

stepped foot inside the dehumanizing darkness of a factory? I was just thinking about that," said Cruz. "He has never once heard the clanking of an assembly line, never stood in line at a bank. In fact, I very much doubt that he has ever cashed a check, or written one, during his whole existence. That's a remarkable thing considering the times we live in. You can be certain that he has never shopped in a department store. That he doesn't know what an office building is and wouldn't believe you if you told him. I can guarantee that he's suspicious of telephones. He doesn't understand insurance or interest rates. Has no idea what a pension is. In all, it's an astonishing combination he brings before us, detective. A man like this is to be admired above other men. In many ways he is not of this century. I'm convinced that in the old days, during the era of crucifixions, he would have been one of Caesar's Spanish legionnaires."

"I reckon so," said Manley.

"You've done very well in bringing him here, and you can be assured I will be most grateful indeed. --Now. Do you suppose one of those hefty fellows there could be persuaded to slit his throat for a thousand dollars? I mean, right now, so that I could watch?"

Manley cocked his head and studied the face of the man in the wheelchair. "I'm not in that sort of business, Mr. Cruz. That's not the kind of work I hire out for."

Alejandro Cruz put his hands together and stretched his arms as if rousing himself from a nap. He rocked his head left and right. Then smiled. "I'm joking, Mr. Manley. I'm just joking. But you have to agree, don't you, that I deserve my little attempt at humor?"

"See," Manley went on, "when I can't tell if a man is joking or not, that's when I start to get a little nervous. People that go back and forth between joking and not joking, they're kinda hard for me to read."

The other shrugged. "I don't believe anybody needs to read anything at present. In fact, I think we're done. You and your people are free to go with my profound thanks." He rang a tiny bell which summoned a man dressed formally and carrying a butler's tray. The man's face gave no sign that he had heard anything other than the bell, but he had obviously known why he was being called. On the tray was a single white envelope, and his master was gesturing toward the detective saying, "Bajardo, if you please." Then Cruz waited for the butler to present the tray, finally adding, "I believe this will more than cover the fee we agreed upon."

Manley put the envelope into his coat pocket and motioned for his hirelings to leave. They went wordlessly through the courtyard and disappeared. The front door opened and closed. Then came the muffled chunking of car doors. Then the sound of an engine cranking, catching, and rumbling to life. And then the low but distinct crackling of tires rolling over gravel.

"What about him?" Manley said. "I mean, police reports, federal warrants, that sort of thing."

"I have something else in mind. And now, if you'll excuse me for being rude."

For the first time the detective sounded worried. He stood up but didn't move toward the courtyard or the front door. "You want me to just leave him here? Like this? Him and you?"

"Oh yes." Alejandro had taken up his cheerful voice once more. "We'll both be quite safe, I assure you. And when we've finished with our little talk, Amedeo will be able to make his own way out. He knows the property, and I'm very sure he can hitch a ride when he reaches the highway. And so, once again, thank you, Mr. Manley. You've been most helpful."

The big man gave a curt and silent nod, affixed his hat, and exited.

After another moment Alejandro made a summoning motion with his right hand.

Amedeo stepped up two, three, four vertical steps and brought himself into the sunlight of the great room, favoring one side as he walked and making slow, arthritic motions, though his face revealed no sign of pain. He wore a long-sleeved chambray shirt and jeans. Dusty boots that matched the deep brown leather of his belt. His hair combed straight back. One arm hanging down by his side, the thumb of his other hand hooked behind the belt's wide buckle.

When Alejandro spoke, his voice had lost its cheer. He put his elbows on the armrests of his chair and folded his hands as if praying. He smiled and leaned forward more until his chin touched his hands. He took his deepest breath and let most of it pulse forth before saying, "Please. Make yourself at home."

"You are enjoying this?" said Amedeo.

"*Joy?!* That's something that I haven't experienced in a while. Although, yes, it's beginning to feel a little familiar. I do believe you're right. But. Our concern this afternoon is with you."

"What about me?"

Cruz looked at the other for a long time before answering. "They say you were king in your own land, something of a tyrant in fact. That's what reports are telling me. And I'm wondering if you think it's true, that you and I are alike."

"Say what you have to say, Alejandro."

"Very well then. You stole from me."

"I did not," said Amedeo Muñoz.

"And I cannot abide a thief. Or a liar."

"I took nothing that was yours," declared Amedeo.

Cruz spoke over the other's words. "You arrogant bastard. Do you imagine for one instant that I will allow you to defile my house? Use my woman as your whore and parade your whelp like a prize? Is that something that in your dim imagination masquerades as a thought?"

"You have a paper saying that I am not the father."

"I can have a paper saying anything I want, you fool. I can turn you into a paper saint. Bury you in a paper coffin. And you've got utterly no understanding of what I'm saying, do you?"

Amedeo could sense something weighty and invisible hurtling toward him. He tried to think of words that could take away the blow, but none came. Maybe the promise he had extracted from the girl had been a mistake. Maybe Reina could not protect her from the poisonous world of Alejandro Cruz. For a moment he thought of rushing forward, knocking over the chair, and trying to escape with Mía; but of course a horrifying memory intervened. The earth itself had collapsed beneath his last escape. In the hollow, senseless present he heard Alejandro saying that he was going to take the girl from him. That he was going to turn Amedeo Muñoz into an irrelevancy, a bad memory that faded to nothing in her mind.

And Amedeo heard himself saying, "You can't take away the past."

"I don't need to," said Cruz. "But I promise you that, day by day, you will become a monster in her memory. Until finally she will choose to forget you altogether."

As if from a great distance, Amedeo listened to himself again. It was like overhearing another conversation when he said, "I'm sorry I did this to you."

"I'm touched."

"You're dying," said Amedeo. "And it's your disease that's talking now."

"We are all dying, my friend. But it is you who are cursed. So let me make you a further promise. That this crime will follow you for all of your wretched life. Whatever you do, I will undo. Whatever you fear, I will embrace. Whatever you seek, I will find. And I will crush it into dust. That will be my joy, Amedeo, and my reason for living."

Alejandro Cruz straightened himself in his chair, wiped at the corners of his mouth as if he had been spitting his words, and then willed himself, with difficulty, into an image of calm. "Now go and be forever cursed," he said. "You don't get forgiveness. You do not get to say goodbye to her. Because you are nothing. And I am retribution. And I promise you that if after this day you step within a hundred miles of her I will have you killed. Do not doubt my word."

"This is wrong, what you are doing," said Muñoz.

"Get out!" Alejandro's face had resumed the color of health, and his body for a brief instant had seemed to fill out his clothing in its old manner. But the illusion was fleeting. Amedeo watched the broken man shrinking back into his body. Watched the pain reassert itself like a familiar, waking routine. And then, after another minute, he left.

Outside, Amedeo stopped at the fountain and dipped his hand into the calm water, taking a sip and wiping the remains over his face and neck. He felt incomplete and unprepared without his hat. Where had he left it? That was the thought that occupied him as he tried to keep the other thoughts from flooding in. He must have left it somewhere. In the tunnel above the village perhaps. Or maybe in Manley's car? You need a good hat. If you're going to work where the sun is hot. Or if you have a long way to go.

Amedeo took the lane through the cottonwoods, squinting when the sun broke through, taking easy strides when the shade allowed. He thought he might go farther north and find work in one of the lumber mills. Or maybe southwest. He had liked Sangre de Cristo. And fishermen made a good living. But Sangre was busy and crowded. Maybe there was something still left for him in the mountains. He had liked the school. He had liked the people who gathered there for meals in the summer and the men who helped with harvesting and carpentry in the fall. The clean air. The view from the valley wall. So maybe the mountains. Maybe he would turn south when he reached the highway. Or maybe north. He would let the sun and the shade decide.

When he had walked several hundred yards from the hacienda, he saw a shape far ahead. It looked like a tortoise that someone had set on the flat line of the horizon, but as he drew closer he could tell it was a car that someone had parked beside the highway. A familiar car, with thick black tires beneath a long hood and a streamlined trunk. Chromed grill and bumpers. A sloping two-pieced windshield. And, when he got closer, a hood ornament shaped like a rocket. Manley himself was leaning against one of the rear fenders. Neither of them spoke until Amedeo had walked all the way to the road. "I thought you might be needin' a ride," Manley said.

Amedeo got into the front seat and rolled down the window. Manley started the engine and turned onto the highway, heading south, shifting smoothly through the gears until the wind and the engine had reached the same pitch. Amedeo leaned into the wash of air and then combed his fingers back through his hair as he had already done several times. "What kind of car is this?" he asked.

The question seemed to surprise Manley, but he answered as if they were old friends who'd been discussing cars for years. "Olds 66. Custom overhead valve V-8 that won't come off the regular assembly line till next year. Four speed hydramatic. And boy you better believe when I say giddy up, she'll go. Best dang car I ever had."

"I think someday I will buy a car," mused the other man.

"Are you okay?" The detective looked in Amedeo's direction.

Amedeo nodded once.

"I figured the least I could do was offer you a lift. He didn't strike me as a happy man."

"He is not. I think his heart is full of poison."

"What happened?" Manley asked.

"He raged. In a way I felt sorry. It was all he could do. When a man does to you what I have done, he must be beaten down. He must be broken with the fists or killed. There is no turning away."

"Hell, Amedeo. You need to catch up with the rest of us in the twentieth century. You sound like a *cholo* throwback, you know what I'm sayin'? I been wondering for six months whether any of you people ever heard of a simple divorce."

"There's nothing simple here."

"I guess the hell not."

"There's a town in about twenty miles," said Muñoz.

"He had to have said something," Manley insisted. "You look like a ghost and you talk like the one guy in the audience who volunteered to be hypnotized."

"He said he would take her."

"That's it?" the detective said. "Hell, you expected that."

"I did," Amedeo allowed. "It just hurt more than I thought it would."

18

THE BOWL HAD A GOLDEN RIM and then a band of flowers set against a pale green stripe and then another thread of gold beneath. It was half full of berries and mixed melons that someone had cut into pieces. Mía sat wondering if they thought she did not know how to eat. The little bowl was perched on a little plate of the same design, and the little plate was nestled within a bigger plate set between forks on one side and a knife and two spoons on the other. There were crystal glasses for each place and an elaborately folded cloth napkin, and silver baskets and platters for the center of the table. While they waited for Alejandro, a maid poured orange juice into the tall glass beside Mía's plate and then asked if she wanted milk. The question baffled her, and Mía blinked at the woman in bewilderment. Milk was for cooking. The maid did not seem to realize what she was saying and stood perfectly still until Leala shook her head and let the woman slip away. Then the same woman was back immediately with rolls of bread, a plate of butter, a carafe of honey, and a small pitcher of cream. While Leala talked, Mía inched her hand into the sunlight just on the other side of her bowl, wiggling one finger where she could see the shape through the white translucency.

After a time Alejandro was wheeled out onto the terrace, smiling and more energetic than he had been the day before. He loved to take breakfast outside whenever the weather was fine he said. "And," he added to Mía, "I pay a great deal of money to insure it is *always* fine. But don't tell that to your mother." Then he laughed and wagged his eyebrows. "Now let's have something to eat." He turned his attention to the maid, who had once more taken up her station by the door. "By God, Sophie, I could use a steak; but I'll take one of those omelets with the peppers and some sausages. And tell Rosarita some sliced tomatoes too."

Without being instructed further, the maid brought a little

bowl of fruit to Alejandro. Mía was afraid that the woman had not heard about the omelet and that he would be angry, but no one noticed. The adults put their napkins in their laps, smoothing them absentmindedly; and Mía did the same, though she was careful not to unfold hers all the way because she wasn't sure she could put it back into its proper shape. Then unexpectedly Leala was asking what she, Mía, would like for breakfast, which seemed to make no sense at all. Here was the fruit directly in front of her for everyone to see, like the juice, and now suddenly there was Reina coming out onto the terrace but standing quietly away from them while just at the same time Alejandro was announcing to everyone that by God he loved taking a meal with two beautiful women on a fine morning in the sunlight, when she got confused by the stacks of dishes and lost in the tangle of words and turned over the glass. It teetered for an instant. Mía watched it, frozen in her seat, as the juice sloshed away and the beautiful crystal shape tumbled over the edge of the table, turned one graceful revolution in the air, and then shattered against the stone.

She could not even gasp. Could not breathe at all. And could hardly distinguish between the heat in her face and the humiliation just beneath. She could feel her skin burning all the way down to her knees, but all she seemed capable of doing was pushing herself back from the table and standing like a fool. They would tell her to go away. To go back to the mountains, to eat with the animals because they could not bear for breakfast to be ruined by a peasant girl. But first they would let the silence grow into a great cloud of anger at their kindness so carelessly repaid. So her tears, when they finally began to flow, were almost welcome, almost a distraction from the fear of what they would say.

And yet here was Leala, now standing too and holding her like a mother, stroking her hair and saying what on earth is the matter child, as if they crashed their dishes every day. Reina, who had instinctively reached out with both arms, checked herself abruptly and resumed her place just outside the family circle. No one else was moving, no one else uttering a sound until still another kitchen maid came scurrying with a cloth and a broom. And Alejandro was asking someone else if the paper had arrived before turning to Mía, as if mildly curious, and saying "Didn't get any on you, I hope. Sophie, be a good girl would you, and bring us another. Good God, Leala, I sound like a movie actor, don't I? One of those British ones. I think that's what I'll be when I grow up."

It was a silly joke. Even cruel at his own expense, but he chuckled and nodded to Mía's chair, indicating that she should sit down again. "Now tell me about the horses," he said. "Did Javy show you around yesterday? Did you see anything you liked?" As though the glass were nothing. As though they did it all the time.

That was the tone of their first morning together. The morning after Mr. Manley had left and after Amedeo, whom she had called her father, had left without saying goodbye and *Abuelita* had stayed but stayed as a different person than she had been in the village. That, in a way, was the most shocking change to Mía. Seeing Reina de la Vega out of her place, no longer the mistress of her domain, not even eating with the family. In fact, the hacienda seemed at times to close Reina out. The child did not need a nurse. The kitchen did not need a cook. The servants did not need an overseer. And while everyone treated Reina politely, the real joy of the household was showered upon Mía. Reina spent a great deal of time standing to the side.

Now people from the kitchen were bringing food and taking it away. There was a new glass of juice. A new topic of conversation as if there were no work to be done in the wide green valley below or in the outdoor kitchen behind the school. Leala said, "I think we should part your hair on the side and give it a bit of a wave. Like Rita Hayworth or Lauren Bacall." Alejandro not hearing her, or not listening, asked Mía how she had slept only to interrupt himself with the same words he'd used the day before. "Let me look at you, Maria Anita. Just let me look at you for a moment, because I never knew your mother when she was your age. And you are surely the most beautiful daughter a man could have." The words seemed kind and generous, but the name seemed terribly wrong to her. Mía wondered if she should tell him what she was really called, but he seemed like a man who had not been happy in years. And she felt so sorry about his legs.

"Her eyes," Alejandro went on. "Have you ever seen such dark and penetrating eyes? And lashes so exuberantly long? I think she has your eyes, *mama*. A chin more like me, though, a sturdy, determined chin, which she'll need, I can tell you that. For the future, eh?" He waved his hand indicating the sweep of all that surrounded them.

Leala said nothing, and the color rose in her own cheeks. He was taunting her, she assumed, about her daughter's parentage; but it was not Alejandro's cruelty that made her want to leave the table. She had expected his scorpion's sting as soon as he had seen the girl. Rather, it was the humiliation, here in front of the servants, that made her want to dash the entire tabletop to glittering shards and then storm away. But she did not move. She smiled, lifted her own chin a bit higher, and pretended to contemplate her daughter's eyes.

Alejandro took no notice of the wife. He was fixed upon the girl. "By God she has that flawless skin, doesn't she?" he went on. "Would you say she takes after me or more after you, in her skin tone I mean? Someone in your family maybe? I want you to dress her like a young lady. None of this, none of this stuff. I want her to look like the daughter of the hacienda."

After breakfast Reina took Mía back to the room where they had both slept the night before. "From now on," she said to Mía, "this will be your room. It was the nursery when you were just born; but, see, a nice new bed and flowers in a vase and your own closet. And I will always be just next door, yes?" Mía nodded without hearing: she was much more concerned that there was another girl, one her own age, who was making the bed. Would they have to share the same room, she wondered? Mía watched the quick brown hands smoothing sheets and could not understand why, when finished, the girl simply stood next to the window and waited.

Reina had busied herself with the contents of a wide closet and did not notice the two girls staring at one another in mutual incomprehension. Finally Reina turned and said,

"These will have to do," dropping several hangered outfits upon the bed. Then, addressing the nameless girl, Reina said, "Have her dressed and ready soon. The Señora will be taking her for new clothes."

When Reina left, the girl immediately began unbuttoning Mía's blouse with the same quick hands she had used on the sheets. It was such a shock that Mía jerked her body away, and the girl pulled back her hands as if she hand been caught stealing. There was a tiny flash of something in her face, but immediately the girl dropped her eyes and said in English, "I'm sorry, miss. I didn't mean to--."

"Why did you do that?" Mía demanded in a burst of Spanish.

The girl thought for a moment, again putting her words into the uncomfortable language of the north. "It's my job, miss. My name is--."

"It's a stupid job."

The girl looked at the door, then at the bed, then at the señorita, trying to think of what to do. She put her hands together in front of her and thought carefully. Raised voices drew attention, and then something worse. She almost whispered, "My name is Daniela, miss. The Señor wishes you to use English inside the house."

Still in Spanish Mía said, "I'm not a doll. I'm not a baby. I dress myself."

"Please, miss," Daniela said.

Then the Señora herself appeared at the door and frowned. "Daniela, for Heaven's sake!" Doña Leala said. And she took Mía in hand, unbuttoning the buttons and tossing the blouse to the floor. Then she pulled the boy's undershirt over Mía's head. "Oh my. We'll need to add a training bra to our list, won't we?" She smiled and kissed Mía's forehead. "Daniela, get a full slip. And do something with her hair." The Señora flipped through the sleeves of the dresses lying on the bed and told the maid to try the yellow one first.

"What am I doing?" Mía managed to say. "I don't know what I'm supposed to do."

"You're supposed to be beautiful. And not worry. And be

happy. It's all very strange right now, I know. But very soon, I promise, you'll feel as if you've been here all of your life. You'll know everyone at the hacienda, and they will know you. Already Javier says you have the horses eating from your hand."

"I like the stables," Mía said.

The Señora laughed while Daniela lifted the yellow dress from the bed.

And so it was throughout Mía's first day at the hacienda. The flashes of color and the blurred daylight hours moved before her eyes as fast as Victor's shuffled cards. That night, however, the bleak hours lingered. The loneliness found her in her room alone, in a hacienda that was uniformly dark and silent, where the familiar flicker of candles and the comforting creaks of the school itself were no more. Mía could not bear the sadness or the fear that even the rustling of her sheets would be heard by a household of lurking strangers. She crept into Reina's room and slipped between the sheets of Reina's bed as she had done for years; and there Mía found a comfort that brought them both to the following day. Again, on the next night, Mía left her lonely room and found her *abuelita*; but in the morning Reina said they should not be sleeping so. It was not the way of her new life. And the girl went away perplexed, not daring to ask questions.

Throughout the fourth night of their return to the hacienda, Reina slept alone, sometimes dreaming, sometimes rising to near wakefulness where she contemplated answers to questions that she knew would come. On the following morning she woke up early, determined to make herself unnoticed during another day. Maybe with time she could become one more fixture that rarely needed dusting. Maybe she could fade into the background of all their lives. That would be the best thing for everyone. To let the routine of living draw a curtain across the past.

That at least was Reina's desperate hope. It was a faith that began to fade as soon as she drew back the covers of her bed, glancing down to see, curled on the floor beside her feet, the form of a sleeping child.

•

The hacienda was low and level, spread out like the signature of Alejandro Cruz upon the ground. And there were unknowable rules that governed her new life. The servants, who came and went like ghosts, spoke of tiny invisibles that they called germs. Mía should not touch objects that the *señor* had touched. And she should stand a respectful distance away from his breath. And speak English only inside the house. And she had to remember that Reina was to be called Reina, and not *Abuelita* anymore.

Then on Monday, her fourth morning in the hacienda, Mía awoke on the floor beside Reina's bed. Someone had laid a blanket over her and placed a pillow beneath her head. She pushed aside the blanket with her feet and listened to the flutter of housemaids cleaning in other parts of the house. The bed itself was empty, and the blanket reminded her of the hanging partition between her old room and her father's room. And thus it reminded her of the man himself who, too cautious to smile in the presence of others, would still tease her and laugh in the mornings. She missed him so.

Mía went back to her own room and slipped into the first skirt and blouse that came to hand. Still barefooted and uncombed, still feeling as powerfully alone as she had felt on her first night in California, she went in search of Reina, who would find her something warm to eat and who would give her a grandmother's comforting words. Mía followed voices through the dining room and farther into the kitchen where Reina stood talking with the cook. And suddenly, without intending for it to happen, without even realizing why she had gone searching, the girl had buried her face against her Reina's breast and had begun sobbing without offering a single word. It was all too foreign, this world of wealth and distance.

Reina tried not to spill her coffee, setting down her cup one-handed and saying, "For Heaven's sake, child, what could be this bad? Was it a bad dream that woke you? If so, open your eyes and see how lucky we are." She patted the girl's back with her forearm and made soothing sounds until there was calm. The cook, at first alarmed, went back to her pots as the blubbering subsided. It was just a girl and her silliness the cook decided. In her maternal voice Reina was declaring, "Just look at this hair. I thought you were the stable boy barging in. Let's get these tangles fixed, and find some shoes, and then you can tell me what's upsetting you."

"I miss him," Mía said. "I miss my home."

"I know." Reina smiled again in the direction of the cook, who was a grandmother herself six times over and knew the ways of young girls. "I know," Reina said. "But this is home now for the luckiest girl in the world."

"I don't belong here," Mía said. "This is not my home."

And in the following instant, without a thought to causing harm, Reina made her fatal mistake. It seemed a small thing at first, like one of the tiny stones that had preceded the earthquake on the day that had changed all their lives. Reina carelessly let loose a single word, uttered in haste and spoken in order to reassure. It was a maternal nothing, but it was a word set free in a profoundly wrong place. She said to Mía, "Nonsense. Of course you belong. And I will always be here with you. And I will always be your mother."

Here was a word that the cook found shocking enough to stop her stirring, a presumptuous, arrogant word in the form of a lie, an insult coming from a former servant and from a woman who had no real place in the hacienda. It was a word that quickly made its way to the real mother of the child.

Then in the early afternoon of Monday, October 3rd, as the routine of the day settled into minor business appointments for Señor Cruz and into a lull for the servants, the *señora* put herself at the piano in the music room, where she began playing something long and meditative. She played until she happened to see Reina's reflection in one of the wide windows overlooking the terrace. And without turning around, Leala called to her old nursemaid, who straightened her skirts and presented herself just to the right of the piano stool.

Leala continued playing but indicated that Reina should take the leather armchair sometimes reserved for Alejandro. They exchanged smiles and waited while the younger woman fingered a few notes with her left hand. In a distracted way she

finally asked if Reina had found her old room comfortable now
that she'd been back for a few days.

"Yes, of course," the other said.

And was the room unsatisfactory in any way?

"No," said Reina. "It is most--"

But Leala spoke over the answer, or simply ignored it, in
order to give her sincere hope that the room was not
disappointing. Leala worked her hand farther down the
keyboard, listening to her own spontaneous composition rather
than to any further reply by Reina. At last she stopped playing
and turned herself slightly in order to thank Reina for her
loyalty and for her faithful mothering to the child. She did not
use Mía's name at first; but as Leala went on, the word *mother*
became a prominent feature of her monologue. My husband
and I wish we could show our gratitude for your acting as the
mother of our child. Being a mother must have been difficult
in a poor mountain village since a mother's work is never done.

Reina sensed the anger before it made its way into Leala's
words. The set of her jaw, the aristocratic remoteness of her
eyes. Reina had seen the same when Leala had been a child.

"What is it?" the old nursemaid eventually said.

"What do you mean?" the young-old Leala asked.

They went back and forth until Leala began playing with
two hands again. "I was just wondering why it was Gabriel,
and not you, who finally contacted me. About my daughter. In
fact, it's been increasingly on my mind. We had no time to talk
there in your village, did we? I mean, first there was meeting
my daughter at the fiesta. And then the next day. It would have
been indecent ... in your grief. But now that you're settled here,
I thought I might inquire. Why, exactly, were you unable to
locate a telephone within a decade or more in order to tell me
that my child was safe?"

There. Leala had set forth the grand obstruction and there
could be no maneuvering away from something so dangerously
large. Reina hoped only to slow down the story and to make
the collision into a glancing blow. She drew a long breath and
began by telling Leala how isolated the mountain village had
been, how impoverished and devoid of modern utilities.

"And yet you could drive to other towns," said Leala.

Reina sat back in the chair, willing herself to show no signs of nervousness or deceit. "It was Muñoz," she said. "He went to Sangre de Cristo just after the earthquake and waited for you for days. He said you had deserted us. That we were on our own."

"And you believed him?" Leala made the question sound innocent.

"In those days we were terrified of him. And of Alejandro."

"And what happened to your arm? Did he chop it off when you disobeyed him? You'll forgive me for not asking sooner."

For the next twenty minutes Reina kept her composure. She began the story again by telling of the death and devastation that came with the earthquake, how the villagers had stumbled about in shock for over a year. She blamed Muñoz for keeping them isolated. The government, she said, had closed the roads into the mountains. And the weather was often harsh. There was no panic in Reina's telling, even as Leala turned aside very excuse. But a change in the conversation gradually emerged. Leala's cold insistence became more trying, and Reina's humility began to wear thin. It was the turn that neither of them had anticipated.

The older woman had prepared for an ordeal but not for the blame that Leala seemed to be heaping upon her alone. The added sarcasm, the false concern over her arm, the dismissal of the village's suffering was more than Reina could finally bear. Her answers grew shorter and less respectful. Finally she recognized something like genuine anger in her own voice.

Then Leala made it worse. Very sweetly and sincerely she said, "Reina. I won't sit here and listen to lies."

And the reply came far too quickly. It was as angry and irrevocable as a pistol shot. "Then step into the library," Reina told her, "where we can close the door. I'll give you this one courtesy that you did not give me." Without explaining herself further, Reina de la Vega, shaking with fury and fear, marched to her room and returned with a single sheet of paper.

"I want to know where this is headed. Now!" Leala
demanded.

At the center of her anger Reina found a frozen calm,
from which she said, "It's headed where it was always headed,
my Leala. From that very first day when you met the carpenter
beneath the great oak and walked him into this labyrinth."

"How dare you speak to me like this," said Señora Cruz.

"Into this labyrinth, and there put a babe into his arms.
From that first caress, Leala, it was always headed to some
awful place where someone would have to hear '*This is not your
child.*' And how bitter it must be to realize now ... that it will be
you."

"You are insane."

"Read it." Reina gave over the letter. Then repeated from
memory the words that Gabriel had written: "'*In this only did I
betray you I told her that her child was well the worst sin of my life.*'"

"What does that mean?"

"It means," said Reina, "that she is *not* your child."

For half a minute, these words stopped everything. There
was neither motion nor sound within the library. But when
words came forth at last, they came from Leala. "You are a
jealous, insane, lying, infertile old woman who would stop at
nothing to save her own--"

"This doesn't save me, Leala. I didn't think it would. It
merely drowns us both."

Under the hands of Leala Anita Sanchez de Cruz, the letter
was torn into halves, and then into quarters, and then into
ragged fragments that fluttered into the open fireplace beneath
a handsome mantle. "I will light a fire with your lies," she
finally said. "And then, you will leave my home."

19

LATE IN THE AFTERNOON, Leala gave Mía the news that Reina was leaving.

"She's decided it would be best if she spent some time with her own family in Guatemala," said Leala. "And I agreed. None of us would want to keep her from that, would we?" These last words were spoken in a tone suggesting Leala had practiced saying them for a child much younger than twelve years.

Mía dashed into *abuelita's* room, throwing open the door without a thought as to what could be on the other side. But there was nothing. An empty closet. A plaid suitcase waiting beside a bed that had been stripped of its sheets.

Following her, Leala said, "Sweetheart, Reina isn't in the house right now. She's gone to say farewell to some of her friends from the old times. But I promise she'll be back to tell you goodbye before she leaves. We both love Reina and want to do what's right for her family and for ours, don't we?"

"Where is she?" Mía demanded.

Leala gave a social smile and made a gesture toward the northwest. "At the house of one of her friends, as I told you. To say goodbye and maybe--"

"But why?" Whatever soothing answer her mother was giving, it was not one that that Mía could hear or believe. She needed Reina to say that none of this was true. She needed Reina herself. "*Why* is she going?"

Leala started to answer but then suddenly stopped. She took Mía's hand as the girl headed back toward the door. "No. Wait," said Leala. "Wait. We can't start out like this."

The woman let out a long and exhausted breath. She drew Mía closer and studied the child's face. Finally she said, "You are my daughter. You deserve truth. And the truth is that Reina and I quarreled. About you. About what you were to be told. And about how you were to be raised." Leala sat down on the bare mattress of the bed and then took both of Mía's hands in hers. "We were both very angry. And so. It really is best now if she visits her family for a while."

Mía felt an odd sort of relief. A quarrel was not a catastrophe. A quarrel could be fixed, and so she brought herself closer to her mother and asked, "Can't Reina just say she's sorry?"

"Yes," said Leala. "Yes, she can. But not just now. Do you understand what I'm trying to tell you?"

"No. Because I don't belong here. This isn't my home. And I don't know the rules. And I don't understand why Reina has to--"

"Ah. Alejandro was right, wasn't he?" Leala caressed the girl's face with one palm, gave a sad smile, and then touched Mía's chin with one finger. "You have that determined jaw and such fierce eyes that you will set men on fire when you are older. And you will defend what is yours, won't you? That's why you *do* belong. Because I am your mother. And because there is no fierceness on earth that can compare to that love. Do you at least understand that? I don't hate Reina. But she will not come between me and my child."

Standing this close to her mother, Mía could see the differences between the photograph she had treasured for years and the real woman before her. The lips that were speaking to Mía now were no longer as full, nor as ready to smile. The eyes, still dark and deep, were no longer as bright or as open as the eyes of the young woman in the picture. The face was fuller now; the hair was shorter, as befitted an older woman; but there were real shadow lines that suggested real pain in her mother's past. The girl nodded, not in agreement with anything Leala was saying, but because the twelve year old Mía was seeing for the first time that life, by its very nature, always demanded change. That it was always turning something new into something old.

"Mothers and daughters," Leala went on, "no matter what their differences or disappointments, are never strangers. Do you believe that?"

Mía nodded again, still unsure of her own feelings.

"Good," said her mother. "Then come with me. I want to show you something, and I *promise* that Reina will not leave before you can tell her goodbye." Leala led Mía back into the great room, stopping her just above the steps that led down into the courtyard. "Stand right here," she told Mía, "and close your eyes."

Mía kept still and shut her eyes most of the way but still followed Leala's movements through the courtyard and out to the wide front doors of the hacienda. Leala opened the doors one at a time. Then her mother's words came to Mía from a distance, as if her mother were speaking from another time and place.

"Your great grandmother," the voice said, "was born in Córdoba, Spain, in 1853. From a very old, very aristocratic family. She didn't want to come to America, but the families had made the match." Leala hooked the doors open with wrought iron latches which held them against the outer walls of the house. Then her voice got nearer as she re-crossed the courtyard. Mía closed her eyes all the way as her mother came up the steps and stood next to her again. "Córdoba is the hottest city in Spain. The hottest in Europe even. It's known for its flowers and fountains," Leala said. "When the Romans were in Córdoba, they would build an inner courtyard, like this one, into each house. It would always be open to the air, like this one. It was called an atrium and was built to cool the house at night."

Leala put her hands on Mía's shoulders and positioned her a few feet to the left, still facing the courtyard. "Are you keeping them closed?"

The girl nodded and then heard Leala walk away in the direction of the terrace doors behind her. Once more the voice came from a distance.

"Your great-grandfather built this house for his bride before he brought her to America. It took three years. Then he stood his young Spanish wife just where you are standing now when he introduced her to her new home. He told her to close her eyes, just as I am telling you. And he said these words to her—"

There was the sound of terrace doors opening.

"'Tell me what you feel.'"

At first Mía felt nothing at all. Then she heard a stirring of leaves from the courtyard. Mía reached out both her hands, half expecting the walls or the floor itself to move. But quickly the cool wash of air was upon her and with it the scent of lilac and orange and rose.

"It feels like ... water!" Mía said. After another minute her face relaxed; a tentative smile came to her lips. "It feels like I'm standing in a stream."

"No," whispered Leala Cruz next to the girl. Then she waited and finally said, "It feels like home. It feels like Spain and family and heritage and honor. It feels like the flow of time. And so this is my promise to you, Maria Anita Cruz. If this house is not *your* house in six weeks, then I will take you back to the mountains myself." The words seemed to have a soothing effect upon the girl who, like her carpenter father, would only nod in acknowledgement.

"Now open your eyes." The voice was still behind Mía, who had to turn around to see her mother and the flowing draperies next to the terrace doors. "The point," Leala said, "is that everything you see, everything, was put in its place for one woman. And she grew to love it more than her first home. A hacienda, Mía, is not a farm or a factory. It is a way of life. And it will take possession of you, little girl, more than the man you marry."

These last words came with such passion that Leala recognized how overwhelming they might be to a child; and so she went to Mía and hugged her in a way that, for the first time, seemed entirely natural. "We're both lost in our new roles, aren't we?" Leala said. "And I'm sorry for that. I realize how strange I sound to you now. But let me have one more chance."

The girl stood still and silent.

"Please," said Leala. She took Mía's hand once more and led her into a bedroom already as dim as early evening. Leala clicked on a lamp, and Mía examined the details of her mother's bedroom while Leala herself knelt before a chest of drawers. From the bottom drawer she was lifting a package wrapped in brown paper and handing it up to Mía. "Open it," she said. "It's for you."

The package had at one time been folded like an envelope; but now the paper was wrinkled and limp, held together with a yellow ribbon. Mía had to untie the ribbon and reach inside in order to pull out a certain affair of fine white cloth, still starched but a bit faded.

"This is for your daughter," Leala said. "I didn't get to use it for mine."

"What is it?"

From the doorway behind the two of them a new voice spoke. "Lace," it said. "From Córdoba. The finest in the world. A gift to you from Gabriel Garcia López Covas. Your friend." It was a woman holding a plaid suitcase in her good hand and nodding formally when Mía and Leala looked up. "Señora," she said. "The car is here."

Mía ran to Reina, and the suitcase dropped to the floor. The forearm patted Mía's back as it had always done when they clasped each other close. The girl put her lips next to Reina's ear and whispered as low as she could, "Say you are sorry. Tell her you want to stay." The old woman pulled back her face enough for Mía to see her smile, and then shook her head no.

Still with her handless arm at Mía's back, Reina took up the suitcase and directed the two of them to the open doors of the hacienda. There was a sedan outside, just to the right of the fountain. It resembled a hearse with a long streak of chrome down the side and a mantle of gray-brown dust. A rear door opened, and a man in a blue suit got out. He stood staring straight ahead, preferring to see nothing it seemed rather than acknowledge the space around him. The driver was only an arm hanging from a window, a cigarette levered between two fingers.

Reina wore neither a coat nor a hat, but there was a woman's handkerchief of cotton and lace that had been hastily stuffed into the pocket of her skirt. She used it to wipe at the girl's eyes and then spoke in clear, unemotional Spanish, "I have something to tell you, child. Something that you need to hear."

Leala stepped toward the old woman but was stopped when Reina raised the stump of her arm with a sudden, determined motion.

In the girl's face Reina saw something that caused her to hold back the words she was about to speak. Was the lie really so hard to believe? Had not God Himself put some of Leala's features into the girl's eyes and mouth? And what kind of truth was it that only caused harm? Reina cleared her throat and then heard herself saying, "What I want to say to you is ... you are the most fortunate of children. Give your new life a chance. And remember that many, many people love you. Remember!"

Reina kissed both cheeks of the girl and turned away before anything further could pass between them. The man in the blue suit hoisted her suitcase into the back seat of the car, climbing into the front with the driver as Reina settled into the back. The hand on the left side of the door flicked its cigarette toward the fountain; and the car eased forward, gathering speed through the cottonwoods and disappearing in dust long before it reached the highway.

20

ON WEDNESDAY, OCTOBER 6, not yet a week into her new life, Maria Anita Cruz was presented to a group of newspaper reporters who had been invited to the hacienda. They came with their notepads and their cascades of questions. There was a photographer too, and then later a news story that sputtered along for days. The papers called her the Lindbergh miracle baby, the Cinderella child.

In the following week there were preparations for a grand celebration, whole categories of guests being invited on different nights. "It's important for you to see all of this and take part," Alejandro told her. So when the gardeners came into the great house itself, Mía thought Alejandro meant for her to watch them cleaning windows and polishing floors. While the carpenters set up a great white tent, Mía herself placed lanterns along the garden paths. The man who tried to straighten her rows was told to work elsewhere. Until at last, on a Saturday evening, when the first guests strolled through a courtyard as extravagantly flowered as any of the great houses of Spain, they found their candle-lit way into the social gathering of the year.

Mía shook hands for an hour it seemed. There were farmers and ranchers and business associates who brought their families in the early afternoon and loosed their children to float sticks in the fountains and to pluck rosebuds that they threw at wind chimes in trees. Mía was ushered from group to group. At the very first cluster of women she said, "Good evening, I am so please to meet your acquaintance." Her mother's hand tightened at Mía's shoulder, but just for an instant, and no one corrected her. It was only Daniela, the housemaid, who happened to notice and to smile.

It was the music that softened any other faltering steps. It brought people to the terrace, where they danced to songs by Frank Sinatra and Doris Day. Mía met identical twin sisters from the Harrison ranch. They were dressed the same and finished each other's sentences with such efficiency that it was like talking to a doubled person. Mía wanted to stay with them throughout the evening, but then their brother asked her to dance when the band played "I'll Never Smile Again." Afterward, some of the other boys found their courage; and Mía's spirits rose each time one of them approached, whether he had been nudged by his mother or dared by his friends. Another one of the boys in particular caught her eye. He was handsome. And spoke to her in Anglo-Spanish when he danced with her, not once but twice. His name was Blake, and he went to a private school in a city that Mía had never heard of, but his family had horses he said and maybe over Christmas break....

Mía did not ask what it meant. Christmas break sounded like an unfortunate thing, but the idea of seeing the boy again couldn't possibly be bad, so she finished the sentence for him, in English. "Maybe, we go to ride?"

"Great," said Blake Buchanan. "That would be really great."

For a time she stayed with a group of girls on the terrace; but the band took up the old traditional music, and when the parents began to dance, the sons and daughters moved away. It was Blake who found Mía in the garden walking with the Harrison girls. This time he took her hand and said, "My dad's talking to your dad in the courtyard. Let's go watch the fireworks."

"Firework?" she said.

"You know, pop, pop, pop, boom." He made raining motions with his fingers. "Our dads hate each other's guts, but they're business partners and they trade horses all the time. You can never tell when they're serious and when they're not."

Blake maneuvered Mía past a boy and girl who were kissing and around tables where the chairs had been pushed back, then through the bright reflections of the great room and into the softer light of the courtyard. There were galleries on three sides, and there was another fountain, this one built into the wall and trickling into a tiled pool. Flowers on every surface. Alejandro spotted Mía as soon as she took a seat on one of the steps. When he motioned to her, Blake dropped her hand and stayed behind.

"Maria Anita," he was saying to a stocky man, "let me introduce you to Buck Buchanan, one of my oldest and dearest enemies."

The man with the gray crew cut and bolo tie reached out his hand to her. "Don't you listen to him, young lady. I'm mighty pleased to see you 'cause I remember when you were born, and I hope you're just right at home like it hadn't been a day. --By God, Alejandro, she's a beauty if nobody else has noticed."

"Thank you," said the man in the wheelchair. "We are glad beyond measure, as you can imagine."

Mía did not know when to let go of Mr. Buchanan's hand but managed to say a clear thank you and "I am very happy and delight to meet you."

Alejandro nodded his approval and, after a few more words about the recent past, steered the conversation to a stack of unframed paintings leaning against one of the gallery walls. "Over here. I want you to tell me what you think, Buck. We got these in New Mexico a few months ago, and Leala thinks they're bizarre. We can't agree on whether to hang them at all."

"Oh no," whispered Blake.

"What is it?" Mía could tell the boy wasn't really alarmed, but any hint of a social blunder troubled her. She didn't want fireworks. She didn't want them anywhere near her waking dream.

"They're being polite," Blake told her. "We may as well go somewhere else."

It was a sentiment apparently felt by the other bystanders as well. The buzz of good-mannered conversation picked up again, and Alejandro Cruz was left alone after Mr. Buchanan looked at one or two paintings. Mía felt a relief to be going somewhere else with Blake. One of the unknowable rules, she was almost certain, had been violated in a public way; but there was no Reina, no Leala, no Daniela even to tell her what had just transpired. There was only the man in his chair, unmoving, as Buck Buchanan and Leala sauntered away into a new conversation.

The wrongness of the moment took hold of her, and Mía told Blake that she would be right back. Then, without a thought that such an impulse could be wrong, she scurried across the courtyard and hugged Alejandro Cruz. "I can show Blake the stables now, okay?" she said. And did not hear the conversations stop.

Those who saw the child were horrified. The tissue of caution that everyone held up against the man's disease had been so utterly torn apart, and so suddenly, that it was a like a child dashing in front of a car. There was nothing anyone could do, no words that anyone could say. One person simply gasped. Another woman turned her back as if she had looked through a doorway onto some obscenity. And there, in the great room itself, was a maid who had obviously seen it all from a distance. She was putting down her tray and rushing in search of the *señora*. What else was there to do? How could anyone scald away that contagion?

Yet in the instant of its happening there was no one as surprised as Alejandro Cruz. Without realizing that he was capable, he lifted up one arm and patted the child upon the back, saying to her, "Yes, of course, my dear. Go and enjoy yourself." Alejandro turned his chair to watch her go. Mía took the hand of the Buchanan boy and led him through the crowd as if she had lived at the hacienda all of her life. And this pleased Alejandro Cruz beyond any expectation.

A light breeze swept across the terrace as Mía and Blake went from the house, not running but clearly eager to be away from the adults and any hint of unease. Mía was thinking of the boy and girl she had seen kissing earlier and feeling that there were possibilities about her new life that could be happy ones. Still holding Blake's hand, she led him toward the stables while filling up the empty space between them with words and words that tumbled out so naturally that she felt she could bridge any misunderstanding.

The two of them followed one path and then another until

Blake and Mía came to the clearing next to the tack room. Heavy mimosa boughs and a hedge partially enclosed the space, giving an air of privacy, an exaggerated distance from the adults. Mía, though, was surprised to find in the shadowy moonlight fifteen or more silhouettes in a half circle, now laughing, now jostling for attention, now cupping a match to a cigarette just as they had learned from the movies.

Daniela was there with a boy from a neighboring ranch. She wore the week-old yellow dress of Mía's, which made her look elegant, more like a woman than a child. And in the same group with Daniela were an older boy and girl who had claimed the choicest seats on the stone wall around the trees. The anonymous couple was watching all of the others and, from time to time, making droll pronouncements or sarcastic asides. The boy held the crown of a beer bottle with the tips of his fingers, swirling the contents in between languid sips. Blake said at once that he and Mía should leave, that maybe they should just stroll through the stable to look at the mares and foals. But no, Mía told him. She saw no reason to walk away. Here it was *her* family, *her* night to assume her name.

But the ones who noticed Mía at all gave her only a single glance and turned back to more interesting antics and conversations. Someone said hi to Blake, but nothing more. When Mía put out her hand and spoke her name to the older couple on the wall, they did not move at first. Then the boy took a long pull from the bottle and said to everyone, "I am so please to meet your acquaintance."

The rush of laughter was enough, almost, to break her down to tears. The words had been spread throughout the evening and repeated in varying accents until they had found their most appreciative audience here, and Daniela's smile was enough to reveal the source. Mía's hand lashed out faster than the thought of her own humiliation. It found Daniela's cheek and whipped her face to one side, and there was another distant accumulation of laughter.

And then Daniela struck her back.

If anything, this response was faster, more ferocious. It met the side of Mía's head and left a ringing in her ear. It was a sound that did not fade in the intervening moments. The two girls flew at each other without another sound, and after several blows, brought themselves down together into the dirt. Someone stepped forward to intercede, but he was himself pulled back into the crowd.

●

On the following day the family and the workers rested. Only the cooks and those who tended the animals went about their usual chores. The day was quiet; and throughout the long, warm afternoon the grounds of the hacienda were as motionless as a painting. Then on Monday, the 18th of October, when the cleaning began, Daniela did not come into the main house at all. The big tent was taken down. The wilting flowers were spirited away. The remnants of Mía's grand introduction were swept into carts or stored in sheds or fed to animals. The unpleasantness between the two girls was simply forgotten by all but a few, and the hacienda fell back into its routine. On Tuesday, the 19th, it was Alejandro himself who woke her. "Up you go, sleepyhead. We still have a few minutes. So why don't you slip into some clothes. It wouldn't do for you to be seen in your nightgown," he said. "But do it quietly. And then meet me at the front door as soon as you can."

It was too early for her to understand. The sky was still pink and gray, and the cooks had not yet arrived to light the stoves.

Mía put on a pair of dungarees and the shirt she wore when she went riding, pulled her hair back into a ponytail and didn't bother with shoes or socks. She wore her old sandals from the village, hurrying through the courtyard where she was surprised to find his empty chair. Alejandro was just outside the heavy doors, calm and smiling when she arrived. He used two canes to help his balance but stood upright on his own, although Mía could not imagine how he had brought himself there without help. He was in a mood for talking and did not bother to look at her as he spoke.

"During the Depression, when the entire country was--."

"What's that?" she asked.

"The Depression?" Alejandro laughed without humor. "It

was the inevitable consequence of greed and stupidity. When people were thrown out of work, then thrown out of their houses, and thrown off their land because they had no money and no jobs. The banks were ruined, and the government was incompetent. That's what the Depressions was."

"Is that when you got sick?"

At this Alejandro laughed more affably and looked down at her. "Maybe. I'm not sure. You have, Maria Anita, a quick and interesting mind."

"Where were you and mama in the Depression?"

"Mmm. Yes. It's what I'm trying to tell you. We were here. And so was everyone else. During all of that time, for more than a decade in fact, not a single family suffered in this place. We ate, we worked, we served the land. That is the way of the hacienda. No one was fired, and everyone shared the hardships and the harvests. No one was told to leave when he grew old." Here he paused to see if she was listening. Then he spoke even more quietly and intently. "This is an ancient way of life, Maria Anita. Some would say it doesn't belong in the modern world because the rules here are rigid and the demands, on the *patrón* and on the people, are great. But it's our way of life, an island in a sea of change."

"You are the *patrón?*" Mía asked.

"On many days I think I am the servant to everyone here." He laughed, but Mía didn't understand. "On some days, yes, I am the *patrón*. Like today. I have responsibilities. Now stand next to me. I believe I hear them."

A truck, heavily loaded, slowed as it turned into the long drive beneath the cottonwoods and headed away from the hacienda. The cab of the truck was crowded and quiet. Next to the driver were a woman and the bobbing heads of several children. An older boy rode in the back, motionless. Mía lifted her hand when she recognized him.

"No," said Alejandro. "Do not wave. It would be insulting. But do watch. This is a lesson for everyone. Especially for you."

Mía looked up, uncomprehending.

"Clodoveo Esparza is a good man. I am sorry for him. He

has done nothing wrong."

"They are leaving?" she asked.

Alejandro nodded. "I think he can find work farther north. It's possible. I'll send a letter if I can."

Mia was incredulous. "But why, if he's done nothing wrong?!"

"Because he has honor. He is loyal to me, and to you, and to this place. In fact I have great respect for him. He has not said a word to me in two days. And I will do what I can for him later on."

"But why?"

Alejandro had this answer ready also and delivered it without inflection, as calmly as he did all of her lessons. "Because his daughter, Daniela Diega Esparza, raised her hand to the daughter of this house. It's something that cannot be allowed."

"No! That's not right! I mean, it's--"

"A hard lesson? Yes. Yes, it is. And so my gift to you, this land and all that goes with it, does not now look so much like a fairy tale, does it? I am truly sorry for that. And for asking you to grow up a bit too soon. But the truth, my daughter, is that animals die, crops fail, machines break down. The people who were invited into this house for your homecoming celebration? The ones who spoke fine words to you and shook your hand? They were not your friends, Maria Anita. These things are all part of the same lesson, one you need to learn."

"It was only a quarrel between two girls," she persisted.

"Shh. Not so loud. You'll wake others, which would be very rude. And, no. It wasn't only a quarrel. That is what Esparza understands. And you were very wrong in what you did."

"But I--."

"And so your punishment is this. Beginning tomorrow, you will manage the stables."

"But that's--"

"Salvador will show you how to keep the books. You will be in charge of feeding the stock, foaling the mares, and selling the overage. You will see that the stalls are mucked. You will have the men repair the fences, and you will assign all of them their tasks. Think of how they will feel being ordered about by a child. You will supply the farrier and store the hay and put down the cripples. Salvador will teach you all these things. And, believe me, you will *learn* your loyalty to him. And at the same time, you will *earn* his loyalty to you. That is how you will be punished and how you will begin to assume your place."

21

IN THE MORNINGS, her tutor Miss Ainsworth did the numbers first because they were Mía's least favorite subject. Then they did the science book and then the reading, which they always practiced together out loud. The other children of the hacienda, the ones who went to the school near the carpentry shop, said that Miss Ainsworth had been to college and knew a hundred languages and a thousand years of history and all the kings of Spain. They met with her in the afternoons. But she met with Mía every morning in the music room, making Mía read in two languages until her ears and mouth were sore. Why couldn't she learn with the other children in the afternoons? Because it wasn't proper she was told. Because, Miss Ainsworth said, you are a bit behind; and it wouldn't be proper for her to be behind among ordinary children.

That, and other oddities, troubled her enough that on one morning, when there was no tutoring at all, she sought out Alejandro. She found him on the lawn beside his bedroom, exercising his legs under Bajardo's supervision. Two wooden canes were leaning against the empty wheelchair, and on the ground beside the wheels were dumbbells with extra weights scattered here and there. Alejandro wore a sleeveless undershirt, like a gymnast, and carried himself between two parallel bars set high off the ground. His long trousers had been tailored for tennis, but the loose fabric flapped against his legs. He wasn't really walking but rather pulling himself along by twisting his hips first in one direction and then in another. It was his upper body that took the weight. The undershirt was soaked, and from time to time he asked Bajardo for a towel. His breath came in labored rasps.

When he turned at the end of his passage, he saw Mía and gave her a smile that she would treasure for the rest of her life. "This *is* a little embarrassing, isn't it?" he said. "I mean, for you to be standing there as barefooted as a laundry girl."

"Tell me the truth," said Mía.

"Ah. Never a good sign from a woman." He turned toward Bajardo. "It's never a good sign when those are the first words you hear." Alejandro was playing with her, she was sure, and still remembering the hug she'd given him during the party more than a month before.

"Did Mr. Manley tell you a secret?" she went on. "About my name?"

Alejandro's lips pressed together, and the head nodded after a moment's introspection. "You are a direct and very serious young lady, aren't you? I do wish my business associates were like you. So I suppose you deserve a direct and very serious reply."

"What is it, really?" Mía said.

"The truth is ... no. I already knew your name. What I needed was your location. And Mr. Manley very kindly provided that information and certain other services for which he was handsomely rewarded. Are we having doubts now about where you belong?"

Mía thought for a moment and then sat herself in a lawn chair. "No."

"Good!" he said.

Still, she could see that it took an effort for him to keep his tone light. He finished turning himself and balancing his torso above his legs before taking several steps in her direction. His hands made patting sounds on the rails. His breath resumed the rasping she'd heard when he first asked Bajardo for a towel. Halfway down the bars, Bajardo brought the wheelchair around but Alejandro waved him away. "Go on," he said. "Have some breakfast. This lovely young lady will help me if I need it, and I imagine we won't wander far, although it's beginning to sound like a solemn conversation. Am I right?"

She said nothing, and they both waited for Bajardo to leave.

Alejandro surprised her by neglecting the wheelchair and walking all the way to the end of the bar. From there he brought himself to the stone wall of a raised planter, keeping his balance with one hand while scooping up the canes with the other. He pointed with one of the canes to the nearby terrace steps and then sat himself there adjusting his legs with his free hand. He wore no shoes, only a heavy pair of socks that did little to hide the high arching curvature of his feet. His calves were as thin and taut as a horse's shanks. He wiped his face with the towel, tilted his chin in the air, and pretended to smoke a cigarette, tapping the ashes in pantomime.

She didn't know what she was supposed to say.

"President Roosevelt!"

She smoothed the folds of her skirt.

"You don't know who that is, do you?"

Mía shook her head.

"Well. No worry. He was somebody who died a long time ago. And I am making a rather tasteless joke at the expense of one or the other of us, I'm not sure exactly--."

"Does it hurt?" she interrupted.

"This?" He tapped his leg with one of the canes.

She nodded once.

For a long time he seemed to concentrate on the near landscape and the gray workers who were as constant and industrious as ants. Then he patted the thigh as if he were comforting a dog. "No. No, for the most part, it doesn't hurt at all. It's like one little part of you goes to sleep, and then can't wake up. I guess that's the problem. But, no, it doesn't hurt. Although sometimes I get a little flicker. A little electric shock from down there. That's why I keep exercising."

"So you can feel?"

"Sometimes," he said. "But mostly not. You'd be surprised how you miss it. Sometimes fear is worse than pain."

"Are you afraid?" she wanted to know.

"Sometimes. But what's all this about? Are *you* afraid? Because that's understandable. It's hardly been three months, and with everything that's happened...."

"No. Everybody's nice to me. It's like a dream."

"Do you miss your old home?" he asked.

She thought about her answer and about the promise she had made to Amedeo Muñoz. "I wake up at night sometimes," she said. "And sometimes I'm afraid it will all go away. And I miss the mountains. And him. And *Abuelita*."

"Ah." Alejandro kept his voice low and calm, as if they were whispering in church. "But he was a very bad man."

"*Abuelita* didn't like him. And some of the others too. But he was always good and kind to me. She said the trouble was he didn't know his place."

"Your *abuelita* was right," continued Alejandro in his cathedral voice. "We all have our place, and we risk a very great cost when we step out of our place."

"She said I was too young."

"I certainly agree." He smiled again. "But too young for what?"

Mía liked his smile. It made him look handsome. She was very sure it made him look the way he had been before the disease took over his life. Smiles came easily to him, and the broad, angular countenance, not yet shaven for the day, still drawn from the exercise, nevertheless held on to some of its old strength and charm. She studied his face looking for signs of herself and thinking how like a dry landscape it seemed, how like a high desert of cliffs and valleys. She wondered if he felt pain behind the mask and if he ever cried out of loneliness. "She would never talk about it much," Mía said. "She thought I was too young to know, I guess, anything, but that one day I would understand like adults. But not now."

"She said that, did she?"

"Tell me. Tell me the secret."

"Dear child...." Alejandro put a hand behind her head, almost hugged her to him for a second time, but then stopped before he had brought her into his arms. "There is no secret." He looked directly into her eyes. "And Reina was wrong if she suggested there was one."

"Tell me the truth," Mía insisted.

And calmly he replied. "I did. Although, I suppose, not all of it. The whole truth, the whole story as you say, is painful; but it certainly isn't secret. First, however, you need to look out there and tell me what you see." Alejandro Cruz pushed down with both hands, turning his body with difficulty until he faced the eastern horizon. Then he nodded directly ahead.

The girl squinted into the rising sun. "Mountains?"

"Yes indeed. Mountains!   And trees. And there's a river back in that direction." He pointed with one of the canes. "Also a hunting lodge. And a small village almost, a few rows of houses over there in that direction, for the people who keep us fed and who work for the hacienda. Then there's grazing land just on the other side of the houses. Farming land to the north and west. And behind our backs, over there, a stable, a corral, pastures." This time he had to lift his legs with his hands, one at a time, until he had maneuvered himself back around. "Then there are also cars, horses, wagons. Gardens and flowers right here in front of us. Fountains. Tractors, plows, combines. A school for your friends. A lovely house with books, paintings, and fine furniture. A safe with silver coins. A collection of old maps and letters in the library. All in all, a very great deal of property."

"It's big. And grander than ... anything."

"Yes," Cruz agreed. "Big enough to be measured in miles. But what I am trying to tell you, Mía, is that from the river in the east to the fence lines in the west, there is much more than you can imagine at present. And. It belongs to you. *That* is the truth. When I die, it *all* goes to you. Until you are twenty-one, it will be held in a trust. And the trustee is a very fine and clever lawyer, Mr. Ian Randall from Sacramento, who will insure that my wishes for you will come true. There are papers that will protect you. I promise. But the very painful truth, my daughter, lies in what people will do when they try to take it away from you."

"Mama? It doesn't belong to Mama first?"

"No. It all goes directly to you. We were so happy when you were born, and so sad when you were taken away. That what we want to do now is try to recover some of that happiness. And we want to do that by making you happy. That's why I will never lie to you. Because that is what I have learned from the doctors. A lie can make you happy only for a very short time."

"Reina said I was the child of misfortune."

"That doesn't sound right to me," said Alejandro. "Do you

think you are the child of misfortune?"

"No," she allowed.

"Are you happy?"

Mía nodded.

"Good. Then I think you can safely skip Miss Ainsworth this morning and come along with me. Tell Javy to bring around the jeep. And give me time to get dressed. Then, my daughter, we are going to drive over some of your property and begin teaching you how to keep it. Because *this*," he reached his arm forth and gave a small wave from the wrist, "is who you are, Maria Anita. And it's who you will be for the rest of your life."

22

AFTER THE NEW YEAR, in late January of 1949, Alejandro began spending days, and soon weeks, within his rooms, wheeling out from time to time to take a meal or to meet with a businessman. "It's an up and down thing" is what he would say. People made their polite inquiries and he had to answer with something dry and signatory, so that is what he gave them. It's an up and down thing. There is always something. Then he would bestow whatever smile was right for them: socialites, businessmen, wives, or kitchen maids. A full-time nurse was hired for Alejandro. The diet changed and changed again. On many days he wanted fire, a great blazing conflagration in the hearth, which was his entertainment and only joy.

A renewed fear of infection made everyone keep a further distance. And Mía especially should not be close to him the doctors said. The nurse will handle medications. The danger now, Dr. Franklin told them, would be from choking. Give him soups and cereals, that sort of thing, but no meat or heavy vegetables. And you might do well to have one of the maids disinfect whatever he touches. A little bleach in water ought to do the trick. Maybe wipe down the floor and walls from time to time. That is, if you insist upon keeping him at home.

Dr. Miles Franklin visited weekly, then another doctor from a clinic in Minnesota because Alejandro made a hacking sound throughout the nights. A second nurse was hired. Soon it was back to silk pajamas throughout the day. Neither sitting up nor lying down gave him much relief. His breath came in tiny gasps. By late February Dr. Franklin had removed his bed and brought in the marvelous machine, situated so that Alejandro could see the flowered steps and the sunshine on the terrace. It was like a huge metal drum with little windows on the side, and it was long enough to contain a man as snugly as his own cocoon. Only Alejandro's head and neck stuck out.

The paralyzed rest they put inside. The doctor was calm and kind, but now Alejandro had to ask for everything, a sip of water, someone to wipe his mouth. But no one seemed to mind. The little pumps made their inhalations, and so did Alejandro Cruz. People moved about the house once more without fear of contamination.

And then, in early March, he died.

Mr. Ian Randall, the trustee appointed by Alejandro, was older than any person Mía had ever known. Still courtly and handsome, he had a head for numbers and a gift for multiplying money. In spite of his gray appearance and his Eastern business suits, he spent hours out of doors with Salvador, the field managers, and Leala whenever he came to the hacienda. He even preferred to meet with Bajardo on the wide terrace where they reviewed household expenses. But most intensely he tutored Mía, translating numbers into words and words into familiar images that she saw before her every day. It was a way of thinking that she finally recognized. And, "Yes," replied Mr. Randall, "you are my third generation at hacienda Cruz."

Mia adapted to the narrative of her life. She blossomed. And like a tree healing its broken branch, the hacienda grew around her. Indeed, until the day she married, there was only one other great discovery, a disorienting surprise in fact, that came to her from out of the past.

Several months after her seventeenth birthday, and more than four years after the death of Alejandro Cruz, Mía found someone in a place where he did not belong.

Perhaps it was because the hat had been pulled low. Or perhaps it was that the passing of seasons had added bulk to his shoulders and arms. Whatever the explanation, he did not reappear to her as the person she had known. True, his sleeves were rolled up, as they had often been, but the hands were veined and leathered. His movements were slower than she remembered, but he kept the shears clipping with practiced ease. Sweat formed a dark V upon his back, although he never paused to wipe his face. He seemed to have been made for the sun. And yet here he was at the end of a row of roses, clipping like a barber while old Normando raked. She would have passed him by if, like the others, he had simply removed the hat.

Mía had taken Kemena, the palomino mare, out to the river and back, a chance for both of them to try the new saddle. Her mother had insisted on it, saying that young ladies did not ride bareback, but Mía thought this puffed up cushion rode too high. It robbed her feel for the horse. And now, after a hard gallop up the lodge road and back past the stables, Mía was letting the mare cool down, turning her into the first of the garden paths and allowing the reins to go slack. Kemena took a long drink at one of the fountains, then ambled down the wide path, perhaps drawn by the fragrance. The first of the men, old familiar Normando, swept off his hat, adding a shallow bow. The second one did not acknowledge her at all.

Mía smiled. Said something social without reining in and gave the other man a focused look. There was a familiarity to his silence. A man who did not search for reasons to talk.

Still, there was no point in being offended. The old ways were dying out. The other families understood. It was, after all, April of 1953. The workers were only workers, and life was no longer a ritual for them. Mía let Kemena walk to the end of the row and take another drink. Allowed the mare to toss her head and sidle into the shade where a rider could stand in the stirrups and stretch her legs. Mía turned at the waist and prolonged her stretches. Then saw that the man was staring boldly back at her.

It was Quentin.

A sudden something rushed upon her. A shiver of recognition, yes, but something more. It was like a flash of happiness and guilt so intermingled that his name would not fully form, would not rise all the way to her lips. Without realizing, she jerked the reins, backing Kemena into branches, the tree reaching around her like the past. She did not sense herself dropping back into the saddle or turning the horse at all. She felt for the first time in her new life a joy that rose above mere gladness. This was Quentin filling up her heart by simply standing still.

Then, still at a distance, he was holding up a rose. "I know where you can get a truck load of these," he said.

And she was off the horse and running into Quentin's arms.

He held her but with a solemn shyness, as if they were cousins separated by time. He was cautious, watching her even as they embraced, to see how much of a stranger she had become.

"How can you be here?" she said.

"I guess you don't remember," he replied. "I have a truck. And a place this big? It's hard to hide."

"I mean, how can you *be* here?"

"He sent me," Quentin said.

There. It was the preface to a hundred dreaded stories that she could not bear to hear.

But Quentin was not sad, only thoughtful. He kept her hand in his while looking back on the scene in his mind. "One morning we were laying up hay for Ordóñez. Me and him. One of those misty mornings, you know, when out in the valley you can look up and believe that you're at the bottom of the sea. And he must have got to thinking. But it seemed to me like something that had been in his mind for a long time. He told me it was time to find my way."

"That's what he said?"

Quentin nodded. "I don't have all the words he said. But you know the way he was, how he would start out talking low and then end up looking at you through your own eyes? That's the way this happened too. He said the world wouldn't wait forever. Else I'd end up forking hay and wondering if."

"If what?" she asked.

"I don't know, he sort of left it hanging. But the thing that came to me, I guess the thing I'd been wondering about all along, was if maybe I should have gone north and seen about this girl I knew. It didn't seem all that hard when I thought about it. But right now.... I mean, look at all this. All the land and water and trees. I think it might be the wrong place after all."

Mía took hold of Quentin's sleeve. "Don't. Don't feel that

way."

"Anyhow ... , you look all right to me. I could tell him. He'd appreciate knowing."

"Is *he* all right?" she wanted to know. "Tell me about him. Tell me everything he said to you. Did he get the letters I sent to him? And why did he not write back to me?"

Quentin nodded again. "I don't know about any letters. We don't get letters in the village. But he's okay: he healed up good if that's what you mean. But the village, it's not what you remember. A wall fell down, couple of years ago. In the old gymnasium. It buckled outward, and some of the people got hurt bad. It took another year to pull the whole thing down and clear it away. And during all that time there were people leaving. That's what grinds him down, the ones that come straggling in and then leave when they get on their feet."

"What else? Why are you really here?" Mía urged.

Quentin looked away, pursed his lips. "I told him I'm no good at this. But you know the way he is. He won't hear what he doesn't want to hear. Anyhow, he said to me just take the message. And I guess I said I would."

"Quentin." She whispered it.

"He said that if I ever saw you again, I should tell you right away. From him. That he loved you so."

"I never wanted to leave," she said. "I only wanted to know who I was."

"So now, do you still hate him? For lying, or for keeping you away from all of this?"

They had been walking, with Kemena a few steps behind, but now Mía stopped to face Quentin with her answer. "No. No, my mother told me who he was, after Alejandro died. And I am not ashamed."

"You mean she told you that he was your father? That Amedeo was. Yes?"

"No," Mía said again. "When I was twelve she told me part of it. And when I was sixteen, she told me that they had been lovers."

"But still," Quentin went on, "he *was* your father. Is that not so? It's the only thing that makes sense. It's what everyone believes."

"Everyone?" Mía turned away and plucked a just-opening bud as she thought about how to answer. She began to peel away the petals and lifted them to her face where she could almost feel the fragrance. "For twelve years," she said, "I was certain who my father was; and then, one day, my mother stepped out of a picture and into my life, a miracle that my first father never bothered to explain. And so I've always thought it was ... polite ... not to question my second father, who gave me this." She let the petals blow out of her hand as she indicated the expanse around them. "What I have here is what I had there. Half a family."

"But you are rich now. And different I think."

"How? How am I different? Because I'm not the person you remember?"

From some troubled place Quentin said, "I think this is no place for a man who can stand up straight, for someone who doesn't bow to the *señorita*."

"Did he say that?"

"No," Quentin said. "But I believe that I may have made a mistake in coming here. It's too much. The space between us, I'm beginning to feel, is too wide."

"Normando is old, and I am loyal to him, as he is loyal to me. Someone taught me to respect that. But you? I think you were taught by Amedeo Muñoz, who does not bow to anyone. And yet, Quentin, I ran to *you*. Just now. As I did in Sangre de Cristo. --Yes?"

He looked down and smiled. "You kicked my jaw," he said.

"Stay," she whispered. "Stay one day more. Please. I know there is a place for you here."

AFTERWORD

WRITTEN IN MY HAND
FOR THE SAKE OF MY CHILDREN,
AND FOR HIM
April, 1982

First, because I was a child and did not know the world.

And, then, because the hacienda had taken possession of me as it had done with Alejandro Cruz. I had children of my own. Employees. Animals. Machines. Crops in the field. One father's ancient enemies, another's enduring absence. Each of these things laid its claim upon me, and I was absorbed by the story that they had made.

The third reason, I suppose, is that I had come to believe that Amedeo Muñoz had at some time committed a crime so hideous that it had severed him from those who would have loved him most. I believed for years that he had been haunted by this offence. Reina used to say that the village was his penance, but no one ever knew what she meant. And during the time I lived with him, no one wanted to know his past as long as bellies were full and blankets were plentiful on winter nights.

So. I preserved our distance for nearly thirty years, and in this way I am no different from many children of divorce. If that is the right word to use.

Now in later years, when I dream of him, I will often wake with a leaden guilt as if I have done him a grave injustice, as if I alone have been the source of some violent wrong to him. I will lie in bed sorting and stacking these dark thoughts, trying to console myself with the brittle certainty that he lied to me for years, telling me that my mother had died. Sometimes I find peaceful sleep again. Usually, though, I stare into the darkness until my husband stirs or until the sun falls upon our draperies and one of our daughters bounds into the room. I will then tell myself that the story of this spectral man is not my story. That his sad conclusion was the sum of his own neglect and sins.

But I know that is not the truth.

He was a silent man for the most part. That is my clearest memory of him. At private moments he could be talkative, but still it troubled me that he could also go for half a day without making a vocal sound. And whenever I would worry him into conversation, it would never last. He did not believe in wasting words any more than he believed in wasting water. Silence was the armor he wore to protect ... exactly what? Some men really are unknowable. That is what I have come to accept. He spent much of his life in silence like the animals he admired. And when he could be coaxed into telling the story of his life or of mine, I could see that he always kept some burning part of it inside of him. I believed then and now that his great and tragic mistake had been in loving someone with a love so fierce it consumed nearly all of his lonely being. But it has been very hard for me to come at last to this one overwhelming thought. That this ferocious love was never intended for my mother. That it was meant for me.

He was the stranger that I longed to meet.

And so.

One day, in the spring of 1981, I found myself upon a road. With me was my husband, another silent man, who could drive for hours without a word and arrive content that you and he had forged a bond. He took us south into the mountains, my husband did. In one sense we simply came together the way a lion and lioness will sometimes wait, belly to the ground, for days and then without a sound or signal rise up to follow the invisible scent. That is how I remember it. But it was not a dream. I drove south with my husband, Quentin Cayetano Ortega, in the spring of 1981. High into the mountains. To find my father's unspoken words.

The name of the village was Catalán.

It is not down on any map. True places never are.

But by following signs that had not existed when we were young, and by driving a road that had been starched and pressed, we came to the sharp-edged mountains by early afternoon. Then up to Zalcupan and, from there, the old road into the clouds. No more desert willow, no more elkweed and ocotillo. Now there were little yellow stars of creeping sorrel along the way, tattered blue tufts of St. Veronica's veil. When we came at last to a broad depression in the shale, Quentin called it the lower valley and relaxed his grip upon the wheel. A half hour later he had found his fields, thick with ruin and burrobush.

Farther on we had to leave the car of course. It seemed absurd, like parking in a corridor of weeds. But we had to remind ourselves that there had never been a road into the village from the south, only a footpath wrenched and carved from granite. We found it. That was my first surprise. The sudden familiarity of those great stone faces brought a rush of happiness that I had not expected. They had hardly changed in our human time except for a thicker growth upon their chins. To me the craggy pathway up was still as elegant and inviting as any sweep of ballroom stairs. Here and there fresh trunks and branches arose from ancient fissures. I recognized most of them as Japanese maples, grown from seeds that he had flung into the air. And the cedars just below my school were now cathedral sized. They hid our view of the buildings higher up.

When we reached the little pool and waterfall beside the two-stone bridge, I was surprised at how well my ear remembered. I stopped and listened to the water's voice. I touched the cedar handrail that the men had fitted between newel stones. The wood was soft as doeskin where the moss had found a hold. Here was where the girls would fill their jars, where I now cupped my hand. The water was as cold as melted snow; and it made music, the same four notes, never quite a chord, falling by ones and twos in such hypnotic rhythm that I was tempted to sleep and dream.

Quentin went ahead of me, climbing the narrow

treadstones two at a time as if he expected discovery, and I lost him at the next turning of the path. I stayed behind in slow reverie. Some of the boulders were higher than our heads, and some of the surface roots looked like crocodiles. Every stride felt to me like a child's adventure, like going back in time. I wondered if anyone but the ancestors had ever reached this height or lived this close to earth. So I went by single steps, imagining myself as one of the girls who made this trek in sandals, carrying half their weight in water jars slung against their hips. At any moment I expected to see their ghosts.

I pulled myself up to the winding turn where there were no steps, just a ragged spiral, and I used both hands to keep my balance. Looked down at my feet like a tightrope walker and almost blundered into him. It was Quentin coming down again, his face a puzzlement of wonder and alarm. He seemed to be bringing me a warning, but he had no words. He just shook his head and reached out his hand. Pulled me up and let me edge past him for the last few steps to the level of the street. It was like flinging wide a door into a familiar room. And seeing nothing there at all.

There was no school.

I looked behind me, I think, to test my senses. There was my husband. There was his hand in mine. The rocky pathway down, the railing, the little puddling stream. I looked again ahead of me. There was no school, only a sloping street and some shells that had once been homes. No children playing. No women tending to their tasks. The world in front of me was not Catalán, but Pompeii.

"Are we insane?" my husband said. "Aren't those, over there, the steps where you sat during the fiesta? Aren't those the foundation stones of the school?"

"What happened here?" I asked, as if I expected him to know.

He shook his head. Then, instead of calling out, he whistled loud and long, but the barking dog did not appear. Nor children. Nor curious women from behind closed doors. At the lowest step he looked back at me, tested the stone with his foot, and went up shuffling like an old man at night. There

were still the remnants of an outer wall. The corner where
Gabriel had sat. The court where the cooking had been done.
The concrete floor of the cafeteria. But no school.

"Another quake?" he speculated. "It was always fragile,
always falling down. Even a little quake would have...."

"Where's the rubble then? Who's cleaned it up? And
look."

The few village houses that remained were the ones lowest
on the slope. All of the upper streets had been cleared
somehow, leveled with soil and stepped down and down like
tea plantations in Darjeeling, like something photographed for
the *Geographic*. There were pillows of earth in three foot heights
pitched against the mountain. The pyramidal steps had been
planted in contoured rows; and the old houses, I suppose, had
been dismantled to build retaining walls. I stood looking for a
long time at the green, just now breaking into color, over the
streets that had been erased. There was terrace after terrace of
them. Roses in monumental rows. A few vegetable gardens at
the lowest levels. A double line of laundry strung between two
poles. The clothes were swaying and twisting in the breeze.
They looked like skeletons dancing. They looked like
something hung up to scare away the crows.

We would have left, no doubt, as poor and foolish as we
had always been, if the man had not found us where we were.
He came up from the tree line I suppose. Neither of us saw
him materialize. He arrived at first as just a sound, a rhythmic
crunching of boots against the ground. Quentin turned and
raised one hand the way that ranchers do, not quite a
salutation, more like a signal that you didn't have a gun. The
man gave a silent nod in return and kept walking in our
direction. He was short and slender, dressed unaccountably in
a starched white shirt on a weekday morning. Pressed jeans and
polished boots. "Señora," he said to me, touching the brim of
his hat with two fingers but coming no further after he had
said the word. His face was familiar and somehow wrong, like
a picture from the distant past. Yet there was no mark of age
upon him, and he showed no welcoming recognition.

"*This* is Catalán?" I said.

He gave no sign that he understood what I was saying.

"We're looking for the people," I went on. "We're trying to find someone, and ... what happened here? What does all this mean?"

But he did not answer me. He was focused on my husband, who was walking toward the man in worried concentration. Five feet away Quentin stopped and said, almost to himself, "Victor?"

The man's eyes lost some of their suspicion. He looked at me directly and then back to Quentin. "My father's name. He die three year ago in the fire." As if that explained it all.

"Amedeo Muñoz?" I touched my breast with my hand. "*My* father's name."

"Amedeo?" The man took several steps toward me. "Amedeo?"

"Yes. Yes," I said. "This is my husband Quentin, Quentin Cayetano. We both lived here. In this place, in this school. A long time ago."

He took off his hat. "Please. Please, you come with me." He gestured down the hill, where two more men were just emerging from the trees. Victor's son made half a twirl with his wrist, like a priest's benediction, and the men stopped exactly where they were, waiting at the edge of sun and shade. They watched us like sheep dogs until we reached the path leading down. Soon we were walking among trees that I had never known, on a path of pine needles and fallen cones. It was not until we reached the slope below the foundation of the school that I recognized our direction. They were taking us to the graveyard where Gabriel lay.

Then it came to me with such force that I nearly lost my breath. The white shirts, the polished boots. A kind of dread swept over me that I had never felt before, and I ran down the path toward the stacked stone wall of the cemetery. I do not know if someone called out after me, but I ran until I burst out into that awful clearing and I saw a sudden swelling of the ground. Twenty faces turned to me, a madwoman in bright pink and blue and yellow. The three men shoveling stopped their work. The boy holding a picture of the Virgin stepped back from the edge of the grave. The women bearing flowers in their arms looked at me as you would imagine. And I wanted to shove them all aside.

But then I saw him. Not lying in a coffin, but seated in a chair. I knew his hands, his sun dark face, the way he still occupied the space around him. I recognized immediately the sadness that had seemed to weigh upon his shoulders all his life. He was there, alive, surrounded by others whom I had never seen. And the years had not been kind. His hair was short and thin and white. There was a tremor in the hand that held the cane, and it was clear that he could not see much beyond the grave, even with his thick-lensed glasses. A girl of ten or twelve whispered to him, and he turned his ear in my direction. One of the happiest moments of my life.

I went to him and knelt beside the chair. Put my arms around him and laid my head against his chest. He patted my back with his hand and then motioned me to stand up. "It's my friend Ordóñez," he said. And I could not be sure if he was speaking to me or to himself or to the little group of mourners. The voice was thin and weak, no more than a rustle among the boughs. His body had not been the least bit startled, as if daughters fell at his feet every day. "We still owe him a prayer. And many thanks." I kissed his forehead with what formality I could manage and then rose up, taking my place behind him where I could keep my hand upon his shoulder.

Quentin came and stood apart from me among the men. They all removed their hats while a man holding a rosary prayed. A boy sprinkled water from a bucket upon the grave. Then the women laid their flowers all about the mound, covering it with a design that looked like a woven rug. The little girl who had whispered into his ear gave me a single rose which I laid at the foot of the grave, and after that the women softened their stares at me. A man played his guitar and sang for a long time. After that there was another prayer, and then it was done. The tiny crowd, all that was left of Catalán, had buried the last of its old men but one.

Amedeo Muñoz stood with the help of his cane. It hurt to see him so. I took Quentin's hand and went close to him so that he could see our faces, but his mind seemed clouded with grief and many years. There were neither tears nor joy, nothing like the homecoming I had envisioned, just a gradual parting of the mist. He looked down at the ground, studied it for a time and then lifted his eyes once more. To my husband he said, "Which one were you?"

"I was Quentin, *Señor*. I drove the truck."

"Ah."

"You sent me north for her."

"Yes. I did," said Amedeo Muñoz. "So. You must be ... the little one."

"I'm Mía," I said to him. It was all that I could manage to say. This time he let me hold him while I cried. His body was no longer made of iron and stone. He had softened into the grandfather of my children, and the mourners must have wondered at such display, but I was no longer with them. I was in the clear and crowded past, where he sat beside me on a stool, elbows on his knees, next to my bed, waiting for sleep to take me away to dreams. I hugged him fiercely. "I'm Mía," I said again. "I've come to pay you what I owe."

And of course he did not understand.

He let me help him as we walked. It was difficult for him, climbing up the hill that had not seemed steep until now. Some of the women hurried on to prepare the meal. The children too, only three or four of them, went on their way. The remainder of the people, though, stayed and listened as we talked. I heard Quentin asking one of the men, "What happened here? The school I mean. What happened to the school?"

"It went away," the other joked. "Stone by stone."

Victor's son was the one who offered to explain. "They are already doing it when I am still a boy, when there is no other work to do I mean. Some of the men, they sell the blocks that had fall in the quake because, you know, they are good stones. Sell them in Zalcupan and some other towns I think. They truck them down, one or two at a time, for a few dollars or maybe for a little bit of trade. It is not a business like the roses. Just a way to buy something nice for the little ones. Then, when the families begin to leave in groups, what is the point of the school? No one ever love it."

"I did," I said. "I loved the school. I think that my father did too."

Victor's son looked at me and then at Quentin as if to say *can you not control this interrupting woman?* And we went a little way in silence until another man prompted, "So. When the church in Casasillo began to build...."

"We need money," said Victor's son. "They pay for stones that are dressed and square. So we cut them free and polish them. Use the glass and beams for our own houses. Some of the wire and copper too."

All of us stopped when we reached where the school once stood. I wondered what Amedeo Muñoz thought when they began dismantling it. I wondered what I would have thought if I had stayed. His face gave no indication. He looked at the level emptiness the way he looked at clouds. Then the other men went on ahead to a house down near the valley wall. We could see them from where we stood, carrying tables and chairs into the street, ignoring instructions from their wives. The four of us came last, Quentin and his wife, Amedeo Muñoz, and the girl who had seen me first, the one who called him *abuelo* and refused to leave his side. The women were ready when we arrived, and we ate outside at the tables they had prepared at a level shady place in the street.

My father remained silent throughout the meal. He had been helped into his chair by one of the women who brought a plate to him without asking what he preferred to eat. She was one of the ageless ones, with skin almost as dark as his, graying hair, and eyes much younger than her years. Her face was full and beautiful, as serene as a mountain morning, but her hands had seen hard work in many seasons. She set his plate before him and urged him to eat when she saw him faltering. He hardly looked at his food and took his meal in bits and sips. When someone spoke to him or called his name, he would reply with a word or two, but I could see that his mind wandered. The thousand questions I had ready on my tongue would have to be surrendered. And I found that I could give them up, all but one.

He held my hand, or I held his. I cannot remember now. We just came naturally into the quiet comfort of each other once again. He did not want to walk or talk, and that was strange to me because he had always been a walking man. I tried to calculate his age and realized I'd never known about his birth. Was he eighty? Was the world taking away the last of him, his memory and strength, before he'd even had a moment's rest?

Once or twice I saw the woman who had helped him to his chair. She looked from a window, I suppose to insure that I was not pestering him. Should I have remembered her? Should she have remembered me? I am not one for faces. There was nothing secretive or furtive in her movements. She watched us openly; and then once, as she laid away a bowl, she nodded as if to say that I had been doing well. The other women came and went until finally they had all returned to their homes, leaving children in the hands of the older girls, and husbands to the mercy of God. The sun began its long descent from mid-afternoon. Before I knew it, the very first of night had begun to gather under eaves and among the thickest branches. In the intervening time, I went somewhere with him.

Maybe it was where he had lived all along. All I can know is that during the last afternoon I spent with him we went somewhere together, and I have been grateful ever since. I was young and old at the same moment, both a woman and a child. The crust of me seemed to crack and fall away. It was just one unending instant, like wading into the gentle flow of a river, deeper and deeper, until finally you are lifted from your feet. You spread your arms, embrace the water, and surrender. You become the river's creature until it releases you on a farther shore. That is how I went with him. It felt like happiness.

Maybe only one of us came back. Maybe a breeze rose up or some material sound came forth that was tinged with sadness. I do not know. Something brought me back to my weary self. There I was beside him but no longer with him. I think that is what it means to die. The sudden recognition that *they* no longer see or hear us. I brought myself as close to him as I could be and gathered all my strength and prayed my words into his ear.

"Do you remember me?" I said.

"Yes," he said from far away. "I think I do."

"Can you say my name?"

He made a silent movement of his lips.

"Papa. Can you say my name out loud? For me?"

"Yes. I believe I can." He looked at me over an expanse of time that could have covered eons. Patiently. Forgivingly, as if explaining to a child. "I remember. I remember now something about you."

"Tell me."

"That when you were with me. I was then at peace."

"And mama's name?"

"Yes."

"Do you remember her?"

"Oh yes, I loved your mother more than you can know."

"I believe you did. She was the woman that you loved the most."

"Yes, she used to hold you," he said. "In this very house. Many years ago."

And there it was, the breaking of the spell. I could see that the questions were confusing him. His past was collapsing into a single story, turning points on a map where the names no longer mattered. Who's to say whether we were in Catalán, or no? I was here, in this peaceful place, inside of his time with him. No need to quibble over names.

The woman from the house came outside and called him Amedeo. At first he did not hear. She straightened the collar of his shirt, made little circles with her fingertips on his head and temple. Then called his name again. He stood up without her help, made a little bow in my direction, and followed her into the house. I wish he had left me with some other sign. A talisman from my childhood, a wink, a photograph. It was so formal, the way he went away, that I wondered if he remembered me at all. I looked about for Quentin but could not take myself from the show of clouds and light. After a time the woman came back and took his chair. "The day has been too much for him," she said. "He'll be better when he rests."

"I'm sorry," I managed. "We didn't mean to disrupt."

"You've done nothing wrong. This is your home. A place where you are always welcome."

"Thank you." I could think of nothing else to say. After another awkward minute, I reached out my hand to her and said, "My name is Mía. I was his daughter. I mean I *am*...."

"I know." She took my hand and patted it. "It was clear to me when he saw you. Clear to me who you were. I think you went away a long time ago like so many families and their children."

"Were you here? Did you know my husband?"

"Quentin? Yes. He was a handsome boy." She seemed on the verge of telling me something else, but she hesitated instead. Watched me trying to imagine the village over years turning into a place without a name. Finally she said, "I was here when Quentin went away."

"Is it true that Papa sent him?"

"It's true," the woman said. "But I think you are here for something more than questions. I think this is not a pleasure trip for you."

Mía folded her hands and propped them against the edge of the table. "Guilt? Is it that obvious on my face?"

"You want to take him with you. You want him to live his last years in the north so that you will not feel bad."

"I want to do what is right for him," I told her.

The woman thought before she answered, and finally smiled. "That is good. Then thank you for your visit." Her smile puzzled me almost as much as her next gesture, which was to reach out and touch my hair, untangling some of the wind's work as if she had done this all of my life.

And I must have stiffened, because I remember the formality of what I said then. "I can't help thinking that he has had a very hard life, that he has never been happy, and that I owe him at least the comfort that I can provide."

"He has been happy," she said. "I promise you. He will be happy here for all of his years."

"I appreciate the care that you have given him. All of you.

But I am his daughter. How can you possibly know... ?"

"Because," she said. "My name is Elisenda. I married him many years ago."

"Then you know...."

"That in this house I cared for you, Maria Anita. Before you had a name, my parents took you in. I held you in my arms, and I placed you on his lap. I know that I was a mother long before I was a wife. But I know nothing that will help you to take him away."

She did not say these words with anger or with any force, but I realized then that I could never know his story. The best I could have of him would be an understanding that his life had not been what I had imagined. And that I could be happy with him and for him during the remainder of his life. There, I have said it. I am not the center of his universe, and what a stunning revelation for any child, no matter what her age. Yet here I am. What does it mean, to be held by a gravity so strong?

Into this wonderful, forbidding place I was born, and I have been lifted here again. It is a blessing just to share a glimpse. I wanted to walk by the little stream again, climb the stony path up to my father's house. I wanted to watch the ocean that washes against the valley wall, see the clouds making islands in the air. I wanted to wade the bed of a truck loaded down with blossoms and go to sleep on the long ride home. But I knew that he did not belong with me in any north that I could imagine. And later, when my husband and I were about to bid goodbye, the same woman came to us and asked, most diplomatically, if we would stay the night. God gave me the grace to say, "Only if you think it would comfort him."

Maybe in the morning he would feel like walking. Or maybe I would visit with my friend Gabriel.

I am Maria Anita Muñoz de Cayetano,
and these are my memories of him.
April 4, 1982

A READER'S GUIDE

The following questions are designed to assist you and your reading group in discussing Randy F. Nelson's novel of love, loss, and identity. We hope they encourage diverse opinions and imaginative answers while enriching everyone's reading experience.

1. *A Duplicate Daughter* features a primary character (Mía) who does not have a real name, identifiable parents, a birth date, or any known relatives. So how does this particular narrative attempt to answer the "who am I?" question?

2. How do we get our identities in the first place? Do we inherit them? Are we born into them? To what degree is our identity the product of a specific time, place, and cast of characters? And to what degree is it, let us say, genetic? The author of *A Duplicate Daughter* seems to suggest that identity is primarily a narrative that we perform or have imposed upon us. Do you agree?

3. Who are some of the other "nobodies" in literature whose identities are supplied by a community, a family, a fate, or a mythology? Who are some of these people in real life? In your life?

4. Questions of social justice in this novel are not framed in terms of huge political or legal issues. Rather, they appear in the story as individual choices made by individual characters. — But which choices specifically? And how do they speak to the larger topics of human rights, equality, responsibility, and class?

5. In the most famous Biblical dispute over a mis-identified baby (see 1 Kings 3: 16-28), King Solomon seems less interested in establishing the literal, legal, or scientific truth of the case than in establishing the emotional truth of the case. Would you say that the same storytelling principle holds for this novel? Does anyone have the role of Solomon? Does he or she get a good result?

6. Is there anyone in this book who is really admirable? If so, does that admiration develop just because good traits outweigh bad traits? Or is it because of a redeeming act? Or some other reason?

7. It's often suggested that *mood* is the reader's attitude toward the subject and that *tone* is the author's attitude toward the subject. Ideally, they'd be the same. Now reread the afterword, where the narration is in a different voice from the rest of the novel and where most readers would agree that the mood changes during the course of that chapter. Where specifically does it begin to change? How would you characterize this change?

8. In an interview, Nelson once called this plot *mythological* in structure, meaning that "one dramatic choice leads to one inevitable consequence and then to another and another until you can almost hear the tumblers of fate clicking into their sequences." Does that sound true? Do characters determine their own fates or merely perform them? How can you tell?

9. What motivates Alejandro besides revenge? What motivates Leala besides loss? What motivates Amedeo besides guilt?

10. How does the external landscape(s) of any given setting compare to the internal landscape(s) of any given character?

11. And just for fun. Nearly every chapter of *A Duplicate Daughter* contains at least one buried quotation. That is to say, a famous line or phrase from another work of literature has been camouflaged in a new context but still laid out in plain view.

For example, the "sudden swelling of the ground" mentioned in the afterword is an allusion to Emily Dickinson's best known poem. Or the line "There is always something," in chapter 22, is part of Willie Stark's cynical mantra spoken a number of times in *All the King's Men*. Did you spot any of the other quotations (from Shakespeare, Milton, Blake, Hawthorne, Poe, Melville, Faulkner, Hemingway, O'Connor, Garcia Marquez, and more)?

ACKNOWLEDGEMENTS

Many thanks to the librarians of Davidson College for their aid in researching the history, culture, and geography of the Sierra Madre Occidental in northern Mexico and especially for pointing me toward the Cumbres de Majalca National Park, which is the imagined setting of much of this book. I'm grateful also to Laney Katz Becker for editorial suggestions with an early version of the manuscript and for discovering the book's title in an obscure line I wrote for my original proposal. The editorial team at Harvard Square Editons have been more than helpful at every stage of production, and I am very grateful for their guidance and professionalism. I owe a debt also to my friend Luis Peña who patiently answered my questions about Mexican history and geography and who introduced me to Juan Rulfo's *Pedro Páramo*, an obvious influence in the afterword.

I used the names of my three good-natured sons for three not-entirely-admirable characters in this novel. And I'm sorry. You deserved better. All of my daughters, alas, are honorary ones; but the bond is no less strong for that. You've enriched my life, and nearly all of what I know about Mía comes from you. Matthew Nelson drew the maps for the front and back endpapers, turning my crude sketches into useable art. Thank you. And finally, I want to reserve a special appreciation and a loving dedication for my wife, Susan, who probably doesn't recognize herself in the character of the wonderful Elisenda. This book is for you, the best person, real or imagined, whom I have ever met.

Readers may also want to know that the legend of Juan Soldado, mentioned in several chapters, is based upon actual events which occurred in and around Tijuana during the month of February, 1938. Juan Soldado is the folk saint name of Juan Castillo Morales, who was executed for the rape and murder of a child. His devotees today believe that his conviction by summary court martial and his execution on February 17, 1938, were part of a cover-up designed to protect important figures in the Mexican army. Thus "Juan Soldado" became a martyr. In using his story as I have, I intend no disrespect to the many good people who believe that he was innocent and who further believe that he performs miracles still today for those suffering injustice or degradation.

Randy F. Nelson
Davidson, 2017

More books from Harvard Square Editions

People and Peppers, Kelvin Christopher James

Gates of Eden, Charles Degelman

Love's Affliction, Fidelis Mkparu

Transoceanic Lights, S. Li

Close, Erika Raskin

Anomie, Jeff Lockwood

Living Treasures, Yang Huang

Nature's Confession, J.L. Morin

Love and Famine, Han-ping Chin

Dark Lady of Hollywood, Diane Haithman

How Fast Can You Run, Harriet Levin Millan

Appointment with ISIL, Joe Giordano

Never Summer, Tim Blaine

Parallel, Sharon Erby